I0652439

Deadly Circles

SIBILLA

Deadly Circles

By
Nelly Chadour

Translated by
Michael Shreve

Based on the characters created by
Pier Carpi & Luciano Bernasconi

BLACK COAT PRESS

Cover illustration Copyright © 2016 Cham/Mosaic Multimedia.

Visit our websites at
www.blackcoatpress.com
and
www.hexagoncomics.com

ISBN 978-1-61227-968-9 © 2020 Published by Hollywood Comics.com, LLC, P.O. Box 17270, Encino, CA 91416, USA, under license from Mosaic Multimedia. All characters of this book are © et ™ 2020 Mosaic Multimedia. All rights reserved. No similarity between any of the names, characters, persons and/or institutions in this book with those of any living or dead person or institutions is intended, and any such similarity which may exist is purely coincidental. Except for review purposes, no part of this book may be reproduced or transmitted in any form or by any means, electronic or mechanical, including photocopying, recording, or by any information storage and retrieval system, without permission in writing from the publisher. The stories and characters depicted in this novel are entirely fictional. Printed in the United States of America.

TABLE OF CONTENTS

Sibilla by Manuel Garcia

Introduction

Sibilla is, without a doubt, one of the most fascinating and sexiest heroines in the Hexagon Comics universe, the successor of Editions Lug. Every month, from the 1950 to the early 90s, Lug published a large array of monthly pocket-sized comic books, with colorful covers and titles beloved by many generations of teenagers: *Yuma, Kiwi, Mustang, Rodeo, Zembla,* etc.

Futura, which also launched the careers of Homicron, Jaleb, the Time Brigade, etc., was nearing cancellation when Sibilla entered the scene in its final two issues in 1975. The least one can say is that she deserved better, because she was the creation of two masters of Italian comics: writer Pier Carpi and artist Luciano Bernasconi.

Carpi, born on January 16, 1940 in Scandiano, in the province of Reggio Emilia, in Emilia-Romagna, passed away on July 26, 2000 in Viadana. He made his debut in 1963 working for the Italian Disney comics. In 1970, along with his friend Alfredo Castelli, the creator of Martin Mystère, Carpi launched the magazine *Horror*, then began a journalistic career which saw him contribute to many Italian daily papers and even to the RAI television channel. Among his most notable contributions to comics are the characters Astorina and many stories for the legendary Diabolik, including numerous novelizations of his adventures.

For Lug, Carpi wrote Dick Demon, Morgane, Sibilla and Bob Lance. Besides his Diabolik novels, he also wrote books on secret societies, Cagliostro, the prophecies of Pope John XXIII, the Kennedy Assassination, etc. For the cinema, he wrote *Un ombra nell'ombra* with Curd Jurgens, Povero Cristo and Irène Papas.

The legendary Luciano Bernasconi, born in 1939 in Rome, started in comics in the early 1960s, working for the Barbato studio with his colleague, Carlo Cedroni. For more than twenty years, Bernasconi was one of the architects of Editions Lug, for which he created a large number of heroes such as Sibilla, Phenix, Count Saint-Germain, Wampus, Kabur, Barry Barrison, Billy Boyd, Bob Lance, the Bronze Gladiator, Jean Girodet, Jeff Sullivan, Kit Kappa, Starlock, Waki, and many more.

In the 1980s, Bernasconi was published in *Il Giornalino*, *Il Messaggero*, and contributed to the erotic comics of Edifumetto Editions in Milan. Then, during the 90s, he created Gordon Linch and published a remarkable comic adaptation of Sherlock Holmes.

In 2000, he returned to Kabur, Phenix and Wampus, and became a founding member of the Hexagon Comics syndicate in 2004.

As for Nelly Chadour, she has been writing since she learned how to handle a pencil, and became a professional writer in 2011. Her works, which have been compared to those of Chelsea Quinn Yarbro and Poppy Z. Brite, have been published by Editions Malpertuis, Céléphais, Le Carnoplaste, and Rivière Blanche.

There is little else you need to know before beginning this book. Elena Drago is a descendant of the sister of the 16th century freebooter Dragut, and the heir to the legendary mage Cagliostro, who once took in Dragut's sister. Under the nom-de-plume Sibilla, she writes a column on the occult for the Italian magazine *Flash*, which is part of the press group of Sir Daniel Wilson. With the help of her colleague Leonardo Verga, she fights supernatural threats.

Jean-Marc Lofficier

Cagliostro's Disgrace

"Tell me again what brings you to Paris, mademoiselle?"

"You have a short memory. That can't be good in your line of work. I'm a journalist and I came to cover the Ready-To-Wear Festival at the Grand Palais."

The customs officer, a young idiot with velvety eyes that were confident in their seduction, had started this mating dance with the lovely Italian with long red hair who had come to register her photography material. To be fair, the pretty girl's gorgeous figure was particularly stunning in her black suit. And she was as patient as an angel with the young hotshot's cooing. Behind her, her friend and colleague, Leonardo Verga, tall, brown-haired, well built and in his thirties, was not so tolerant and was shifting from one foot to the other.

"Could you speed it up a little?" he raised his voice. "I'm waiting here."

"It's true, we have to cut our lovely conversation short," the Italian said with a little sass. "But we'll certainly see each other again when I go back to Milan. Unless, of course, someone perishes from your cute dimples before that."

"I love your accent," the customs officer muttered as he literally melted behind his desk. "Have a nice trip."

The young lady thanked him with a dazzling smile and left holding her friend's arm.

"You're too much, Sibilla," Leonardo said. "When a young creep is hitting on you, you always have to overdo it."

"I love light appetizers, especially when the rest is looking so spicy," replied Elena Drago, a.k.a. Sibilla, a journalist with *Flash* and an occult investigator. "According to Sir Wilson the case we're interested in involves Interpol as much as… as the past of a person I owe a lot to, or so he said. I don't like it when he's vague."

"Interpol is no small matter! Let's hope we're not getting mixed up in politics. And for your meeting? Is a driver waiting for us or are we on our own? Just getting out of the airport is going to be a mess."

"Look."

Sibilla pointed to a tall, thin man, impeccably dressed in a black suit. He was holding a sign on which the names of the two Italians were printed. His blonde hair was brushed back and his expressionless face could have belonged to an English butler, but a butler whose respect you had to earn to give him orders.

"If that guy isn't a Brit working for Interpol I'll eat my Leica," Leonardo mumbled, then he raised his hand to show that they were the expected party.

The stranger smirked when he saw them coming up. He held out a firm hand in a leather glove that Sibilla and Leonardo shook in turn.

"Miss Sibilla and Mr. Verga, welcome to Paris. I'm Graham Carter. I'm the one who contacted your boss. I'm part of a special section of Interpol, but I'll tell you more on the way. Please follow me."

The Englishman turned around and without looking to see if they were following him he marched through the teeming crowd. Even the passengers in a great hurry stepped aside to let him pass.

"What presence!" Sibilla whistled in admiration at the natural authority emanating from their contact.

Leonardo grumbled.

The trio left the crowds behind to wind their way through the vast parking maze. A black sedan was waiting for them. Leonardo was a little disappointed by the car that looked nothing like James Bond's Aston Martin. Graham Carter let them get settled in the comfortable leather seats, then sat behind the wheel.

Before starting the car he turned to Sibilla, "As Sir Wilson must have explained to you, we're going to be staying in an apartment in the Marais. The place should be familiar to you. During part of 1785 Count Cagliostro lived there."

Sibilla's heart beat faster. To be within the walls that had sheltered the man to whom she owed her occult powers was an exhilarating prospect. Without a doubt and despite the short time he spent in the rooms the magnetic presence of Cagliostro ought to have seeped into the place.

"Would the case have anything to do with him?" Leonardo asked.

"Let's just say that Cagliostro was the unlucky hero of what we can call the prologue to our story. Incidentally…"

The Englishman opened the glove compartment and took out a document carefully wrapped in brown paper. He handed it to Sibilla who felt her hair stand on end as if she had just got an electric shock. She tore off the paper and held a very old, bound notebook. Her fingers drummed on it. She looked at Carter as he finally turned the ignition.

The Englishman smiled in the rear view mirror, "That's the journal the Count kept during his imprisonment in the Bastille. The story he wrote is really fascinating. It should make for good reading during the drive."

Sibilla opened the book gingerly. The yellowed pages were fragile. Having consulted the grimoires countless times the magician was familiar enough with Cagliostro's handwriting to authenticate the work she held in her hands.

While the sedan sped through the traffic and honking horns, the pretty Italian learned about the dreadful disaster of the famous case of the Queen's necklace.

August 13, 1785

"A nocturnal visit might play against you, Your Eminence. And it's all the more dangerous if the king's spies are watching you."

"That's exactly what I said," the cardinal's young secretary affirmed, "but he refused to listen to me. And when I begged him not to go to the rendezvous supposedly set up by the Queen, he did as he wanted. Now you see the unfortunate results!"

"That's enough, Louis!" Cardinal de Rohan shouted. "There's no need to twist the knife in the wound. I came in spite of the dangers because I couldn't wait any longer to show you, Count. Oh, have pity and save me! I think I'm being followed. I feel like one of those big deer being attacked on all sides by relentless hunting dogs."

"Worry is making His Eminence poetic," Louis muttered.

Count Cagliostro gently pushed Cardinal de Rohan into a comfortable armchair and went to fetch some wine for his guests. The churchman was Cagliostro's patron, who had been witness to his magical talents when he had healed the prince of Soubise by a simple laying on of hands. The Cardinal was amazed and eagerly sang the magician's praises all over Paris. At first embarrassed by the sudden interest that he attracted in high society Cagliostro finally realized that he could turn an honest profit from his powers. But only the least spectacular of his gifts and the least susceptible of incurring the wrath of the clergy. Unfortunately some of his patients were so generous that the Count could not stop tongues wagging and calling him a cheat.

But tonight, what de Rohan brought was harder to define than a simple attack of gout or kidney stones. As the Cardinal's personal secretary Louis was responsible for explaining the particulars of the affair: his boss had been involved in a large-scale fraud and he was the main victim. Someone pretending to be Marie-Antoinette had kept up a regular correspondence with him. Then they had urged him, in order to prove his "friendship" with the Queen, to acquire a necklace worth the extravagant sum of two million pounds! Of course, the crooks had pocketed the money without giving anything to the artisan who was supposed to make the jewelry. When no money came the craftsman went to complain directly in Versailles. Already shaken up by the scandal Rohan was now filled with terror on learning that the King had requested his sworn enemy, Baron de Breteuil, to look into the affair. The situation was really desperate for the Cardinal whose naivety could land him in prison and made worse by the fact that the Queen hated him with all her heart. She would certainly not lose the chance to heap scorn and disgrace on Rohan.

"I didn't think you were so candid, Your Eminence," the Count said once Louis had finished his story. "You really thought that the Queen wanted a quick and easy reconciliation after that grievous dispute that pitted you against her late mother? And you never doubted that the letters apparently signed by her hand were fakes? Breteuil must be in seventh heaven."

"My friend, your chiding only makes me feel worse. I came to you because you are the person I trust the most. I was counting on your intelligence and your uncommon gifts."

Rohan waved to Louis to hand a document to the magician.

"I wrote down the names of the swindlers," he explained. "We know that some of your talents involve bending even the most contrary minds to your will."

"I see. I can't guarantee a complete absolution with the Queen, but it's true that loosening a few tongues will be the only way to soften your fall."

A great weight seemed to lift off Rohan's shoulders. He took Cagliostro's hands in his own and squeezed them. With tears in his eyes he said, "Thank you! Thank you! I owe you so much!"

"Wait to see the results before you start thanking me," Cagliostro replied. "Tomorrow night I'll pay a visit to a few scoundrels."

"Louis will go with you. Everybody respects him for his intelligence and his virtue. His presence will play even more in my favor."

If Cagliostro was offended by the unspoken suggestion that the word of a magician was of little value, he did not show it.

"Do you really want to go with me, Louis?"

13

"These rogues and their little schemes make me sick," the young man answered. "I'm ready to sacrifice a good night's rest for it."

"I hate getting such a noble soul mixed up in such a dark affair, but so be it," the Count sighed.

"Great!" Rohan sounded confident. "My friends, I'm counting on your discretion, your ingenuity and your very special talents."

The first person to receive a visit that night was a skillful forger by the name of Marc Rétaux de Villette. He was the one who had written the letters perfectly imitating the Queen's handwriting. His reputation was more of a ladies man than a reasonable man and he would give his all to enjoy their generosity.

Cagliostro had the carriage stop a few streets away from the scoundrel's lodging. The two men walked calmly, like all good people, up to the house. Rétaux de Villette lived on Île Saint Louis. The three-storey building had seen better days. Cagliostro and Louis walked around the side looking for the servant's entrance. It was not locked. As the two men snuck in, the magician had a morbid feeling that turned his stomach: death had struck.

Louis saw him turn pale all of a sudden and grabbed his arm, afraid he might pass out, "Count?"

"It's nothing. I was just taken by surprise. Quick, let's find the cur... even if we can't get much out of him."

Worried about the physical change in the thaumaturge, Louis did not dare say a word. They tiptoed upstairs. Although modest the house was well taken care of. The servants were certainly on the top floor but it was better to be careful. They stopped before a door that was left ajar. Cagliostro opened it slowly and was blasted by the stench of death. A painful, desperate death. Merciless.

Candles burning in the tarnished silver candelabra cast a faint light in the room, a scene of total chaos: sheets of paper and inkwells lay on the wooden floor, books were piled up on the shelves, disheveled wigs were hanging off the backs of chairs, open bottles of perfume and cosmetic powders added their heavy scents to the shambles.

And slumped in a high-backed chair, a motionless king in the middle of his chaotic realm, Marc Rétaux de Villette stared at the ceiling in disbelief. His corpse showed no trace of violence. However, the agony of his death still filled the room. Cagliostro smelled it like the sharp odor left from a deadly fire days later.

Trying to hide his disgust, Louis examined the dead eyes and hands. "I don't think he was poisoned. And yet it looks like he had horrible convulsions."

"Here's a death quite convenient for our thieves but at a bad time for the Cardinal," Cagliostro muttered.

He nervously twisted his strange ring in the form of a snake pierced by an arrow, which he never took off and whose brilliance always fascinated Louis.

"My friend," the magician said, "You've already seen some of my... tricks, as the skeptical call them. You've seen the relief I brought to those in suffering."

The young man nodded without saying a word, waiting patiently for his companion to get to the point.

"I know that you're a sensible, rational person, not so gullible," the Count continued as he circled around the chair in which the dead man lay. "That's why I'm sorry to have to rattle your beliefs, so to speak. I could make an excuse to get you out of the room but I need a witness of your standing. You're going to see some magic that would earn me the gallows if word got out. But there's nothing else I can do if I want to learn more about our criminals or whoever's in control. So, in the name of our mutual trust, please don't be afraid and don't scream bloody hell."

Louis felt his throat tighten. It was hard for him to swallow. "I will prove worthy of your trust," he croaked.

Cagliostro gave him a warm smile, glad to hear his answer. Then his face went hard as he turned toward the forger's remains. Slowly, he raised his hand. The ring on his finger shined in a glow of jade, lighting up the room that the candles had kept in morbid shadows.

"By the power of the Twelve, I order you to appear and reveal to us what is hidden, Marc Rétaux de Villette. Show yourself, wretched lost soul, and find peace once your duty is accomplished."

All of a sudden everything went dark except for Cagliostro's ring. Then a figure stepped out of the shadows. Louis struggled not to pass out in fear: before them stood the spectral form of Rétaux de Villette. His dark-ringed eyes were jumping out of their sunken sockets, his mouth was gaping open with mute, unbearable sorrow. His milk-white body twitched in a dance of suffering like a glowworm held over candle flame. One bony hand clutched his chest.

"Tortured spirit, poor, tormented soul," Cagliostro murmured, "eternal rest will be granted you when you have revealed to us who it was who used you to harm Cardinal de Rohan and how you died."

With this said, the ghost moaned long and low, which shook Louis to the depths of his soul. Then, slowly, the pale lips exhaled such weak grumblings that the two men had to hold their breaths to hear.

"Jeanne... la Motte... she dem... to imitate... the Queen... Jeanne plan... all... London, the jewels... My heart! My heart!"

These last words came out in a heart-rending cry. The ghost twisted in pain, opened and closed its mouth searching for air that it would never breathe again.

"What's happening to your heart, Marc?" Cagliostro asked compassionately. "Are you sick?"

"No, no!" the ghost said. "Jeanne... the pin..."

The ghost reached out its trembling arm toward the small desk by the door. Cagliostro went over and opened the drawers one by one. When he finally found the strange object, his blood froze. But his voice was calm when he addressed the phantom for the last time.

"Marc Rétaux de Villette, by the power of the Twelve, may your poor soul be free of the sufferings of this world. You can rest in peace."

A bright, green light sprang out of the ring and enveloped the sad, spectral figure. Louis watched on, frozen in both fear and amazement, as the forger's spirit dissolved. There was just enough time to see Rétaux de Villette close his eyes, peacefully, before the ephemeral figure vanished in a glowing whirlwind. When everything was back to normal, the young man finally let his legs go. He dropped to his knees on the floorboards, utterly stunned by the sight he had just witnessed.

"Come on, Louis, this is not the time to pass out," Cagliostro told him.

But he was not looking at his young companion. His eyes were captivated by the object found in the' desk drawer, which he was holding out in disgust. It was a small, wax doll bound with a lock of hair. Sticking out of the middle of it was a long, silver pin.

"I wouldn't be surprised if this hair belonged to our host," the magician said. Then, to Louis who was still dazed, "Get hold of yourself, my boy, we have a very interesting clue to follow here."

"Huh?" Louis looked up and slowly pulled himself together but he was obviously fighting against the fear of going crazy. "Yes, yes, I remember. He mentioned a name and the city of London."

"I'll bet my precious ring that the stolen jewels are in London. But do you know this Jeanne la Motte?"

"Jeanne *de* la Motte," Louis corrected. "I'm afraid yes. She's the Cardinal's mistress."

Cagliostro swore. "That explains why he was so easily manipulated. Rohan kept you from adding her name to the list of suspects while she was the ringleader. A criminal who knows black magic to boot!"

"But... and you? What you did..."

"I have never used my gifts to hurt anyone. In the name of our friendship, Louis, don't think of me as one of those cheap necromancers squeezing riches out of helpless grieving families... nor like a sorcerer who would sign a pact with the devil. I get my powers from an ancient civilization that is now extinct, from an age when the devil was a light-bearer and not a tempter. But we have to get out of here fast. Maybe the depraved woman has not had time to get rid of all her accomplices.

All night long the magician and Louis walked the streets of Paris, silent shadows lost in the twists and turns of a dark tale, searching for other people on Rohan's list. Twice they could only join the onlookers crowded around a house, mumbling about the freshly discovered corpse. Cagliostro and Louis had no doubt about the identity of the deceased. On the other hand, they were the first on the scene of the lifeless corpse of a prostitute named Nicole Leguay. Looking at her delicate face frozen in death, the two men understood why Cardinal de Rohan proved to be so remarkably naïve.

Except for a few small details the young woman bore a troubling resemblance to Marie Antoinette.

It was easy to imagine the secret rendezvous set up between the fake queen and the cardinal. Rendezvous that took place in suitably deceptive shadows.

Despite Louis' obvious reluctance, Cagliostro called upon his dark magic once again. Whereas the ghost of Rétaux de Villette had been sad and sorrowful to a pitiful extent, the aura of Nicole Leguay's ghost was a mixture of tears and anger.

"Jeanne, that damned witch!" she shouted while ectoplasmic tears ran down her marble face. "May God forgive all my sins but I hope He soaks that harlot in the flames of hell!"

Then she pointed to an object under her bed. Cagliostro was expecting this but he could not stop the shiver from running down his spine when he pulled out the wax doll like the one found at the forger's.

Nicole Leguay's ghost was not finished, "Look for the Count de la Motte in London. The jewelers Clifford and Parrels."

Cagliostro would never forget the ghost's unflinching eyes drilling into his own when his ring flashed and freed her from the terrestrial purgatory.

The clues they had now were enough to form an action plan. The day was dawning when the two men went to Louis' home to prepare for his trip. Nine o'clock had not yet tolled when the Cardinal's secretary jumped into a carriage headed for Calais with some light luggage. He had to find the stolen jewels as soon as possible. Rohan's disgrace was no longer a question of days but of hours if one could judge by the way Jeanne de la Motte was disposing of the most compromising witnesses.

Once Count Cagliostro was alone he shut himself up at home. He slept very little. He sent a message to the Cardinal that summed up the investigation but without informing him of Louis' departure, which had to remain confidential. For the rest, the magician shared his worries and advised the greatest caution because evil sorcery was at work.

The two wax dolls were put on a stand, looking like they were observing the magician emptying his bookshelves and thumbing madly through old tomes that exuded a sweet, musty odor. These dolls, obviously the instruments of lethal black magic, reminded him of a wicked person whose evil influence on history was seen in the massacres of Protestants.

Thus Cagliostro spent the day, a day of suffocating heat, reading and cussing under his breath whenever his fears were confirmed. The sun was sinking behind the roofs of Paris when he closed his last book and turned his eyes toward the two little, wax horrors.

"Now you're going to take me to your real creator."

Late at night when honest folks are snoring soundly in bed a shadowy figure was sneaking through the streets, as dark as the other shadows and as quiet as a cat. It would have taken a very careful observer to spot the two tiny creatures leading the prowler. Without any hesitation the two things jogged down the road, jumping over holes and puddles. With his hand held out in front of him, as if he were trying to catch the weird pixies, the man trotted lightly behind them. Look closer and you might see a shiny ring with a jade glow on his finger and a thin ray of light coming out of it and surrounding the two dolls.

With his magic Cagliostro had animated the wax dolls and turned them into guides toward the real mastermind behind the crimes. The farther he went through the dark night, the more sure he was of his conclusions: it was not just Rohan who was the target but also the royal couple's reputation. Getting their names mixed up in such a sinister fraud, already being so unpopular, could very well make them lose all credit with the people. Jeanne de la Motte's interest was not in the money she would swindle or else she would be in London with her husband. She was one of the last descendants of the royal family of Valois but had always been poor. Only vengeance could make her form an alliance with a demon that everyone thought was dead.

When he got in view of the tall column next to La Halle aux Blés and topped with a big sundial, Cagliostro knew that he had arrived at his destination. Because of the nearness of Les Halles market to the old Holy Innocents' cemetery, he became doubly cautious. Even in the darkest hour of the night chance encounters could happen. Thieves, murderers, beggars, road workers, early peddlers, all kinds of people were already pounding the pavement close by.

With a wave of his hand Cagliostro broke the ray of light that energized the wax puppets, which plopped quietly to the ground. Then he slipped behind the tall column that rose up to the stars. A relic of the reign of Catherine de Medici, it had been used to watch the heavens by the magus Cosimo Ruggieri, the queen's official astrologer and a fervent practitioner of the darkest magic. It was said that on stormy nights you could see a gaunt figure on top of the column, flashing in and out of sight with the lightning.

Cagliostro perked up when he heard distant rumbling. Here came the answer to the heat of the day.

"A perfect night to invoke certain ghosts," the thaumaturge hissed.

The quality of the air changed abruptly. Everything became smothered under a lead weight. The nocturnal birds flew off from the roofs and screeched out wild songs.

Cagliostro was about to cross the few yards between him and his goal when he saw a figure wrapped in a dark cape dashing towards the little door at the base of the column. With one hand on the door and other holding a lantern the stranger looked around to make sure nobody was following. The light from the lantern revealed the pretty face of a common woman but with a noble features marked by extreme cunning. It could only be the Countess de la Motte.

Once she had closed the door behind her Cagliostro stepped out of hiding and snuck up to the building. The first drops of rain hit the pavement when he reached the column. The Countess had locked the door so she would not be disturbed in her dark intrigues. The magician took a skeleton key out of his jacket pocket and picked the lock. The hard rain that was pouring down on Paris drowned out the creaking door as Cagliostro slipped into the column. The winding stairs were lost in almost total darkness. But a faint light came from above, changing the black into a dark gray.

The violent storm was the only noise to be heard. The Count did not know if Jeanne de la Motte was alone or if other people were already waiting for her up above. But the magician was fully aware of another presence besides the woman. An insidious presence full of powerful magic. It was seeping out of the walls, soaking into the stones.

It had been waiting for two centuries.

The magician had goose bumps. To give himself courage he fiddled with his ring, which had always protected him from evil spirits. Then he started climbing up the stairs of the Medici column. The rain might have covered the voices of anyone present but it also covered the Count's footsteps. The climb was long and tortuous because the magician was listening for signs of what was happening up above and also keeping an ear on downstairs so he would not be surprised by a newcomer.

As he neared the top he heard the woman talking passionately. A shiver ran down his spine when he heard the answer in a deep, cavernous voice devoid of all kindness and especially of life. He ducked down when he got to the top of the steps. He did not want to show himself right away and he could easily be seen in the flames of the thirteen candles, each placed at the points of the strange symbol drawn with red chalk on the gray marble floor. Jeanne de la Motte was in the middle of the cabalistic sign, on her knees, looking up, frozen in an attitude of ecstatic devotion. A dark figure, darker than the night, rose up before her. Two points of absolute blackness in the middle of a shadowy face seemed to be staring at the woman.

"The unwanted witnesses are gone," she said. "Everything will trace back to Cardinal de Rohan and I will corroborate the accusations against him. It will be so scandalous that the King and Queen will have their reputations tarnished forever."

"I know that, my child, I have seen it," the dark figure whispered.

Hissing laughter like the slow beating of an eagle owl's wings crept over the stones.

"The fall of the Bourbons is written in the stars. It's an impure dynasty that deserves to be wiped out. We will establish a kingdom enlightened by magic and prosperity. Like the great Catherine wanted."

"And for that you're ready to use the most disgraceful means, Mage Cosimo Ruggieri," Cagliostro spoke slowly as he stepped out of his hiding place.

He was pointing his ring and a jade light flashed out, lighting up the whole space, followed by a loud thunderclap that shook the column to its foundation. But this did not drown out the laughter of the ghost who looked exactly like on the day of his death: an old man with a thick beard, dressed in black, wearing a dark cap and his eyes were shining savagely under his heavy eyelids. Cagliostro had encountered many spirits, some so weak that they were no more tangible than a wisp of smoke, and others so full of anger and energy that even the living could see them. All of them, however, were disturbed or terrified by the magic emanating from the ring.

Cosimo Ruggieri was the first to scoff at the demonstration of its power. "You're finally here, magician!" the ghost clapped its bony hands joyously. "Did you like our little treasure hunt?"

"Treasure hunt?" Cagliostro could not believe it.

"You're smart but too proud of it," Ruggieri said. "Those wax dolls were meant for you. My disciples talked a lot about the healing sorcerer who was hovering around Rohan and the court. I knew it was one of the Twelve Immortals. Yes, I know all of you, my dear Count, and you alone have the power to thwart the projects that even Death couldn't stop. So, I decided to kill two birds with one stone."

Hurried footsteps could be heard on the winding staircase just behind Cagliostro. To his surprise he had not heard the door creaking open down below. The magician was caught in a trap! Determined not to go down without a fight, he pointed his ring again and raised his voice, "By the power of the Twelve, I order you to return to the Beyond, Cosimo Ruggieri."

In the magic ray of light the ghost dropped his insolent attitude and twisted in pain. Seeing this, Jeanne de la Motte, who had not budged the entire time, ran screaming at Cagliostro. He pushed her away easily but suddenly felt his arms and shoulders seized by strong hands. Ruggieri's backup had arrived.

The Count desperately kept his ring aimed at the slowly vanishing phantom and shouted at the top of his lungs, "Disappear! By the power of the Twelve!"

At the same time, he was hit in the face. Then a fist landed in his belly, knocking the wind out of him. They threw him on the ground and attacked. In spite of the pain Cagliostro kept his eyes on the ghost. In one last frantic move he shot the jade light at Ruggieri whose shadowy figure was evaporating like poisonous gas in a gust of wind.

"No! Save the Master!" Jeanne de la Motte cried out in despair.

A heavy boot came crashing down on the ring, cutting off the exorcism. The magician howled when he felt two of his fingers broken. Even through the shooting pains he saw the ghost vanish and every ectoplasmic fiber soak into the wet stones.

They yanked him to his feet. The hateful look in the eyes of his attackers left no doubt that they wanted to tear him to pieces. One of them stopped the others when they were about to finish him off.

"That's enough! Master Ruggieri wanted him alive so he could be blamed for the crime of treason."

Cagliostro blinked, not believing his eyes as they stared at the man standing before him. He had seen him with Rohan at the court.

"Baron de Breteuil…"

It really was the Minister of the King's Household, responsible for finding the culprits of the fraud, standing here grinning at him with morbid delight.

"In person, my dear Count, if your title is not stolen. But it doesn't matter, you're nothing now. The Cardinal is finished. As for that stupid Bourbon and his Austrian wench…"

The Baron laughed scornfully. "They will end the Age in purifying violence."

Then he turned to his henchmen, "Take this vermin to the Bastille! He is officially under arrest. You too, Madame, I'm very sorry to say."

"I have my role to play, Baron," Jeanne de la Motte sighed. "But our Master?"

"He knew the risks. Don't worry, though, he will never abandon his disciples. From now on it's up to us to set the wheels of History in motion."

Cagliostro fought against his abductors but there were too many of them and they were too strong. They forced him down the stairs and dragged him outside in the pouring rain. A carriage hitched to four black horses was waiting for them. The magician's cry for help was so unsettling that it froze the blood of his torturers. Then he was thrown head first into his decline.

When tears fell on the yellowed paper Sibilla realized that she was crying. Completely absorbed in her reading she had not noticed that they had arrived at their destination. Graham Carter parked the car in an inner courtyard. Leonardo was watching his friend attentively. With a tissue he wiped the beautiful green eyes of the young lady. Sibilla's distress affected him so much that for once he did not even try to deny the reality of the strange facts he had read at the same time as she did. But always the skeptic he was already imagining alternative theories to explain vengeful ghosts.

Carter kept silent, giving the investigator time to recover from the emotional upheaval caused by the reading. Then in a soft voice he concluded the story:

"The affair of the Queen's necklace was an explosive scandal. Public opinion was persuaded that Marie-Antoinette was involved. You could say, without being completely wrong, that it triggered the French Revolution, just as Cosimo Ruggieri had predicted. Jeanne de la Motte was branded and sentenced to life in prison. But she managed to escape, no doubt with the help of the old mage's disciples, and fled to England. Despite Cagliostro's revelations, Baron de Breteuil cleverly hid his involvement thanks to la Motte's testimony. He escaped the revolution's violence by emigrating to Hamburg and dying there peacefully in 1807. However, he did not manage to completely disgrace his enemy, Cardinal de Rohan. Thanks to Louis, who found the stolen jewels in London, the

Cardinal was acquitted. He, too, had to get far away from the royal court but he died surrounded by friends many years later. The young Louis followed him into exile, then returned to Paris where he barely escaped the guillotine. He had a brilliant political career and died in 1823. As for Cagliostro, after a year in prison they kicked him out of France. Nobody knows if he's really dead but they lost trace of him in the prisons of the Inquisition in San Leo. In many ways the victory of Ruggieri and his accomplices is undeniable."

"What do you want from me?" Sibilla asked. "You want me to make sure that the evil old sorcerer is totally destroyed?"

"In fact, I'd like you to finish the work," Graham Carter said. He handed a briefcase to the pretty Italian. "Here's proof that the disciples of Ruggieri are still plotting dark deeds."

He motioned for her to open it. Sibilla obeyed and right away felt a pit open up in her stomach. Her heart raced when she picked up the little wax doll wound around with a lock of hair. A silver pin was buried in the soft chest.

"We found it near the corpse of a shady English immigrant. A talented forger suspected of imitating the writing of the English Ambassador in Paris on some compromising letters. The subject in question is Sir John Saint-William, currently being interrogated by the French police about an indecent affair of which he's obviously innocent. Other British subjects are likewise worried by the threat."

"What could happen?" Sibilla asked.

Graham Carter lowered his eyes, "A rupture in the friendship between France and England. Pure and simple."

"So, this is where the famous Count lived," Leonardo shuffled on the floorboards to hear them creak. "I was expecting more, uh, space. The Cardinal must have paid him a pretty penny for his services, right?"

"Cagliostro accepted money from the people he helped really just not to offend them," Carter said. "Beyond the splendors of the court he led a modest life made up of study and solitude."

"I know what you're going to tell me next," Leonardo snorted. "*Cagliostro was a great man who preached world peace and love power, blah blah...* I've seen groupies before, in particular on the day I met Sibilla."

Speaking of the she-wolf, the pretty Italian had not said a word since she stepped into the house. She walked from one room to another absorbed in her thoughts. The place was empty and renovated but it still gave off energy, a force that was stronger than others. Sibilla touched the walls. She felt a tiny shock that brought a metallic taste to her tongue and made her hair stand on end.

"He's here. Or least a part of his spirit," she murmured.

"I thought he was haunting the Villa Verucchio." Leonardo was referring to the place where Cagliostro had appeared for the first time. "It really gets around, this ectoplasm."

"I'm not surprised," Carter said. "We always leave a part of ourselves in the places that made us welcome. Hmm... Mr. Verga? I'd like to ask you about the Villa Verucchio. I know a café nearby where the waitresses are particularly fond of Italians."

"Yeah? Well..." Then seeing that his friend obviously wanted to be alone in her spiritual mentor's former lodgings, he shrugged and said, "Why not."

"Great!" Carter's enthusiasm was a little exaggerated. "You can tell me all your rational theories. Sir Wilson has already mentioned it and I'm curious to know your take on all these stories of werewolves and ghosts."

Sibilla did not even turn around to watch them go as Carter's voice faded down the hallway. She knew what the Englishman was expecting of her and she was sure that her invocation was going to be the most moving experience she had ever had in her career as an occult investigator. She, who had never feared facing the most perverse and heinous spirits, could feel her courage melting. She had discovered a vulnerable side of her mentor and she did not want to know it.

Perhaps that was why she ended up kneeling down like a penitent when she invoked Cagliostro's spirit. With her eyes lowered and a knot in her throat, fiddling with the ring bequeathed by the magician, she muttered the words that she had always pronounced with confidence:

"By the seal of the Twelve and the Ring Infinite, I ask the spirit enclosed within these walls to manifest. Show yourself. Speak to me."

The stone carved into the serpent symbol reacted strangely. The magic artifact had always been a jade headlight in the darkest spaces. But here all light was absorbed. The ring sucked in the evening glow of the setting sun, then the whiteness of the walls was swallowed up. Only her body escaped the annihilation. In the blink of an eye Sibilla was surrounded by darkness so thick that even her tight black suit looked bright in the void. However, she also suffered a disturbing transformation: her skin turned white as bone.

Sibilla still felt the floor under her knees and she had to lean on her hands to steady the dizziness washing over her.

When she saw her ring sparkling with a warm, green light she tensed up, on alert.

He appeared then, quite naturally, as if there were only a thin curtain between them. His pearly white hue was nothing like Sibilla's sickly coloring in this dark world. His brown eyes blinked joyously at the sight of her. Cagliostro smiled and motioned to her to get up.

"Why demean yourself in a posture so unworthy of you, my heir?"

Sibilla stood up, afraid that her legs would betray her. But she knew that she was firmly planted on the invisible ground. She stared at her spiritual mentor. His dark eyes emanated so much life that she could not stop a question from slipping out, like a swarm of butterflies out of a greenhouse left open.

"Master, are you dead or just hiding somewhere ready to reveal yourself at last?"

Cagliostro's smile widened. He shook his head slowly like he was dealing with an impatient child, "Death is nothing. And I've lived thousands of lives. It's all a matter of perception."

"I should've figured that you'd speak like the sibyls," the Italian muttered without noting the play on words she unwittingly used. "Since you don't want to answer me directly, I guess I should just get to the point. Master, we think that Cosimo Ruggieri wasn't sent to limbo. I know he was the cause of your unjust downfall and I'd like to avenge you…"

Cagliostro held up a hand to quiet her but the smile was still plastered on his face. "It won't be a matter of vengeance here, my dear child, but a task to fulfill. And it doesn't just concern me but perhaps the whole world. Ruggieri is a powerful entity who has wreaked havoc for thousands of years. He is of my race and not a simple, mortal ectoplasm. Even though you are one of the best magicians that I've seen, without my help you won't be able to defeat the evil being. Are you ready to let me guide you body and soul to victory?"

Sibilla was not sure what this implied. She shuddered and accepted her mentor's request, looking him straight in the eyes.

As his face suddenly turned serious Cagliostro held out his hand to the young lady. She grabbed it. The pact was sealed.

The first drop of rain splashed on the cigarette that Graham Carter was holding between his gloved fingers. A cavernous rumbling filled the sky at the same time as the dark veils of storm clouds.

"Ah, our stay in Paris is starting off great," Leonardo said, wiping off another drop that had fallen on his nose.

"I think it's going to be shorter than planned," Carter replied and he crushed out his cigarette in the ashtray.

The shower rained down on the city. Another clap of thunder, closer this time, made the glasses tinkle. The other customers on the terrace on this warm summer evening hurriedly picked up their belongings grabbed their drinks and went to stay dry inside the café.

"You go back to Miss Drago and I'll pay for us here."

Without waiting for the Italian to answer Carter dove into the bar. Knowing that he was out of sight of the journalist he took out his cell phone. It was time to ready the response team.

Leonardo did not wait for Carter. The rain was pouring down now. In a hopeless attempt to stay dry he ran from one awning to another until he reached Cagliostro's former lodging. He was soaked and shivering. The wind was also picking up, stripping the trees of their leaves and the pedestrians of their umbrellas. Leonardo ran inside and up the stairs, trying to shake the water out of his hair.

"Sibilla!" he called out in front of the door upstairs. "Can I come in? Carter'll back in five minutes."

The door creaked open slowly. Leonardo took a step then stood frozen in the doorway. White candles, hundreds of white candles, flickered on the floor. The apartment, however, was completely empty when they were there before.

Sibilla was sitting cross-legged in the middle of the web of wax and flames. Her eyes were closed and her breathing deep.

"Sibilla," Leonardo whispered slowly, uncertainly, as if she were sleeping.

The young lady opened her eyes and smiled at her friend. Something kept Leonardo from returning that smile. He was not sure but her attitude seemed different. Still, the kind look she gave him was reassuring enough—he had not disturbed her meditation.

The pretty Italian stood up and brushed off her tight-fitting suit. Her hands lingered a little over her round hips well accentuated by the cut of her skirt and her smile got bigger, clearly enjoying the moment.

"I'll never get used to these curves."

"What?"

"Oh, it's nothing… The storm is unleashed, so it's now or never to confront that damned sorcerer!"

Leonardo was totally baffled. What did the storm have to do with Cosimo Ruggieri? Carter hinted at this too when he said their stay in Paris would be shorter than planned as soon as the rain started.

"Maybe we should wait for the Brit…"

"Here I am! I hope I wasn't too long. It's a real flood out there!"

The Englishman was standing just outside the door, as soaked as the journalist. Even with his hair dripping wet he was as calm and cool as usual. But it seemed to Leonardo that he was looking at Sibilla with a certain respect that he had not shown before."

"If you wouldn't mind," he said as he courteously showed the young lady the door.

"We take the car?" Leonardo was hoping.

"Nothing more refreshing than a little rain," Sibilla replied. "Let's go."

Leonardo let his friend go first. Even her walk was different. Her steps were longer and the gentle sway of her hips less pronounced. She and Carter had already reached the stairs so Leonardo had to follow them despite all the questions mulling around in his head.

To keep up appearances he shouted, "What's the storm got to do with Ruggieri?"

The British agent answered, "Cosimo Ruggieri, or rather his ghost, gets his ectoplasmic power from storms. The lightning's magnetism and electricity help him materialize. Lots of witnesses have seen his shadowy figure on nights like this."

Carter had to almost yell to make himself heard over the downpour. Leonardo imagined them on a sinking ship. Everyone had taken cover. The street belonged to them alone. And Sibilla was marching forward as natural as ever. Even Carter was having trouble keeping up with her. However, a strange, wild smile was etched on the formerly impassive face of the Englishman. Leonardo plodded behind them with a very bad feeling that they were heading straight for disaster.

It was all coming together to make this night a hell. Rain gushing from the heavens, transforming the streets into rivers of leaves and garbage. Bright lightning flashing in the black sky. One bolt even striking a tree on the sidewalk. The journalist jumped aside and screamed. Sibilla and Carter were still striding onward, unfazed.

When they finally arrived at the square where the Bourse du Commerce stood, they were already waiting for them. Six people joined them. Four men and two women who must have come from all corners of the globe to form this motley group.

The tallest of them was a Sikh wearing a wet turban. He said to Carter, "The storm's here just like we expected. It's time to go into action. They're about to start the invocation ceremony."

"Perfect, Singh. And we'll use it to help us. This is Sibilla. She's accepted to be the receptacle of our own master."

The men and women surrounding them suddenly looked like they were struck dumb.

"Master Cagliostro, is it really you?" a young black man sputtered. "It's a great honor."

Sibilla turned to him with the same kind but unusual smile on her charming lips, "Please, drop the formalities. We're brothers in arms here tonight. And it's also an honor for me to be side by side with such brave men and women."

It was not the clap of thunder that made Leonardo jump but rather the sudden realization of what was happening to his friend. He swung around and grabbed Carter's drenched coat, "You brainwashed her with your nonsense! She thinks she's possessed by that stupid sorcerer! You hypnotized her!"

Leonardo was shaking him but the Englishman kept his cool. He took off a glove and put a bare hand on the Italian's fist. When his hand suddenly felt burned the journalist let go. The skin where Carter had touched him was red and smoking.

"It was only a little warning," the agent said, taking off his other glove. "Tomorrow there will be no trace of my contact. And to answer your passionate accusations, no, we didn't hypnotize her. Cagliostro is really here with us tonight. I knew what his heir would have to do but I was sure Sibilla would let his soul and consciousness borrow her mortal coil."

Leonardo wanted to protest, to rant and rave against the trickery, but he was fascinated by the Englishman's hands. They were glowing like red-hot glass. Purple and yellow tattoos snaked over his skin. The rain evaporated on contact.

They hypnotized me too, the journalist thought in a panic.

"Look!"

Sibilla, or rather the part of her that thought it was Cagliostro, was pointing to the top of the dark column next to the round building of the Bourse du Commerce. At the top there were orange lights battling against the electric shine of the storm. Figures were dancing before a fire being threatened by the rain.

"Cover me!"

The young lady ran to the building, her high heels clicking and splashing over the wet cobblestones. Suddenly a brighter flame sprang out from the top of the column and a red lightning bolt shot out at Sibilla. But a crackling ball of fire crashed into the lethal ray before it could reach the pretty Italian. She ran faster and got to the door at the foot of the column.

"Did you see that?" Leonardo's eyes were popping out of his head. "I think they've got rocket launchers!"

"I saw it because I was the one who stopped it. But it wasn't a rocket."

White steam was coming off Carter's glowing hands. Leonardo stood gasping.

"Stop looking so surprised and take the gun out of the holster, Verga. I can't give it to you because I'll heat it up. Protect your friend. I'll stay here and get them busy. Go!"

Leonardo took Carter's gun and ran to join Sibilla. His logical mind was running wild trying to find explanations for the chaos. Lightning ripped through the clouds, joining with the bright, colorful bolts of energy that were flying through the air. The Italian journalist barely saw the figures on the ground dodging the fireballs launched from the Medici column. Several times he felt the heat go whistling by like fireworks. Yes, that was it! They were fireworks!

Partly reassured by his theory Leonardo paid no attention to the prickling sensation that tickled his neck and fingertips. He gave no thought to the smell of ether mixed with ozone and sulfur. Under different circumstances Sibilla would have explained that this was all normal when magic was being used.

Speaking of the beauty, when Leonardo finally reached the door his friend had already started up the stairs. Her heels echoed in rhythm on the stone steps. Someone pushed him gently through the doorway. Even in the dark Leonardo recognized Sikh. An Asian woman and a black man followed them in.

"With all this Harry Potter madness on the top of a protected monument, we're going to end up in jail," the Italian grumbled.

The three others ignored his fussing. They were already climbing the stairs. All of a sudden the whole column trembled and pieces of stone came tumbling down. Right away Leonardo thought of Sibilla, in danger in a body she could not control, and he immediately ran after the other three. Halfway up a man jumped out screaming at him and grabbed him by the throat. In the dark the reporter could not see the attacker's face, but without thinking he stuck the barrel of the gun in the guy's ribs and pulled the trigger. A yellow flash revealed a figure wrapped in a black woolen robe who fell backward, hit the wall and dropped head over heels down the stairs. Without turning around the Italian kept climbing, but his stomach turned as he tried to forget that his survival instinct had just killed a man.

When he finally reached the top of the stairs his lungs were hurting. He was not used to running up hundreds of steps and his body was making it painfully clear that he was out of shape. But he had no time to listen to it: if it looked like war on the ground, at the top of the column it was the Apocalypse.

An infernal storm had unleashed on the summit. Leonardo had to shield his eyes to see what was happening. Bodies were lying around, mangled or horribly burned. One of Carter's partners, the young black man, was sitting in a corner holding his bloody shoulder. The Asian woman was protecting him against men armed with swords dressed in the same outfit as Leonardo's attacker. She was thrashing the air in front of her with long, sharp fingernails. The tall Sikh was standing over a robed man on the ground. The hood had been knocked back, revealing the ruddy face possibly of a person of note. And in the middle of a tornado of flashes, rain and smoke was Sibilla. Her hair was whipping her pretty face. She stared with cold determination at the dark, snake-like figure that was twisting around menacingly above her, ready to strike. A black face was grinning at the top of the wicked twister, the face of a bearded old man with eyes glowing with hate.

Leonardo rubbed his eyes. The effects of the hypnosis would not go away. But he had enough presence of mind to raise his gun when one of the hooded men came at him with a sword. This time the bullet went through the attacker's hand and he dropped his weapon.

"Nobody move! I've got a gun!" the journalist shouted.

The Sikh and the clawed Asian woman used the surprise announcement to overpower the evil henchmen. Now it was a duel to the death between the ghost of the old sorcerer and the possessed magician.

With a quick lunge the monstrous specter wrapped around Sibilla and squeezed her in its black, vaporous coils.

"Cagliossstrooo," the Ruggieri-snake hissed as it crushed her. "I defeated you in the past and I will beat you again. Then nothing will stop the reign of my black magic. The leaders of the world will be my devoted disciples."

"Your disciples are just blind and stupid puppets, you fiend!" Cagliostro/Sibilla cried out. "They know nothing good or just. Without their puppet master your disciples will collapse."

With these words the jade ring shot out a blinding light that enveloped Ruggieri's snake body as it started fuming and crackling. The ghost opened its huge jaws full of fangs and screeched, shaking with rage and pain and wild panic.

"No! How can you hurt me like this? I'm stronger than before! I put all my power into the lightning!"

"I can destroy you because this time we are two against you. This body belongs to my most devoted heir. Our spirits and energies are united against you. By the power of the Twelve and the Infinite Ring, Cosimo Ruggieri, demonic creature, I order you to go back to the hell that spawned you!"

"Be struck down, stupid magician!" the ghost yelled back.

And at the same time two lightning bolts flashed. One from the sky and the other from Cagliostro's ring. Everyone watching the scene was thrown to the ground by the shock when the two forces collided. The whirlwind around Sibilla and Ruggieri transformed into a blinding maelstrom of pure energy. When the light finally faded everyone saw the body of the magician glowing with a green aura. The explosion had slightly singed her hair and clothes but she was more beautiful than ever. Ruggieri's ghost, on the contrary, was in miserable shape, its ethereal flesh was sizzling and falling off its ophidian body. It had lost the duel.

The Italian only had to point her ring and when she spoke there were two voices coming out of her mouth, her own and Cagliostro's, "Goodbye sorcerer!"

The purifying ray from the magic seal wrapped the ghost in green light. The ectoplasmic remains peeled off Ruggieri and were blown away by the wind. Phantom cries of pain faded as the creature crumbled. He who was once the personal astrologer of Catherine de Medici was gone, swept away in the gusts of wind and rain. One final howl rolled around the survivors of the battle before disappearing forever.

The surviving henchmen groaned pathetically as they watched the black particles dissolve in the puddles. The Sikh and his two partners looked up triumphantly at the rain, happy with this outcome.

Leonardo saw Sibilla wobbling and caught her just in time before she dropped to the ground.

Sibilla was floating in serene bliss in the middle of a rejuvenating night. She did not know how long she had been cradled in this sweet drowsiness but she was enjoying the rest because even if Cagliostro had been in control she had still been aware of what was happening.

She was not alone.

"Elena Drago."

She opened her eyes reluctantly. Count Cagliostro's face was smiling over her. A sweet but sad smile, marked with regret at having used his heir like a common tool. He took her hand and touched the ring on her finger. The snake pierced with an arrow sparkled briefly for an instant.

"I'm so glad to know that my heritage is in your possession. Take care of it like you've always done. Lead your life the best you can. I'm proud of you. Maybe our paths will cross again. Goodbye, my child."

The Count kissed Sibilla's forehead then disappeared. The young lady reached out, grabbed empty air and cried. She had not told her mentor that she forgave him for using her as a flesh puppet. She had not told him how grateful she was for the precious knowledge he had given her.

She let her tears flow and the wet contact on her cheeks woke her up, this time for good. She blinked, trying to get her eyes used to the daylight flooding the room. She was lying on a bed and a breeze felt cold on her tears. Graham Carter had opened a window to smoke without waking the sleeper. He put out his cigarette in the ashtray he held in his gloved hand when he saw her waking up.

"Sibilla, what a relief!"

Carter sat at her bedside. His usually impassive face was exuding joy. His superficial scratches and burns managed to camouflage his English butler look.

"Leonardo?"

He nodded at the journalist sleeping in an armchair, curled up in a way that was going to make him hurt when he woke up.

"He hasn't left for the two days you've been asleep. We've been facing off like porcelain dogs for something to do. He's really mad at me for what happened to you."

"It was a trying ordeal... and kind of devastating," Sibilla said.

She pulled up the covers, fearing and hoping at the same time that it was Carter who had changed her into the silk nightgown that felt so soft against her skin. But she had one important question to ask.

"Are you really an Interpol agent, Graham? I saw why you never take your gloves off and what you and your friends are capable of."

"I belong to a special branch of Interpol. We deal with investigations that involve the occult and black magic, just like you. My colleagues and I have special talents. Mine is the gift of pyrokinesis, something I've had since I was fourteen. Interpol set up this section at the same time that a manuscript was found in monastery dating to the 18th century. It was a kind of moral treatise on the good use of magic. We called our section after the author of this work. He's become a kind of spiritual guide."

"Let me guess," Sibilla's heart was racing. "You're called the Cagliostro Section."

Carter nodded with a smile, "And we are his humble disciples."

Fan Mail

A huge bag plopped down on the desk of Leonardo Verga. "Hey, watch out!" the journalist shouted.

"Very zorry, sir, but thiz thing weighs a ton," the mail clerk replied. "All thiz is for Sibilla."

Before Leonardo could say a word the rude creature had scurried out of the newsroom, grumbling to himself the whole way.

Zeno Arbini, a short guy in holey sneakers and a worn polo shirt, only at *Flash* for about three months now, leaned over the bag, his eyes sparkling with curiosity. At the moment he was editing the short articles covering local news but Leonardo knew that the kid dreamed of landing a better paying, more rewarding assignment like his experienced colleagues.

"So, this girl's a star or what," the kid said. "And all because of her fairytales."

Even if Leonardo shared his skepticism he felt obligated to defend his friend. "I used to say the same thing, you know, once upon a time. Then I went on a few investigations with Sibilla and even with my doubts about the authenticity of the weird things we've witnessed, I know she isn't messing with her readers."

"Wow! And you know her well?"

Leonardo bit his tongue. He had sworn to never reveal any compromising information about Sibilla. He was about to tell Zeno to go back to his squashed dogs when the editor-in-chief's office door opened, letting out a cloud of smoke. A brown-haired head came peeking through the toxic mist and two piercing eyes scanned the newsroom.

"Verga! Come into my office and don't break your back with that mail bag."

Leonardo felt the weight of the world come crashing down on his shoulders. The world plus the load he had to carry into the office of Maria Carpi, their smoking, venerated, grand poobah.

Zeno stood there with his mouth open, apparently waiting for an answer to his question.

"Go back to writing instead swallowing flies," Leonardo said before lifting up the burlap sack. Aye! Forty-five pounds! At least!

When Leonardo came grumbling into the office Maria Carpi closed the door.

"Put that on the table, Verga, and give me a hand with these letters."

Leonardo raised his eyebrows, "Don't you think I have something better to do than pick through the advice column."

The editor blew a huge puff of smoke out of her nose. Her angry bull imitation was so expressive that Leonardo figured it wise to simmer down.

"All right. Anyway, I've already finished the first page of my 100-page article for tomorrow."

Carpi opened the bag. A flood of colored envelopes poured out. Without a moment's hesitation the editor-in-chief started examining them one by one.

"What exactly are we looking for?" Leonardo asked, picking up a handful of letters, all addressed to Sibilla.

"Red envelopes with a heart-shaped stamp. The address is written in gold ink."

"At least it's specific."

After ten minutes the pile of mail that did not meet their requirements was up to their knees. But no envelope fit Carpi's description. The editor shook the bag upside down. She had chain-smoked at least three cigarettes and the ashes from the last had fallen on her blouse.

"Nothing? Maybe he finally got it?"

"Who's he?" Leonardo asked.

"For two months someone's been writing love letters to Sibilla. I didn't pay attention at first, figured it was some romantic fool. Then they started coming in like the proverbial hotcakes. Our jilted lover started sending in three a day, more and more impassioned, but really more and more disturbing."

"How's that?"

Maria Carpi opened a drawer in her desk and handed Leonardo a package of red envelopes.

"Take a look."

He read through the letters one by one:

"Sibilla, my love, queen of the strange, your last case left me breathless. I want you to be mine. Such great things we could accomplish together. I'd be the happiest creature in the world if you'd answer me in your next article…

"To the prettiest, bravest journalist, I throw myself at your feet. You solved the case of the ghost of Saint Mark's Basilica with such intelligence…

"My beloved Sibilla, you would make me the happiest of poor wretches if you would deign to answer me in your next article…

"My love, my Sibilla, you still haven't answered me and I can't sleep. You're making a big mistake…

"When will you stop making me suffer?

"Girl, is this how you thank your most devoted reader?

"I will kill you! I will cut your throat on the altar of Mammon, you harlot!

"Divine Sibilla, sorry for what I wrote, I'm just a worm enlightened by a fiery-haired star, a sun to which you owe your sweet name: Elena. My sublime Elena."

Leonardo could not believe it. He read this last letter over and over and sputtered, "He knows who she is."

"Exactly," Carpi said. "Even after everything we've done to protect Sibilla's anonymity, this… sicko managed to discover a secret that I'm hiding as carefully as my birthday."

Leonardo was careful not to blurt out that he knew her birthday. "Does Sibilla know about all this?"

"Of course. I've been giving her all the letters, harmless or not."

"And today, nothing…"

"I don't know if I should be worried or relieved. Maybe the article we wrote to him paid off."

"You mean the one next to Sibilla's column a couple days ago? I was curious about it."

"That's it, the one talking about stalkers, guys falling in love with celebrities and harassing them. I pointed out the excellent police work and possible prison time."

Maria Carpi bent down to pick up a piece of mail and put it back in the bag. "Now that you know, I think I'll let you go back to the work you didn't have time to finish. But watch out, keep your eyes and ears open. I smell a rat here. I think there's a leak at *Flash*."

"At least I'm not a suspect."

The telephone on the desk rang. The editor-in-chief snatched it up. "Hi, Sibilla. Leonardo and I were just talking about you."

Carpi's face suddenly turned gray as ashes. Her umpteenth cigarette dropped out of her mouth and fell on the carpet."

"Uh… hold on, I'm putting you on speaker," she muttered.

Sibilla's voice came ringing out, clear and strong, "Hey Leo. I was just telling Maria that I got letters from my mysterious fan *at home*. I'd be glad to read them together if you want."

"OK," her friend growled thinking of the alarming messages. "Don't move. I'll be there in a jiffy."

As soon as they hung up the journalist ran to his car and sped through the streets, ignoring the honking horns and traffic cops who recorded his license plate to send out a fat fine. He skid to a stop in front of Sibilla's gorgeous home and jumped out of the car. He gritted his teeth when he saw that the front gate was unlocked, but without stopping he dashed up the walkway and rang the bell. His friend opened the door almost immediately. Dressed in a long, purple, flowery dress and barefoot, she looked perfectly relaxed. The ring with the weird jade stone that she never took off sparkled on the middle finger of her right hand and her long, red hair shimmered around her calm face.

"Don't you even ask if a lunatic is at the door?" Leonardo blurted out as a greeting.

"Hello," is all the young lady said. "The fact that you're worried about me doesn't excuse you from being polite. Come in."

Leonardo followed her, a little ashamed at his bluntness. Frightening, primitive statues stood guard in the hallway. If only these exotic talismans were real...

Sibilla brought Leonardo into her bright living room that was always cheerful despite the assorted combination of African masks and astrological maps, the odd engravings on the walls, the shelves full of old, bound books, the heavy candelabra of tarnished silver and the clearly ancient book stand on which sat a huge grimoire whose decorative script had faded with time. A tray with fresh lemonade and two glasses was waiting for them on the mahogany table sculpted with oriental dragons. And next to the drinks was a pile of red envelopes.

Leonardo recognized them thanks to Carpi's description. "You got all those this morning?"

"My secret admirer was very excited," Sibilla replied calmly. "Probably the joy of having found where I live."

She was taking things with surprising serenity. The letters, however, were not just love letters from a bashful suitor. The stranger had threatened her for real. Leonardo picked up an envelope from the pile and read the outrageous prose.

"Elena, my beloved, I finally know where you dwell. You can no longer escape me. You will be mine. Forever."

"He wants to kill you, that's obvious," Leonardo was boiling with anger.

"Indeed," Sibilla said. "The other letters there promise me a gruesome end. I'm bound to be sacrificed to Mammon in two days time."

She poured some lemonade and offered it to Leonardo. He paid no attention to it.

"What?"

"Take the drink and please sit down," she pleaded gently.

"How can you be so calm? A maniac is out to kill you!"

"We've seen worse."

"This threat is much more real than your ghosts and werewolves. We have to call the police."

Sibilla shook her head, "My anonymous admirer wouldn't like that. Besides, he might be a creature of flesh and blood but he uses black magic. So, we're still dealing with the occult—my specialty."

The look Leonardo gave her said all that was needed for her to explain.

"I had a weird feeling when I touched the mail for the first time and then he started talking about Mammon. So I analyzed the paper and ink with a divining pendulum and my knowledge of alchemy... quite meager I have to admit."

"Zeno Arbini, the little intern, was right: it's all fairy tales," Leonardo grumbled.

"But I don't write fiction. Anyway, I found out that the ink is a mixture of pure gold, linseed oil and a little blood. The paper is hand colored with a purple dye blended with red rose petals. Well, magicians always make their ink and paper or parchment themselves. And as for this Mammon I'm supposed to be sacrificed to, it's one of the seven Princes of Hell."

"That's great. A crazy fanatic of black magic and infernal demons. I feel so much better. And what's all this magic ink and paper supposed to do?"

"Love charms. If I answered the letters through my column at *Flash*, my heart would've been stolen and I would've offered my throat willingly to the sacrificial knife. That's why he was so upset by my ignoring him."

Leonardo could not decide if he should feel relieved by Sibilla's calm or disturbed by the obscurity that she was once again delving into. That a maniac believed in black magic was one thing but that she apparently took it seriously was something else. It was nice that she felt able to confront the madman but her little pendulums and magic ring were not going to be much help when her dangerous fan came knocking at the door in two days.

"OK, you don't want to call the police, fine, but I'm staying here to protect you," the journalist declared and jumped to his feet.

"As you wish," Sibilla said. "One of my friends is coming from Chicago to keep me company as well. The trip was planned a while ago and I didn't have the heart to cancel it."

"Not too smart of you. The whole story might frighten them."

Sibilla shrugged her shoulders and smirked, "Maybe not."

A loud noise made them jump. One of the windowpanes in the living room was cracked and blood was trickling down the glass. Sibilla and Leonardo went out into the yard, walked around the house and found a dead dove, its head smashed in. The reporter picked up the little corpse but dropped it right away, screaming in disgust: wriggling among the soft, white feathers, making them twitch, was a horde of maggots. The foul scavengers seemed to be multiplying exponentially in the remains. As the two horrified friends looked on, the dove was picked clean in a matter of seconds.

Encaged in the frail ribs was a blood-red origami, folded into the shape of a heart. Sibilla bent down to pick up this new letter delivered in the most unusual way. Leonardo was dumbfounded trying in vain to understand the weird phenomenon.

The same gold letters were written in capitals on the paper:

"Dear sweet Elena, this is a warning. If you don't answer me you will lose something precious."

"Obviously," Sibilla said, "he's growing impatient."

"But… but it's disgusting," her friend almost choked. "I don't know how this psychopath managed to send this crazy thing but he succeeded in scaring the crap out of me."

"I admit that he's pretty good at magic. And my impending sacrifice will only help increase his powers. Or the power of his master, Mammon."

For the first time Sibilla's Olympian calm seemed to falter. Her hands were trembling slightly. This new show of force by her mysterious fan was very impressive.

Leonardo was glad he did not believe in all that nonsense. It was up to him now to show a cool head. He put his hands on his friend's shoulders and said, "Listen, I'm not going to let anyone hurt you. I won't let you out of my sight. I'll watch over you day and night if necessary, but this creep will have to deal with me if he comes anywhere near you, okay?"

"Oh, Leo," Sibilla sighed, "I don't know if you're really up to it. There are forces in the world that are beyond you. Your courage alone isn't enough."

"Nonsense! You said yourself that we've gotten out of worse scrapes, right?"

The beautiful redhead smiled and nodded.

"Right. So, the two of us have to kick Mr. Heart Letter's ass. I'll go back home and get some stuff. You go back inside and lock the doors. Booby-trap the place if you have to. When I come back I'll ring and go stand by the living room window so you know it's me."

Sibilla patted his arm. "Very good. I'll do as you say. I know I can't get rid of you anyway."

"I'll be back within the hour."

Leonardo turned around and ran to the gate. Sibilla walked around her house, thinking, gripping the little red heart in her fist. When she reached the heavy front door she heard tires screeching to a halt. Then screams. Prompted by a terrible intuition she ran into the street.

Her friend was lying unconscious on the ground. His head was in a puddle of blood and one of his legs was twisted so horribly it was painful to look at. A young couple was already next to him giving him first aid. Dark skid marks scarred the road. Farther along a car had stopped with its front bumper dented. The driver was out of the car, terrified, a hand over his mouth and his eyes popping out.

Sibilla wanted to yell out for Leonardo but the shock had frozen her throat shut. The red paper dropped out of her numb fingers.

...If you don't answer me you will lose something precious...

When Maria Capri got to the emergency room Leonardo was already in the recovery room. Sibilla was waiting in the corridor, pacing back and forth. Her face lit up when she saw the editor-in-chief.

"Well?" is all Carpi said.

"It's not as serious as I feared. He had a broken knee and a concussion but no edema. They're going to keep him a few days for observation to make sure there're no internal injuries. But even after the fracture heals it'll be a long recovery."

The editor took out a toothpick from her raincoat and bit down on it fiercely. "I knew we should've taken that sicko's threats seriously. I heard from the police that the driver was completely sober. A university professor with a clean record."

"I know the guy's innocent. He stayed there till the ambulance came and looked more shocked than me. This is no simple stalker fan, Maria. I saw what he's capable of and I'm going to have to fight him with the darkest means at my disposal."

"If there's anything I can do, Sibilla."

"Yes, you can publish an article I'll send you for tomorrow. Right now I have to get back home. I have a friend coming in tonight."

Maria Carpi was astonished. "You really think this is the time to be visiting friends?"

"It's a friend who will be a great help to me but I still need you. Here, take this."

The magician handed her a small, green, velvet bag.

"And follow my instructions very carefully."

As promised the suitor went into action the next night. Horror films often set the scene with a pale moon, in all its fullness, rising in the sky to better illuminate the bogeyman. This night, however, was as black as ink. The nocturnal pollution in Milan obscured all the stars and even the moon had waned into obscurity.

A beautiful night for anyone attracted to the powers of the dark.

The car with blacked-out windows stopped in a dark alley right near Sibilla's house. Three figures got out. Two of them were wide-shouldered, bald and thick-necked. The third shady character wore a long, tailored coat and his distinguished bearing set him off from the two gorillas. But his long hands could not stop fidgeting. Without checking to see if his companions were following he strode straight for the house. The two tough guys rambled stiffly behind him. The streets were deserted. Night owls rarely ventured into residential neighborhoods like this, especially when it was late on a chilly night.

The man in the elegant coat stopped in front of the wrought-iron gate. A beautifully manicured hand hovered over the handle but would not touch it. The gorillas waited patiently. Their boss stepped aside and said, "Eh 'ad, break it!"

One of the brutes stepped in and grabbed the latch. There was a smell of ozone in the air and his palm sizzled. Keeping his blank look the giant twisted off the lock and the gate creaked opened. At the same time, the brute's hand crumbled to dust.

The elegant man nodded. "She put a spell on it, of course… but this magic only works on creatures of flesh and blood. Eh 'ad, you go first. Shnyim, bring up the rear."

The two goons started wobbling forward, still without a word. Eh 'ad did not even look at the little pile of dust that had once been his hand. The trio went up the alley in silence. They went through the same process as the gate: on his master's order Eh 'ad broke the handle on the huge door. Smoke, a little magic sparkle and the brute's flesh burned to ashes and fell off. Still staring blankly the giant pushed the door open with his stump. The well-dressed man snickered when he sniffed the air: all her magic for nothing. The beauty was at his mercy! She had finally answered his letters. She had taken her time but it was all right. He should have taken out her little friend at the beginning. He felt around in his coat pocket. The article crinkled in his fingers. He had read it and reread it until he knew it by heart.

"Let me start this column with a personal message. I don't usually address individual readers but this one has to know that he's been in my thoughts. His letters, his persistence got to me. And as a result of certain events I can ignore him no longer. I realized how your determination and stubbornness pushed you farther into the domain we are both interested in. And now I entreat you: stop before it's too late! You cannot yet handle the risks you are running, the dark territories you are exploring. I know there is still time. You can still turn back. For your salvation."

"Heehee…" He giggled again. It turned out so well but the stupid girl! He certainly was not going to turn back now when everything was coming together. He ordered Eh 'ad to go first and he followed him down the big hallway.

A door was ajar and a golden, flickering light filtered through the crack, inviting them to enter. Cautiously, the intruder pushed in poor Eh 'ad who seemed completely unaware of being used as cannon fodder. But this time when he pushed the door open the hinges creaked softly without any sparkling magic and the obsessed fan could look freely around the room lit by tarnished silver candelabras. African fetishes, unsettling paintings and eyes painted on a big sarcophagus propped against the wall across the room, everything looked like it was dancing and trembling in the flickering candlelight. And sitting calmly in the middle of the motley decorated room, on a wooden chair whose high back was carved with disturbing faces, his beautiful, redheaded Elena was waiting for him. Dressed in emerald green leather she seemed to be having trouble keeping her eyes open and her head was bobbing up and down. A small pistol in her limp hand shined in the light.

Seeing her at his mercy the fan finally gave in to a fit of loud, victorious laughter.

"At last! My dark princess, you are mine!"

"What… what?"

The fan knelt down at the feet of his prey and put a trembling finger on her rosy lips that were trying in vain to ask a question that he could guess.

"Shush, my love, don't say anything. By answering my enchanted letters you finally surrendered your will to mine. You tried my patience but, yes, it's over now. We are together at last."

He kissed Sibilla on the mouth and held back a sob. He finally had her and it was best that they separate. How sad! If only she had answered him sooner, they could have spent months together. But tonight was the very night appointed by Mammon for the sacrifice. And the books were explicit: to get the eternal treasure the Suitor had to separate himself from what he cherished most. He kissed Sibilla one last time and stood up.

"I'm going to prepare the offering," he whispered affectionately. "You did well to sit here like this. It makes the scene all the more touching."

He grabbed the bag that Shnyim was carrying. With half-closed eyes Sibilla watched the ritual. She noticed that the two goons were really clay golems. She should have been scared because this showed the extent of the madman's talent but the spell keeping her paralyzed also numbed her emotions. The fan took the gun from her hand and put a crown of red roses entwined with gold wire on her red hair.

"It's real gold so don't drop it."

Then the Suitor drew a circle around the chair with ashes. He had burned cash and peonies. Love and money combined. Tonight he was going to renounce one to get lots of the other. Then he took out a strange object from the bag: a knife with a short blade engraved with rose-shaped symbols. He tilted back Sibilla's head and held up the weapon.

"Mammon, my master, my guide, accept this offering. Because we cannot honor two masters at the same time I renounce Eros to live in luxury. Because everything can't be bought I renounce the riches of the soul. Because I can't have eternal life I will know the absolute joy of a wealthy life. Take this mortal female and bless me!"

At the moment when the Suitor brought down his ceremonial knife, there was a loud bang and something weird struck his wrist. The weapon fell to the floor. The man cried out in pain and looked around for the attacker. A young woman looking like Bela Lugosi was standing in the sarcophagus whose cover had slammed into the wall. The boomerang that had hit the murderer's arm whistled back into her hand. She was wearing a black suit molded to her athletic, statuesque body. Her eyes were hidden behind dark glasses and her long, black hair was tied into a tight ponytail that cascaded down her back.

"You want to cut your ladylove's throat on your first date?" she said with a strong American accent. "A real love-hate relationship you got there!"

The Suitor's cheeks turned red with rage. How dare this stupid girl interrupt him during a primordial ritual and then make fun of him! "Eh 'ad! Shnyim! Destroy her!"

The two golems obeyed the order and threw their massive bodies at the intruder. They were fast despite their size but the mysterious young woman was as agile as a cat. She dodged the first clay giant, jumped on the other's massive shoulders and gave him a strong, swift kick to the neck, which sent him hurtling into the open sarcophagus. The ancient casket and the golem crashed to the floor. The strange woman landed gracefully a few feet from the furious fan. He had picked up his knife and was already threatening Sibilla again. The beautiful brunette disarmed him again, chopping his wrist. The man screamed in pain and anger.

"Red is definitely not your color, Romeo. Oh, let me introduce myself—Phenix at your service."

The Suitor only stamped the ground in rage. The young woman was disappointed. So, her reputation as a tough crime fighter had not reached Italy yet? Criminals usually turn pale when they hear her name.

Too bad, but I'll still ruin his life.

With a flick of her foot she sent the knife skidding under the mahogany desk. Then she turned to Sibilla, who was still struggling under the spell, but the two golems were back on the offensive. She barely dodged a big, whirling arm by jumping to the side when Eh 'ad rushed at her. In his excitement he crashed into a bookshelf that buried him under a pile of yellowing tomes.

"Sorry, Sibilla," Phenix smiled humbly. "I promise to clean up afterward."

Since Shnyim was coming at her again, the pretty brunette ducked and rolled between his legs. In the meantime the Suitor was crawling under the desk looking for his precious knife, so tricky Phenix jumped on top of the huge piece of furniture and started dancing. The fan knew what was about to happen and yelled, trying to get out, but it was too late: Shnyim pounced on the woman in black with all his might. Phenix rolled over the back of the monster as he fell onto the desk and the Suitor yelped helplessly, crushed under the combined weight of the furniture and his artificial servant.

Phenix burst out laughing with her hands on her hips, "I wonder who's the bigger creep, these soulless gorillas or their master."

"Phe… Phe…"

Sibilla tried to get up but her muscles felt like marshmallows. Phenix rushed over, took the gold garland off her head and looked at her straight in the eyes. "Try not to forget: it's okay because it's you but I'd rather just stay friends."

With that she kissed her friend on the lips before backing away from the sight of Eh 'ah shaking paper and parchment off his shoulders. The golem ran at Phenix with as much grace as a steam engine. Sibilla dizzily caught a strong whiff of earth as the monster sped by her. She was slowly regaining her senses but the result was the unpleasant sensation of pins and needles in all her limbs. Thousands of burning specks along her arms and legs and even behind her eyelids. The spell was lifting like a veil of toxic mist.

And now that the redhead was back to herself she was going to help her friend who had finished sacking her living room and was now running down the hallway with Eh 'ad hot on her heels. But a groan behind her meant she had another clay robot to deal with first. Shnyim was slowly getting up from the wreckage of the magnificent mahogany desk.

Half crushed under the debris the jilted Suitor was whining in pain, "Shnyim, get me out of here."

Just when the brute was stretching out his huge paw to help his master, Sibilla strode over to them smiling. Shining on his flat forehead were Hebrew letters forming the word *emet*, which meant *Truth*. The Suitor was certainly gifted but his art of giving life to inanimate objects still required old magic that the young lady was familiar with. She reached out and wiped off the first letter, significantly changing the word from *emet* to *met*: *Death*.

The artificial man crumbled to dust with a weird, rattling sigh, leaving nothing but red powder and empty clothes behind.

"Shnyim!" the Suitor choked out. He tried to crawl out of the debris. He stopped on seeing Sibilla's ring pointed at him and glowing menacingly.

"It's… It's not…"

"Possible?" the magician kindly finished his sentence for him. "And yet… I still don't know your name and so you're still one up on me there but I think you're still a neophyte in magic. Gifted, sure, but you can't have been practicing for more than… a few months?"

"Two years!" the Suitor squealed, grimacing in pain as he sat up. His shoulder was visibly dislocated but Sibilla kept her eyes and Cagliostro's ring trained on him.

"But I thought you were in my power," the guy moaned. "How'd you do it?"

"It took a simple kiss," Sibilla answered. "Just a selfless gesture like that was written in the book of spells written by the historian Jules Michelet in secret. Yes, Jules Michelet was adept in magic and had tried to reeducate magicians with his excellent work, which I highly recommend. That's how I was able to break the evil web you wove with your letter bombs. Against the selfish, possessive love in your heart I set forth the sincere love of Phenix."

Of course the beautiful Italian and her crime-fighting friend had not come up with this strategy trusting only on their hearts. All their research to trap the Suitor relied on theories gotten from dusty old books. The only reliable part of the plan was the American's skill in martial arts to fight the inhuman brutes.

Speaking of Phenix, a dreadful ruckus made the magician clench her jaws. "I have to leave you and go save my house from my clumsy friend."

"Sure, great," he snickered, "leave me alone so I can esca…"

A jade light suddenly shot out of Cagliostro's ring and struck the Suitor between the eyes. He sat there frozen, an expression of surprise had replaced his sneer.

"I didn't say I'd leave you willing and able," Sibilla said before running into the hallway.

Everything was topsy-turvy. The primitive statues were lying on the floor and holes the size of giant fists riddled the walls. At the foot of the grand staircase, the twisted body of Eh 'ad was trying to shake loose of Phenix who was beating it with a huge mask from Papua New Guinea. Pieces of clay were flying all over the place.

"Well, you're finally here," the crime fighter said as she smashed her improvised weapon into the golem's jaw. "I don't know what your lover boy gave this guy for breakfast but he's invulnerable."

"Magic and a lot of love," Sibilla answered.

She walked over to the golem on the ground. He must have fallen down the stairs while chasing Phenix because some steps were cracked and his legs were broken. But it was not enough to kill him, of course…

As she did with Shnyim, Sibilla wiped away the first letter carved into the golem's forehead. Within seconds he disintegrated into clay dust leaving nothing but clothes.

Phenix whistle in appreciation. "They die like the aliens in The Invaders. A once-over with the vacuum and not a trace!"

"We'll need a lot more than a vacuum to clean up this mess," Sibilla hissed.

"Don't get in a fit," Phenix waved her hand casually, "I've got enough money to buy you two new villas. Even Bruce Wayne is jealous of my fortune. Did you abandon your groupie?"

The groupie was still under hypnosis from Cagliostro's ring when the two young ladies got back to the ruined living room. Half-sprawled over the former desk, his shoulder hanging loose, he was rocking back and forth with drool in the corners of his mouth. Phenix figured it was just desserts for what he had done to her friend.

"What's the plan?" the crime fighter asked.

She already had her own idea after her years of chasing down all kinds of criminals, but the decision belonged to Sibilla.

"I'm going to interrogate him, for starters, then make him forget about me and everything he knows about magic. For that I prepared a little concoction that the magicians of old called the drink of Lotus-eaters."

"Pretty name, very poetic. Does it keep?"

"Yes, but it has to stay below fifty degrees. Help me tie our friend to this chair, then go and look for a small, blue bottle in the fridge, please."

Once he was tightly bound the Suitor woke up with another flash from the ring. He shook all over and cried out in pain because of his deformed shoulder.

"Don't worry," Sibilla told him, "we'll take you to the hospital when we're done with you."

"You've got a heart of gold,' the Suitor muttered. "An angel. Worthy of all my praise and love! That's why Mammon would've rejoiced if I spilled your blood and deprived myself of your sweet presence. What a wonderful sacrifice you would've made, my Elena!"

"We don't always get what we want in life, Mr..."

"Mr. Your Greatest Fan!"

"That doesn't help me."

"He's called Araldo Arbini," Phenix strutted in with a bottle in one hand and a wallet in the other. "I searched him when he tied him up."

The Suitor finally given a name started spitting like a cat sprayed with cold water, "Bitch!"

"Arbini," Sibilla wondered, "where have I heard that name?"

"From my father, Senator Arbini!" Araldo shouted. "And he's going to sue your asses when he finds out you two molested me!"

"Even better," Phenix giggled. "I didn't think I'd find this kind of sue-happy crap in Italy."

"Arbini is super rich. Why would you want to sacrifice me to the demon of riches?" Sibilla asked. "Don't you have everything you want? Your family is swimming in luxury."

The Suitor looked away, pursing his lips.

"I'll take this one, my friend," Phenix intervened. "In the world of finance where I like to swim with the big sharks, everything comes out in the end. So, I've heard about a certain Italian businessman and senator who disinherited two of his sons, young good-for-nothings who were arrested for sniffing some white lines in a Roman cemetery. I'm talking about your old man, right, Araldo?"

The Suitor did not answer but he started trembling with rage so badly that the heavy, medieval chair creaked under him.

"I believe he's ready to taste the house cocktail," Phenix turned to her friend triumphantly.

To her great surprise Sibilla had turned pale. "My car is in the garage and the keys in the glove box," the magician's voice was shaking. "Warm up the engine and I'll meet you after giving him the drink."

Phenix put a hand on her shoulder, "You sure you're alright?"

"Yes, yes, but we've got no time to lose. I just remembered where I heard the name Arbini."

There was just one hour left in her shift and the young nurse on duty, Bianca Pastore, had rubbed her eyes red. She hated working at night, the perfect definition of Ennui. Yes, with a capital E. The patients were all knocked out with drugs and rarely broke the monotony of the night. She was just wondering if she should ask to transfer to the emergency room, which at least would give her a dose of adrenalin with the aggressive drunks, serious injuries and evangelical schizophrenics, when a man came bursting into the lobby.

Bianca immediately forgot about her dreams of hospital adventure to call out to the guy. How the devil did he get in without being stopped by security?

"Hey, you! Visiting hours are over!"

The man turned slowly to look at her. He was grinning from ear to ear, making his face a demonic mask that looked creepier in the shadows of the overhead lights. All of a sudden he ran at her.

Bianca yelped and jumped out of her chair to pick up the telephone. But the man was on her and grabbed her hand. He blew a stinging, blue dust into her face.

"Good night, carita mia."

Bianca coughed, choked, then her eyelids closed and the young nurse collapsed to the ground, her body as limp as a wax doll in the sun. A faint snore made her parted lips vibrate.

The man snickered. These little magic spells certainly made life easier! He went to examine the computer and easily found what he was looking for: the room number of Leonardo Verga.

Soon to be the deceased Leonardo Verga in room 48.

Without wasting a second the man marched down the corridor whose linoleum floor made his tennis shoes squeak a little. He passed by one door after another, glancing at each number until he saw the ones he was looking for stand out in black against white. The stranger snuck in.

The room was bathed in half-light that was disturbed by the light from the outside, glaring over the whiteness of the bed where the *Flash* journalist was sleeping with his head wrapped in a bandage and one leg in a cast up to the knee and propped up on a pillow. An IV tube came out of his left arm, hooked up to a bag full of transparent liquid. The intruder studied his victim for a moment before closing the door silently and entering farther into the room. A big smile, full of cruel joy, stretched across his face as he took a small flask out of his coat pocket. He only had to dip one index finger into the cat's blood and draw a magic figure on the sleeper's forehead and then it was goodbye Verga!

The thing about head wounds is that they are unpredictable. A simple bruise might prove fatal…

The man wet his finger and reached out for his victim.

But he hit an invisible wall.

He backed away hissing in both surprise and anger. He had touched something hard to define, a kind of supple distortion of the air, solid but very elastic too. He reached forward again, his finger dripping with red and pointing at Leonardo's forehead. Again his hand was stopped.

It was then he noticed the circle of white rose petals and ashes surrounding the bed.

"The bitch!" he growled.

"Be polite, Zeno, you have to talk nice if you want to save yourself."

The man spun around. At the same time the neon light in the bathroom turned on and the cast a cold light on the intruder like an improvised but quite effective spotlight. Maria Carpi was standing in the doorway, one hand on her hip and the other pointing a gun at the prowler. The *Flash* editor looked relaxed but a shiver ran down her spine when she saw the face of young Zeno Arbini. He who had always looked so naïve and kind was now grinning like a predator, baring his fangs and glowering with cold, calculating eyes. But did he really exist, this kid who complained after only a week on the job about the stupid articles they made him write?

"You don't look so surprised," the young man whispered.

"The love letters started coming in right after our first meeting when you hassled me about getting the same kind of work as your more experienced colleagues. And the next day I noticed that someone had been through my stuff. You know there's a huge difference between stubbornness and perseverance? Leonardo had to wait two years before I assigned him front page material."

"Two years!" Zeno burst out laughing. "You think I had nothing better to do than wait around for two years? With my jerk brother to take care of, who couldn't slow down his crazy life even after father cut us off? You don't know what that does to go from the lap of luxury to pure and simple survival, picking through the trash cans!"

"You don't know anything about my life, Zeno," Carpi replied calmly.

She glanced at Leonardo who was still sleeping off the medication. Good. The magic circle that Sibilla had asked her to draw was protecting him from the nefarious intentions of this young man.

Zeno was watching the editor-in-chief and a mischievous smile crossed his lips. "I guess it was your star witch who came up with the idea. Well done. Too bad my brother had to kill her to get our riches back."

"So putting your souls in danger by using Black Magic is for nothing but money!"

All of Carpi's muscles tensed up. She did not want this demon to see her tremble. She did not want to cry over the possible fate of Sibilla. She had to have confidence in the magician.

Zeno shook his head, "My brother, sure, Baal bless his poor, measly soul, is only interested in money. But I'm more like our father, more ambitious. What I want is power. and your little newspaper might be one way to get it."

He took a step toward Carpi who was pointing her gun at his grinning face.

Arbini clicked his tongue, "You wouldn't dare, Signora Carpi."

"Don't fool yourself, kid. I haven't had a smoke in hours and I'm ready to tear the throat out of anyone who gets under my skin, which you're starting to do. Besides, I don't know what you have planned for my newspaper, but you're fired!"

"Tsk, tsk, tsk, after I kill you, it'll be *my* journal."

Carpi did not have time to pull the trigger. Zeno was already on her and had slapped the weapon out of her hand. The gun slid over by the door. The young man raised his blood-red finger and pointed it at her forehead.

"In the end, your death will be more useful to me than Verga's. I'll take over your paper and get all the way up to Sir Wilson."

The *Flash* editor tried to push him away but her ex-employee had her by the throat to keep her head still and his nails were biting into her skin. His finger came closer. The neon light was casting eerie shadows over the two of them.

"It'll be quick," Zeno whispered. "After all, a stroke can happen to anyone."

The door of the room flew open. Carpi used the surprise to shove Zeno away from her. "Sorry, but I decided on lung cancer a long time ago!"

The wicked young man did not fall onto the bed but hit the protective circle that held him trapped like a clumsy trapeze artist in a net. Then a strong hand pulled him out by his lapels and stood him up. Zeno found himself face-to-face with a young, pretty brunette whose eyes were hidden behind dark glasses that reflected his own face back to him, a face twisted in anger. And just her was someone whom Carpi was hoping desperately to see again.

"Sibilla!"

The beautiful magician was safe and sound, looking worried, of course, but very much alive. She ran over to check on Leonardo, who was groaning now, woken up by all the noise.

"You followed my instructions to the letter, Maria. You're the best."

"I usually try to stay away from this magic stuff," the editor said, "but this was an emergency." Then she nodded toward the creep being held by Phenix. "I just fired this freelancer for willful misconduct. I'll leave him to you. I really need a cigarette."

All of a sudden Phenix yelled. Her sleeve was sizzling and smoking. Zeno had gotten free and was standing with his two hands raised up, emanating a noxious, purple phosphorescence.

"Bunch of bitches! I'm going to annihilate all three of you even if I die of exhaustion while doing it!"

The walls shook and the paint cracked as Zeno started chanting three syllables more and more frantically. Sibilla recognized the Hebrew word *Abaddon*... Destruction.

Phenix saved herself by jumping on the bed when the linoleum floor warped under her feet. The noise and the shaking finally woke up the wounded journalist for good and he sat up and screamed. The IV popped out of his arm and a little blood spilled on the sheets. The whole room was deforming under the effect of some monstrous pressure.

Sibilla pointed Cagliostro's ring at Zeno. The young man just grinned at it evilly. The purple light from his hands had spread down to his shoulders now.

"By the power of Cagliostro whose heir I am..."

A section of the wall caved in, covering the magician with debris and almost crushing her. At the same time, tentacles of linoleum wound around Maria Carpi's ankles and knocked her off balance. The concrete groaned and the glass trembled, shaking the window frames. The whole hospital seemed to be endowed with chaotic life and the irrepressible need to uproot itself from its foundations.

With her hair powdered white from the plaster Sibilla pointed her ring at the sorcerer again, "Zeno Arbini, I order you to stop all magic at once, in the name of the Twelve..."

Leonardo's sheet flew up, passed the protective barrier with no trouble and wrapped around the magician's head like a Manta Ray, muffling her words. Verga was still groggy as he tried to get up to help his friend but the mattress had melted to putty and the journalist was stuck.

Phenix was on the bed fighting against linoleum tentacles that were trying to snatch her. "For unwanted magic I have a homemade solution."

Without further ado she leapt, somersaulted in the air and landed two feet on Zeno's chest. The impact threw him back into the window. The shatterproof glass had been weakened by the black magic and burst into splinters. Zeno fell out with an expression of horrified disbelief painted on his face. A glittering shower of broken glass followed him down. He crashed on the visitor parking asphalt forty feet below. Phenix leaned out the missing window to see the results of her homemade solution.

The bed, walls, ceiling and floor were returning to their normal immobility. But the scene had left its scars. Carpi was shaking her feet out of the limp linoleum and Sibilla threw off the sheet. Both of them joined Phenix in gloomy contemplation of Zeno's corpse.

"It's all very troubling," Maria Carpi pushed away her empty plate.

She lit a cigarette and looked at Phenix in her civilian clothes and known as Patricia Hope. She had swapped her crime-fighting suit for an elegant, low cut, charcoal gray dress and invited Sibilla and the editor-in-chief to a five star restaurant on a sumptuous terrace decorated with marble columns. Leonardo was still under observation and must have been thinking of them as he swallowed the tasteless hospital food.

"I don't want to ruin this wonderful dinner, Miss Hope," Carpi continued, "and God knows I hate sounding ungrateful, but I'm really afraid that your way of solving problems is just going to create more for us."

"And yet the police seem to accept your version of the facts," Phenix said. "And by the way, you barely even scratched the truth. The reputation of your rag is probably going to suffer a little though."

Carpi's account to the authorities was missing all supernatural aspects and especially the presence of Sibilla and Phenix. The two of them had taken off after making sure that Carpi and Leonardo were fine without them. Then it was just a moral tale of little disinherited Richard and his insane ambition trying to squash the famous journalist. But he had not figured on the heroism of the editor-in-chief of the respectable publication.

"The police aren't the problem, it's old Arbini," Carpi snapped back at the word 'rag'. "One of his precious runts is dead and the other barely remembers his name."

"I admit that under the dire circumstances I went a little heavy on the amnesia spell," Sibilla humbly confessed.

"A contagious amnesia apparently, since Signor Arbini has completely forgotten about his sons' misconduct. He's determined to take vengeance on *Flash* and find out the truth about what happened to those two creeps."

"I wish him luck," Sibilla said. "Sir Wilson's fortune, our generous benefactor, can match his any day. No, I'm more worried about how those young tyros could reach such a high level of magic."

"You'll get to the bottom of it, I know," Phenix said. "As for the infamous Signor Arbini, he'll also have to deal with me. I'm ready to put my money and my fighting skills at your service. And I promise, I'll try not to kill anyone... unless I have to." The pretty brunette raised her glass of wine, "Long live *Flash*!"

Sibilla did the same, "To *Flash* and to friends!"

Maria Carpi crushed out her cigarette in the porcelain ashtray, filled her glass of chianti and raised it up in turn, "I'll drink to the longevity of *Flash*, to friends and to the health of poor Leonardo who has to make do with gnocchi swimming in bland sauce, a piece of rubbery meat and sugarless apple sauce."

"Poor thing," Phenix laughed. "A small raise might get him back on his feet."

"Fat chance," Carpi said. "He'd become lazy! Cheers!"

The three women clinked their glasses.

Deadly Circles

1.

A little red Fiat came swerving down Via dei Serragli. Despite the late hour there was still traffic in Florence and the pedestrians in the path of the crazy car owed their safety solely to their reflexes. But a few people were going to have an ugly surprise the next morning because the car kept swerving and sideswiped some parked cars, denting the doors and knocking off the mirrors. Glass splinters littered the Via. The driver was trying to control his left hand while moving his right arm all over the place; his face was twisted in fear and disgust. Then he slapped himself hard and yelped. Another tug on the wheel followed by screeching tires and the car started spinning around. A young man on a scooter screamed when he saw the blinding headlights heading straight for him; he hit the sidewalk as the car swung away. The spinning car finally crashed into the concrete balls lined up on the edge of the parking lot across the street from the Porta Romana.

The young scooter driver struggled to his feet. His helmet had protected him but his right arm was bleeding and his elbow had turned into a knot of pain. "The guy must be crazy!" he yelled as he felt for more injuries.

He approached the car that was leaking oil like a gutted cow. The engine had been completely destroyed by a concrete ball. The reckless driver was doing some ridiculous dance inside the Fiat. When he finally figured out that he had stopped he opened the door and fell onto the pavement. But right away he jumped up screaming, his eyes popping out of his head. The scooter driver was stunned to see that it was a priest whom everyone in the neighborhood knew. His robe was soaked with sweat despite the mild spring evening.

Father Celestino trampled the squirming mass of worms that had cushioned his fall. Their sticky little bodies exuded a black, foul-smelling pus at every step. He tried to run but he slipped on the maggoty carpet. To his horror he had almost forgotten the incessant buzzing of flies and wasps that had started plaguing him when he left the church. He had tried to outrun them in his car but a bunch of insects had got in and the rest of the evil swarm followed him through the streets. Now that he was out of the Fiat the little abominations were assailing him even worse than before. His vain attempts to chase them away only made them angrier. Father Celestino howled out when a wasp with a shiny belly landed on his cheek and stung, immediately imitated by another vicious one attacking his neck. The burning sensation was unbearable. The flies were hanging onto his eyelashes and hair. One crawled into his ear and buzzed incessantly. His screams got louder when wasps flew into his open mouth and injected their scorching venom in his gums and tongue.

Adriano, the young scooter driver, backed away. He was taken aback by the raging madness that had seized Father Celestino. The priest was rolling on the ground, howling, slapping himself so hard his nose and mouth were bleeding. The metal gate on the café rolled up and Cesira, the manager, came out. She was over 50 with graying hair but she was strong and moved with energy and assurance. She ran over, horrified by the cries that had interrupted her cleaning. She froze before the sight and grabbed Adriano's arm.

"What's happening? Has Father Celestino gone mad? Call for help!"

"I... I broke my phone when I fell."

"Go into my bar and use the phone behind the counter. If you try to swipe anything out of there, I'll know about it, Adriano Lanzi!"

Without another word, Adriano obeyed. Cesira bent down and tried to hold the priest still by the shoulders like she saw wrestlers do on television. As strong as she was it was no use. The mad priest was kicking and bucking too hard every which way.

"Get them off me! Get them off me! Arrgh!!!"

Cesira gritted her teeth. Father Celestino's face was covered with red, swollen spots. He looked like he was being martyred.

Lights came on in the windows around the square and heads popped out.

"Hey, Cesira," an angry voice yapped. "I called the cops and they'll take care of your drunk *subito*!"

"It's not a drunk," someone else shouted out. "It's a bad trip. Drunks don't scream like that."

"What have I got myself into!" Cesira was losing patience. She barely avoided getting kneed in the face. Father Celestino was doing anything he could to free himself from the woman's grip. "Come down here and help me! This isn't a movie here!" she yelled when the possessed priest hit her in the ribs.

Adriano had phoned for help and run out of the café. But on seeing the purple, bloated face of the priest, he refused to come any closer. The poor man's eyes were full of tears and his gaping mouth revealed a monstrously swollen tongue. The kid felt his stomach turn. He swallowed hard.

"They're on their way," he said without needing to say who.

His tongue grew fatter with every sting. They were holding his hands down and he could not defend himself. He screamed again when a wasp stung his eye. He felt his eyeball throb and his vision turned red. The flies snuck up his nostrils, into his mouth. All the stings were slowly cutting off his breathing. Soon he could not utter a sound. But the pain, the horrible pain and suffering still gave him energy to fight.

"Help me hold his arms!"

67

Adriano knelt by Father Celestino and tried to hold him with one hand. His injured elbow was shooting pain every time he bent it. "I think he's choking."

Cesira swore. The kid was right. The priest was gagging and his chest was jerking up and down as he tried to catch a breath. His tongue had grown to nightmarish proportions. Cesira put her fingers in his mouth to open the trachea. She could feel his throat was swollen too. Adriano's eyes were full of tears of disgust as he watched the devastated face of Father Celestino whose puffy eyelids covered his eyes with a veil of grotesque skin and purple rashes scarred his cheeks and nose.

A crowd had gathered around them. At the sight of the black robe all talk of drunks and drugs addicts on a bad trip was immediately silenced. A few of the bystanders crossed themselves. One of them, a young man, was watching the scene with keen interest. He had snuck out of the back of the crashed Fiat where he had been hiding the whole time, without even the priest knowing. His round, moon-shaped face was rapt with attention.

When help finally arrived and parted the crowd Cesira was trying to blow a little air into the priest's lungs, which were no longer breathing. Despite her brave efforts and the tracheotomy that an EMT performed skillfully, the man of the cloth died in the middle of the onlookers.

Everyone stood still for a moment, stunned by the events. Only the moon-faced guy dared to sneak away without looking back. He breathed deeply and went up the Via dei Serragli.

"One down," he whispered.

2.

Milan, three days later

While the residents of Milan began their day in the generous morning sunlight, a man limped across the yard of a beautiful, mysterious villa. Groans of pain slipped out of his mouth ringed by a bushy, black beard. His grimy bare feet were bleeding in spots. The pedestrians who had crossed his path wrinkled their noses at the filthy stench emanating from the vagrant's clothes. He stopped at the heavy door of the villa, raised his hand, which was almost as dirty as his feet, and rang the bell before leaning his forehead against the door. His belly was grumbling. It was obvious that the poor man needed a bath, food and bed, preferably in that order.

Someone opened the door and the homeless man almost fell inside. Sleep had overcome him in that brief wait. The young woman who had answered caught the filthy visitor before he crashed to the floor and set him back on his bloody, bare feet.

"You're finally back!" she said, a little disgusted by the slovenly appearance of the newcomer. "Ciao, Leonardo!"

Leonardo Verga, a reporter for *Flash* and a friend of Elena Drago, known as Sibilla, grumbled a weary "hello". He felt repulsive in the company of this beauty whose long, bright red hair framed a lovely face that was fresh and rested. The columnist was wearing a simple, comfortable outfit that was a nice change from her shadow-thieving leather suits: a white, short-sleeved shirt and black jeans that hugged her magnificent legs. Impeccable and clean. His own clothes had long since lost any definable color. The driver who had stopped to pick him up must have been a saint.

"The bathroom is upstairs, second door on the right," Sibilla smiled graciously. "I'll get you a big cup of coffee, croissants, pineapple juice… hmm, I even have some strawberries in my garden… with some cream."

Leonardo's stomach voiced its approval. The journalist had to keep his mouth shut so that he would not start drooling. But he did finally start to feel a tiny bit better after the awful week he had just spent.

Half an hour later a presentable man joined Sibilla in the big living room. His brown hair was still glistening from the shower. His face was closely shaved and his feet were disinfected and bandaged. He had found clean clothes, folded and ironed, sitting on the dresser in the bathroom. They were a little big and old fashioned but what a relief after wearing stinking rags for days on end! It was perfect until Leonardo could go back home. At least until he could call his cleaning lady who had a spare key because his keys were probably rusting in some crevasse in the Alps.

The full breakfast Sibilla had promised was waiting for him on the big, oak table, which had replaced the mahogany desk that had been destroyed by a golem. Sibilla had cleared off enough space for the food, pushed aside a pyramid of books, stacks of manuscripts and piles of letters. A few primitive statues were used as paperweights.

"Sit down and fill up. When you're done you can rest in one of the guest rooms."

"Thanks for everything," Leonardo said. He poured himself a big glass of pineapple juice and downed in. "And thanks for the clothes," He added as he heaped a spoonful of whipped cream on a cup of fresh strawberries. "But I have the feeling that the guy who wore them first was bigger than me."

Leonardo studied Sibilla's reaction as he bit into a butter croissant. She did not even raise her head from her laptop. He had already asked if his friend had been married. He had also never hidden his attraction to her but she seemed or pretended not to notice. The journalist knew that his hint about the presence of men's clothes would get no response since the girl was absorbed in reading her emails. Once in a while she would study a bunch of papers with photos. The laptop was one of the few concessions to modernity in the villa that looked more like an annex to the Museum of Tribal Art in Paris.

Leonardo pointed to the letters, "Your fans are still writing letters when you can be reached by email? Some of them obviously don't believe in the benefits of technology."

Despite his feelings for the beautiful woman Leonardo still considered the columns that Sibilla wrote as lovely nonsense only good for making her thrill-seeking readers tremble.

At the mention of "fans" the young lady finally looked up from her laptop to answer her colleague. "They aren't *my fans*. A lot of them were as skeptical as you before being faced with the supernatural. So my role is to give them answers to their questions when they find that our world is not a comfortable, Cartesian sphere."

"The world is scary enough as it is," Leonardo said with a bitterness that even the strawberries and cream could not sweeten up.

"You're talking about your report in the Alps, aren't you?"

The journalist grumbled, "Where even you didn't want to go with me. My great guide turned out to belong to a bunch of highway bandits stuck in the Middle Ages. They took everything from me, papers, money, camera, phone, keys, even my shoes! I wandered around the mountains for a week eating ants and sucking pebbles. In the only village around no one would help me, not even the police. I got back to Milan by hitchhiking."

"Be happy you're alive. I'm sure our chain-smoking editor is going to love the story of your misadventures. And the readers too."

"I'll get a nice article out of it but I almost lost my life!" Leonardo raised his voice." One of those bastards even put a knife to my throat!"

"You weren't in any real danger," Sibilla stated matter-of-factly.

The reporter slammed down his coffee and spilled some on the table. "How would you know?"

"Those bandits may have had nothing to do with the supernatural but I followed the case with Gebelin's tarot cards and the runes of Armanen. All the signs were clear: material losses, wounded pride and a rough trip home were on the program. But the cards and runes also showed what would happen to you in future. Therefore…"

"No, no, stop! Time out!" Leonardo blurted and jumped up. "Enough with the superstitions. I have a hard time believing you could sleep peacefully just because your pieces of cardboard and pebbles said I'd pull through! Stop talking about this fortune-telling nonsense! Look, open your mail and find a nice, weird mystery that I can solve thanks to my practical, down-to-earth mind."

And Leonardo wrapped up his passionate rant by swallowing one last spoonful of strawberries and cream.

"Okay, okay," Sibilla said calmly. "Well, I have the pleasure and honor of presenting you with my next case."

She held up the pack of papers that she had been studying while Leonardo recovered his strength.

"It's a whole file that a journalist in Florence by the name of Dalia Barbieri sent me. She thinks she's onto something: a series of weird deaths that the police have blamed on psychotic fits. Three deaths, three nights in a row, around the same time of the day. The M.O. is different every time but weirdness abounds. You might want to digest a little before looking at…"

"I've seen worse, I'm sure," Leonardo said. "Show it to me."

The past few years in the field in search of a scoop had hardened the journalist. It took a lot to shake him up. The first big photo, however, made him wince. It showed an older man naked on a dissection table. His hands, face and neck were gnarled by swollen growths. His face had turned dark purple and his huge tongue stuck out of his mouth. The poor guy must have choked to death.

"Father Celestino," Sibilla explained. "First victim of the series. One of the first witnesses, a Cesira Martino who manages a bar next to the incident, happens to be Dalia's aunt. So, she told her every detail she could about the priest's death."

Leonardo read the account and shrugged his shoulders when he was done. "The poor priest must've eaten a bad host, a wafer infected with a fungus or something."

Sibilla laughed, "Oh Leo, the police came to the same conclusion as you but their explanations weren't quite so colorful. Luckily, for me I mean, our friend Dalia managed to get a copy of the autopsy report. The blood tests did show the presence of a neurotoxin in large quantities: apamin."

"Hah, see! Well, well… but what exactly is apamin?"

"It comes from bee venom, wasps in particular. According to the report it seems the priest was attacked by a huge swarm of them. Even the inside of his mouth and throat were stung. That's what killed him."

"Sorry? A swarm of wasps? But Signora Martino didn't say anything about that in her account!"

"And the police didn't find a single insect in the priest's car. So that's where the case looks interesting to me."

Sibilla's eyes were sparkling when she handed a second set of photos to her friend.

"Here are the victims on the next night. Not so spectacular but just as intriguing."

3.

Florence, the next afternoon

"Giuseppe Lado, Donato Solima and Frederico Garcia. They're known around the neighborhood as the Three Philosophers. Donato, the oldest, was nicknamed Virgil. Aunt Cesira told me they could spend all night sitting on a bench arguing about human nature, politics and the existence of God. Donato always had crazy stories to tell. People liked them and even though they were homeless they were taken care of by folks in the neighborhood. I met them a few times in my aunt's café. Real characters…"

Dalia Barbieri's high-pitched voice echoed under the vaulted ceiling of the small church of Santa Elisabetta delle Convertite where they had found the three corpses. She was a very young journalist who blushed easily. With her straight, black hair falling halfway down her back and her long nose she looked like a young Anjelica Huston. Like a lot of shy people her style was a little outrageous—eyebrow and lip piercings, her forearm covered in tattoos and wearing a 50s style red dress with white skulls printed all over it.

When Sibilla and Leonardo met her at the scene of the second tragedy, farther up the Via dei Serragli, young Dalia turned the same color as her dress when she shook their hands.

"Madame Sibilla, it's an honor. I've read all your articles and I owe my career as a journalist to you."

"Oh, well... I'm flattered," Sibilla was embarrassed. "But between colleagues, let's stay informal."

No need to call me "Madame," the ghost-hunter said to herself.

Despite being tired Leonardo smiled kindly. He noticed his friend's embarrassment and he was not going to forget Dalia's "Madame". The girl was ecstatic to be considered an equal by her idol as she explained with exaggerated gestures the circumstances of the three deaths.

"What got me first was that they were killed on the same street as the first victim. And almost exactly twenty-four hours later according to the coroner. They were found early in the morning by Father Corbucci who was going to celebrate a mass in memory of Father Celestino. No trace of a struggle and no visible wounds."

"You apparently know the coroner pretty well," Sibilla remarked.

Dalia turned red again. "Sure... he's... my boyfriend, Dr. Francesco Taddio. He's taking a big risk telling me about the results of the inquest. So, in order not to betray him I have to write my articles in a way that hides my sources."

Sibilla nodded and smiled, "One of the crucial rules of our job—always protect your sources."

At these words Dalia proved that it was possible to turn beat red by blushing. Leonardo thought the girl was having a stroke with all the blood rushing to her cheeks. He took the file from Sibilla and picked out a photo. It showed three men lying in positions that looked like a Pieta. One man, still relatively young, had his head lying on the knees of the oldest. The third victim, with his sharp features, was on the elder's shoulder like a pillow. From their ragged clothes and dirty hair it was obvious that they were homeless. What was especially troubling to Leonardo, however, was the intense sadness that was frozen on the dead faces. The photo was strangely beautiful and expressed profound melancholy.

"They killed themselves together," he said at last. "I understand why you were so affected by their deaths."

The girl hopped from one foot to another, looking from Sibilla to Leonardo. "Oh, it's… it's not just that. They all died of a heart attack even though they were in good health considering their precarious situation. And they died one by one. The expression that you see on their faces might be a clue. They found lots of traces of tears on their clothes. I think they died of sorrow, which is weird enough, right?"

"You don't die of sorrow," Leonardo sighed.

He sat down on one of the pews because his knee and his chafed feet were still hurting him. Sibilla took the photo and examined it herself, then the church to find the exact spot where the three men had breathed their last—behind the altar, just under the golden altarpiece representing the four saints. The magician touched the ground. The ring engraved with the emblem of Cagliostro the mage glowed faintly. Behind her Dalia was trying to make Leonardo listen to reason.

"Sure, it sounds wacky, but I'll tell you another weird fact: they got into the church when it was still locked up tight in the afternoon. And as usual the guardian had checked the place thoroughly before closing up."

"He did a bad job but would never admit it," Leonardo replied.

Good Luck, Dalia, Sibilla smiled sarcastically to herself.

But her smile was immediately wiped away by an intense feeling of deep sadness. An empty, hideous, abysmal impression as if all of a sudden her existence was completely worthless and was teetering on the brink of a bottomless pit of dread. Cagliostro's ring sparkled more brightly.

Then she heard muffled sobs, distant but nearby echoes mingled with a constant litany: *Oh, we have lived our lives abandoned by God and Man. We have walked through Limbo without hope of every seeing the light. Why do we need to keep on living? Let's snuff out the spark that keeps us in this aimless existence and be free of this burden of life.*

Sibilla knew that she was hearing the psychic remains of the three men's sorrow. And these occult traces were now clutching her chest, forcing tears into her eyes.

"By the power of the Twelve, O suffering spirits, I order you to appear."

Nothing happened. Just a wave of gloomy sadness a little deeper than before. Nothing else mattered except for the comforting, black arms of Death. It would be so easy to just lie down on the cold ground and stop breathing.

Sibilla choked back a sob and stumbled back tearing herself out of the grip of the supernatural sorrow. She turned her moistened cheeks to Leonardo and Dalia who were still arguing.

"You're wrong, Leonardo," the magician coughed out. "You can indeed die of sorrow."

The two others stopped talking, surprised by the interruption. On seeing her face still affected by the strange, psychic attack, Leonardo jumped to his feet, worried.

"What's going on? Did you see something?"

"I felt it. I heard it. But I'm not sure I understand exactly what it is. Cagliostro's ring can't bring back the souls of the dead but a kind of trace remains, like the echoes of weeping. It's both here and elsewhere. And I felt the awful grief of those three men."

"I knew you were sensitive but come on, you're exaggerating a little." As usual Leonardo tried to minimize the mystery.

"I know what I felt and I know something infused those poor men with such despair that they let themselves die. Let's get out of here, please. The sunlight will do me a world of good."

Once outside the gorgeous redhead breathed deeply. The sound of traffic on the Via dei Serragli brought a note of reassuring normality. Sibilla filled her ears with the sounds to chase away the echoes of the desolate voices still moaning in her head.

"Madame Si... sorry, uh, Sibilla, if you'd like... If you want we can postpone our investigation till a little later."

"No, it's okay, thanks Dalia. This case looks like it'll be frightening but also very fascinating."

Sibilla's cheeks had gotten their color back to the great relief of the two other journalists. The occult investigator even had the strength to smile, trying to dispel the sorrow that was stuck in her throat.

Let's keep going. Let's see the place where the young couple having an affair died.

4.

"I'll tell you again that I didn't want to kill them, Inspector. I wasn't in control. I went up to them and I pushed them over the edge but it wasn't my hands... it wasn't me!"

Giorgio Malatesta looked confused in his dim cell. Sitting on a cot, his thick, silver-framed glasses next to him, he rubbed his eyes with trembling fingers to hold back the tears. He was barely thirty years-old but prematurely balding and a little fat and red for his age with rings around his eyes. His tuxedo was crumpled. He had spent two nights in jail since the gruesome night of his wedding but he did not want to change his clothes.

Straddling a folding chair facing him Inspector Bonelli, a tall man in his forties with graying hair, was trying to look friendly and sound considerate in order to relax Giorgio. Without much success. Most of his questions got only tears for answers.

The Florentine cop turned to man leaning casually against the wall across the cell. The foreigner was spinning a pack of cigarette in his gloved hands. Bonelli wondered again why this Englishman from Interpol constantly wore leather gloves despite the nice weather. Then he turned back to the interrogation.

He knew that the alleged murderer was going to repeat the same story, which he had heard *ad nauseam* from the start:

After the wedding, which was as beautiful as the bride, everyone went to a restaurant at the end of Via dei Serragli that had a great view of the Arno. It was a friendly celebration. The laughing and singing, more and more inebriated, gradually drown out the band. Then Francesca disappeared. After ten minutes or so Giorgio started to worry and got up to look for her. He searched everywhere and asked everyone if they had seen his bride. Just as he was headed back to the reception room he heard a voice like someone was whispering in his ear. "You'll find them upstairs." He swung around. Nobody.

The groom first blamed the good wine and his being tired. But then why did he feel pressure on his back as if someone were pushing him. Why did the door to the stairs unlock and open up all by itself?

The invisible hand pushed Giorgio towards this new goal. The voice kept whispering to him to look on the top floor. It was insistent, insidious, like an obsessive thought driving him mad. He climbed the wooden steps silently. All the way to the fifth floor. He knew what he would find before seeing them—his wife with her arms around the neck of Piero, his younger brother, and Piero's lips pressed hard against Francesca's. The two of them sitting on the sill of the open window. A gust of wind raised the bride's veil as she embraced her lover to stay warm. Their mouths were still plastered together in a kiss, more and more passionately. They did not notice the newlywed husband standing there.

Giorgio collapsed in tears at this point in the story. His mouth opened and closed but no words came out. Tears poured down his crimson cheeks.

Bonelli pursed his lips. This happened every time they questioned Malatesta. This part of the deposition was the hardest for the alleged murdered to get through. He had to stop every time, shaking with sobs. The Inspector pitied the poor man. He hated pressuring this kind of guy.

"Breathe, okay, slow and deep," the cop patted Giorgio's shaking shoulder.

The Interpol agent chose this moment to come over to them. He offered Giorgio a cigarette. "If you'll let us, Inspector, we can bend the rules a little about no smoking in the station," he said in English.

This seemed to calm Giorgio for an instant, enough time for him to understand the foreign language spoken spontaneously. The young man came from a well-to-do family and spoke three languages fluently. He had no trouble adapting.

"Thank you," he said in English, holding out his hand. But he stopped and looked at Bonelli.

The Inspector gave his blessing with a nod. Giorgio stuck a cigarette in his mouth and the Englishman lit it with his Zippo. The prisoner coughed with the first puff.

"I stopped smoking for Francesca," he explained in English before taking another long pull.

"In that case you're better than me," the other said, lighting his own stick of nicotine and tar. "I've never been able to quit, even for a day." He blew long plumes of smoke out of his nose and smiled. "Excuse my rudeness for coming to this interrogation without introducing myself. I'm Graham Carter. I work for Interpol. I'm pleased to see you speak my language so I'll ask you again to tell your story in English. Even though I'm familiar with this beautiful Italian tongue, there are still some words and phrases that escape me. Would you mind telling me everything one more time?"

Bonelli saw through Carter's ploy and found it interesting. Retelling the painful story in another language would allow Giorgio to distance himself from it. The mental effort would push his emotions into the background. The accused started again slowly from the beginning. When he got to the most sensitive part, he stopped again. Carter and Bonelli waited anxiously.

Giorgio just asked for another cigarette, then he continued with a knot in his throat but a determined look on his face. And for the first time the widowed killer spilled his guts, reassured by the kindness of the two men and the victory over his own grief.

"Do you know the worst part of this whole thing? It's that I wasn't really surprised to find my wife in the arms of my brother. I know what I look like and most of the time a woman like Francesca would never look twice at me. Thanks to my family's influence I got a lot more. Except that when she said yes to my proposal, I didn't kid myself. But still I saw myself as saving a penniless student, a Pygmalion who would be able to blossom in society and end up loving me for my generosity. I forgot that you can't buy love. It's tragically naïve, isn't it? And my handsome, funny brother, so full of energy, was the fly in the ointment."

"If you weren't kidding yourself, why did you commit such a rash crime?" Carter asked.

Giorgio crossed his arms as if he had suddenly felt a chill and whispered, "The one who led me to them... my invisible guide... he told me such awful things that drove me crazy."

Carter leaned forward. The glowing tip of Giorgio's cigarette reflected in his pupils. "What did the voice say?"

The young widower furrowed his brow. "I can't remember. But I can still see everything else about that day very clearly. Even minor details are engraved in my memory. But when that voice started telling me to push them out the window, everything gets blurry like a confused dream. I don't remember the exact words whispered in my ear but they made me raging mad... they burned me! As if all the frustration and bitterness over the years suddenly erupted. A volcano of hate. And I pushed them."

Giorgio exhaled one last quivering puff of smoke and crushed out the butt on the bottom of his expensive shoe. Bonelli thought for a second about how that one shoe would cost him a month's pay.

"Their screams when they fell snapped me out of my reveries. I tried to reach out for them. I thought I could save them at the last minute. I still see my brother reaching out his hand while hugging Francesca close to him. But they were sucked out of reach."

"Sucked?" Carter inquired.

"Weird, eh, to say it like that?" Giorgio almost giggled. "But I swear that something pulled them away. There was a huge gust of wind that made the whole building shake. Ask the guests, I'm sure they'll remember that muffled roar of the wind. It got hold of my wife and brother and spun them around so violently that Francesca's veil and part of her dress were torn off. It mangled them, threw them around like rag dolls."

Giorgio stopped again. His eyes were wide with fear and disbelief when he stared at Carter.

"I swear to you that over the howling storm I heard their bones break. I swear that blood poured out of their nose and mouth and flew around them like they were sucking it in. I know they were both dead already when they hit the scooters parked on the sidewalk 30 feet below."

The poor guy pressed both hands against his mouth. He felt his stomach turn as he recalled the scene.

Carter put his hands on the young man's shoulders. "Breathe slowly. There's nothing more we can do for them except try to figure out what killed them. Justice will be done in their memory."

"I don't know if I'm much use to justice," Giorgio dried his eyes with his sleeve.

"Knowing will help you get through the grief, you'll see. But I'll need other witnesses of the strange phenomenon. And we'll keep looking."

"So you didn't find the guy?" Giorgio asked.

"What guy?"

"I didn't get a chance to talk about him… I break down every time like you saw… but I saw a man on the street a few feet away from the bodies. He looked pretty young. And what strikes me now is that he was just watching my wife and brother with his hands in his pocket. Or maybe I'm just imagining his attitude. Then he turned around and strolled away."

"Well, his attitude does sound weird. Can you describe him?"

"Hard to say... I was crying and didn't see much. But I think he was really covered up and wearing a kind of black hoodie. His face was round and pale, I think. Sorry I can't tell you more."

"Don't be sorry. I thank you for the help you've given."

"So, you believe me?"

Carter looked Giorgio straight in his desperate eyes before answering, "As crazy as it probably sounds, yes!"

Giorgio thanked him silently. He waited for the two men to leave his cell before he broke down in tears again.

5.

A few hours later, while evening cast its shadows over the bustling streets of Florence, Dalia brought Sibilla and Leonardo to her apartment on Via de Mezzo. The place was a shelter from the tumult of tourists but not from the buzzing of Vespas. Like a lot of buildings in the museum city this one had passed through centuries and the forest green shutters, like wooden eyelids, were closed over the windows to keep the heat out of the apartments.

A man was waiting at the entrance. A young thirty years-old, average height, casually dressed but with a neatly trimmed beard, his face lit up with relief on seeing the three of them. "Dalia, my little flower, you're finally back! I've been hanging around here for half an hour because your crazy roomie won't open the door for me."

"This is my boyfriend Francesco," the young journalist explained by adopting once again the color of her namesake flower. "Dear, this is Sibilla and Leonardo Verga from *Flash*."

"Oh, I could've guessed," the beard smiled. "She talks about you all the time, Madame Sibilla. I feel like I've read all your articles."

"Just Sibilla is fine," the magician forced a smile.

Clearly this Florentine escapade was becoming more and more amusing to Leonardo.

"So what's wrong with Sandra now?" Francesco asked. "The new love of her life dumped her? She didn't get enough 'likes' on her last Facebook post? You didn't pretend to drool over her latest culinary monstrosity?"

Dalia did not look amused in the least. "Sorry. Sandra is my roommate and things are a little touchy between us. Right now she's having a tough time. There's a nice little restaurant not too far from here. Francesco can take you. I'll just grab a few files for our investigation and join you there in no time. Sorry again…"

Dalia unlocked the door whose paint was flaking off and disappeared behind it.

Francesco was all smiles. "My little flower doesn't seem it but when trouble comes knocking she turns into poison sumac and no mercy! I wouldn't be surprised to find Sandra's guts spread out on my dissection table someday."

When he saw the two journalists looking a little shocked he added, "I'm joking, of course. Follow me, you're going to have the best *panzanella* in the world."

Dalia, on the other hand, was hopping up the stairs after taking off her high heels. She lived on the top floor in a loft with creaking floors that was built by knocking down the walls of the old servants' quarters. Before her relationship with Sandra went sour it had been a little paradise.

As soon as she entered she clenched her fists: the table in the dining room was still covered with dirty dishes from breakfast and sexy lingerie was hanging from door handles and even from the old chandelier. After giving up on a number of dead-end projects, like journalism, balloon sculpture, radio DJ and playwright, Sandra had decided to become a stripper. From the looks of it this was just an excuse to avoid doing housework while her roommate was already overwhelmed with her studies and internship at the paper. And to think that at the beginning the two young ladies got along so well together with the same taste in music and movies. Then, little by little, Dalia realized that you could not burst the little dream bubble that Sandra floated in by reminding her of her domestic responsibilities. Things only got worse when the budding journalist started going out with Francesco and getting paid for her work. Sandra who suffered setbacks in her professional and personal life could not hide her jealousy of her roommate who was ten years younger than her.

Really upset by the mess Dalia went into her room and found Sandra leaning over her desk. She almost fell over when she spun around. Her career as a dancer was going to be short-lived if she could not control her pirouettes. Short but curvy, she had long hair dyed black and big blue eyes that had too much make-up. A big, embarrassed smile showed off her crooked teeth that ruined her face.

"Oh, my Dalia, I was looking for my Kiss CD."

"If you paid attention to anybody besides yourself, you'd know that I hate Kiss. And I'm not *your* Dalia."

Sibilla and Leonardo would have had a hard time recognizing her stone-cold voice. Too shocked to reply, the intruder ran out of the room. The young journalist took a deep breath to cool her cheeks that were burning with anger. That little parasite was searching through her stuff! It was time to kick her out. When this case was over she would ask Francesco to come live with her. They couldn't smother each other because they were both too involved with their work.

Once she was calm Dalia gathered up the documents she needed and went back downstairs with the files pressed against her chest and her laptop under her arm. She went down the street to the restaurant where the others were waiting for her. She had no idea that Sandra was spying on her from the apartment window. In truth, she had been spying on her roommate for a while. She had decided to bring a big story to the papers that had the audacity to refuse her a job. And what better way than to get revenge on Dalia by stealing her story.

With a big smile showing all her crooked teeth she put her hair up in a bun and hid it under a cap that she had just bought and then she changed her clothes, wearing the ones she rarely put on. Dalia had to be on a new trail and she wanted to get the jump on her. It was about time that her ambitions were rewarded and too bad if she had to trample someone else. She had waited long enough. So, she grabbed her i-phone and the photos she had taken from Dalia's desk.

"Let's just see where the trail of these murders leads."

Francesco had already ordered a bottle of red wine when his girlfriend arrived. The place had the faded charm of those family restaurants that offer a limited menu with no fuss but delicious. The walls were painted ochre and purple rings (traces of all the glasses of wine over the years) decorated the old, wooden tables. After ordering, they started talking seriously. The four investigators went over each victim again while looking at the photos, which were so familiar by now that their appetite was not ruined... except for maybe the fourth:

Sibilla, Leonardo and Dalia had gone over the crime scenes on the banks of the Arno and the traces of blood still visible inside the police tape but it left only a vague idea of the carnage that had taken place. A man, Ciacco Iacopo, had his face ripped off by his great dane, who was usually calm when taken for a walk in the same place every evening. The passers-by had heard the animal howling like mad with its chops dripping with its master's blood.

"Poor old thing," Sibilla sighed, "I'm sure something pushed him to kill."

She had not tried to learn more with Cagliostro's ring. The frightening experience in the church of Santa Elisabetta was almost too much. On the other hand, she had probed the sidewalk where the bodies of the lovers had crashed and the result was... troubling.

"Could be," Francesco said. "They still don't know if they're going to put it down because it's so sad and docile now. It shows no symptoms of rabies. Signor Iacopo's widow loves the dog so much she wants to get it back."

"The irony in all this," Dalia added, "is that this guy Iacopo was a pretty well-known food critic in Tuscany. Given his size he must have loved his work."

"All that fat must have been too enticing for his dog," Leonardo piped up.

His mood was dark. All these deaths had no connection. Even if a stroll in Florence to discover its nice restaurants was a lot nicer than his expedition in the Alps, he felt like he was wasting his time and would rather be resting from his adventure. And to top things off his knee was killing him.

Sibilla glared at him, "Please, let's not see who can make the most morbid comments."

"Sorry," Dalia babbled and blushed.

The waitress, a "mamma" whose round belly and breasts filled out the sagging red apron brought them their anchovy panzanelles and gnocchi with ricotta. After a mouthful of salad with bread, olives and tomatoes, Leonardo admitted that he was not completely wasting his time. Francesco was not exaggerating about the good food. And he had more surprises up his sleeve.

"You might have suspected but last night there was another weird crime."

"Yes!" Dalia blurted out. "I wanted to talk to you about that. So?"

"Seeing that the photos of Father Celestino and Signor Iacopo didn't ruin your appetites…"

The young coroner took a file out of the bag hanging on his chair, moved the bottle of wine and the bread basket, then opened the file. The three journalists leaned forward. Leonardo almost choked on a tomato when he saw the new horror. He cursed his intuition for being right: the corpses were swollen and covered with bruises. One had its skull cracked open; the other its ribs smashed in.

"What happened to them?" Sibilla asked. "Looks like they got hit with a heavy weapon."

"Indeed," Francesco said. "This one deserves a Darwin Award. It started off simply enough with two guys having a fender bender. The Mercedes of the first guy bumped into the second one's Porsche. As you can see from the photos the two drivers didn't stop at insulting each other, they went at it with fists. And when their fists weren't enough they smashed the pavement and used it as crude weapons to slaughter each other. Nobody could stop them."

"And I suppose," Sibilla said, "that neither one of them had a reputation for violence."

"Exactly. Pietro Alvaro was a business owner who was hard, strict, no fun managing his olive oil company with an iron fist. He could fire you on the spot with his pulse not rising in the least."

"No!" Dalia was so surprised that she spit out her gnocchi. "I know the other guy, it's Prodigo Nero!"

"And the second person recognized by my sweetheart, this Prodigo Nero, was as generous with his donations for the restoration of historical monuments and works of art as he was with the croupiers in his casinos."

"What a mess!" Dalia was worked up. "Uh, sorry, but this force Sibilla talked about is turning Florence upside down by killing such high-ranking people. One of my colleagues was supposed to interview Nero, his first big story... He must have cried all night long."

"That's the line we should follow," Leonardo said. "A kind of organized terrorism. They must have drugged them or brainwashed them somehow to make them commit these insane acts."

"And what about the three homeless guys, Leonardo?" Sibilla asked. "Collateral damage, perhaps? And Father Celestino and Francesca? Why were they so important that someone would kill them? The same insidious force pushed them over the edge. Or a third party killed them like with Malatesta. I felt very strong residual energy at the crime scenes we visited. Intense, disturbing emotions like fear for Father Celestino and despair for the three homeless... sexual desire where Francesca Malatesta and her lover fell."

To her great relief Leonardo made no inappropriate comments about the third point. But Dalia's boyfriend looked terribly interested.

"I don't believe in the paranormal… not really… but I am a believer and I think that lots of things in this world are beyond our understanding. And it really does seem that the last things the victims felt have pervaded their theater of death. I wonder what emotions you would feel in these last two cases."

"I don't think I want to know right now. But time is short because another victim will be struck at midnight."

The restaurant manager looked over to see that they were taken care of, then went to clear another table.

"We know when but not who," Leonardo said. "And no idea where."

"I have an idea," Dalia offered. She took her phone and brought up Google maps to see a satellite picture of the city. "Father Celestino died near Porta Romana, then the death road led up Via Serragli to the banks of the Arno. From there turn right and you find the corpse of Caccio Iacopo near the Santa Trinita bridge, right? Next, where did Nero and Alvaro kill each other?"

"In front of the Ponte Vecchio," Francesco answered.

"So that means the next crime of crimes will take place around the next bridge," Sibilla said.

"Could be," Leonardo mumbled. "It's just a theory though."

"The only one we've got," Sibilla shot back. "Tonight we patrol the bridge and if there's any black magic around I'll feel it."

"Yeah, sure," Leonardo whispered. "If you get a whiff of sulfur and goat shit it means we're on the right track." And to the frustrated faces of the others he said, "What? Do you know any smells more evil than that?"

He knew that his mentor was behind him before he felt the long, bony hand on his shoulder. Guido pretended not to notice his visitor. His moon face reflected no emotion as he leaned over the ruby-red card and wrote a message with silver ink, his tongue darting between his flaccid lips. He was no longer surprised by the other's visits even though his studio apartment was locked. His patron could come and go as he pleased. He was used to this by now. He knew that a simple door could not stop such a person. He caught the faint odor of old parchment when the stranger leaned over his work. Out of the corner of his eyes Guido thought he saw the head nodding with satisfaction.

"Already at work on the sacrifice for tomorrow night," a raspy voice said. "Good!"

"Well, if I were lazy I'd end up like the priest," Guido said.

Hoarse laughter caused an involuntary shiver run down his back.

"And yet, my little friend, and yet! What were you doing with your life before I showed up? You were nothing but a hibernating larva watching the sands of your life run out in the hourglass of passivity."

Guido did not answer but his round face turned slightly red. The naked truth was hurtful but there was no denying it. The young man had been doing nothing with his life. At almost thirty years-old he had dreamed of drawing *fumetti*, comic books, and imagined that his brush would revive a genre that had become obsolete. But his lack of willpower and perseverance had, in the end, landed him in the lowly, boring job of assistant shopkeeper. But under his bland, insignificant appearance Guido hid a bitter heart gnawed away by malice. He blamed his repeated failures on those who did not give him a chance—his parents, the timid publishers, the people who could not encourage him—without ever thinking it was his own fault. So, when this stranger offered to fulfill his deepest desires at the price of a few human sacrifices, Guido did not waste any time listening to his scruples.

However, some part of his humanity not yet anesthetized by his mad ambitions whispered to him to beware, to quit this crazy project. But it was too late now. He had too much blood on his hands already.

One final period with the silver ink put an end to his musings. The young man blew gently on the ink. The next name was written with an artful hand. Guido slipped the card into an envelope already addressed to the next sacrificial victim.

The aspiring illustrator turned to his visitor, "I just have to put it into a mailb…"

The mysterious man had disappeared without a sound. The floorboards had not even creaked. Guido shivered. Yes, for sure, it was too late to turn back now.

6.

The current made the reflections from the streetlights dance on the river. Sibilla ran her fingers over the railing of the Ponte alle Grazie while scrutinizing the passers-by who were enjoying the beautiful Florentine night. Many of them stopped to take a picture of the old, historic bridge downstream. The lights were still shining on Ponte Vecchio even if the stalls along its sides were all closed now. Unlike the other bridges spanning the Arno, which were destroyed by the Germans in '44 and rebuilt on the old stones, the Old Bridge had been saved from the Nazi bombs because it was too narrow to let the English and American tanks across.

"The people are walking around so carefree," Sibilla said. "Hard to believe that this city has such a bloody history and right now an occult menace is looming over its inhabitants."

"Oh, I can believe in the punishment of Savonarola out in public, in the Pazzi conspiracy, in the Guelfs and Ghibellines knocking each other off and all that crap," Leonardo said, standing next to her and smoking a cigarette," but an occult menace…"

He let his words trail off and took another puff.

"I thought you quit smoking."

"I'll quit when my goddamn knee lets me play sports again," he snapped back.

An uncomfortable silence fell over the two friends. Sibilla knew that the tall journalist had been very short-tempered since the accident that left him seriously wounded. And for his part the reporter was sorry for being so gruff.

Dalia and Francesco were not with them. They were posted on the banks. The young coroner was walking along the south side and Dalia was on the north pretending to fix her friend's old scooter. There was no bar or restaurant nearby and staking out the enemy was a little depressing despite the beauty of the buildings and lights.

"It shouldn't be long," Sibilla said. "It's five to midnight…"

"What's your super magician sense telling you?"

She held her breath for an instant at his sarcastic tone and fiddled with Cagliostro's ring on her index finger.

"It's pretty weak, like a distant signal. Our killer is still far away but he'll be here. According to the autopsies everything happens around midnight."

"Forensic science at the service of the supernatural, eh?"

Leonardo leaned back on the railing and pointed to a little old lady shuffling along and mumbling constantly to herself. "Look at her. I'm sure she's invoking Satan. Burn the witch!"

Sibilla's eyes shot daggers at him, "Why do you always have to throw your skepticism in my face like you're spitting on me?"

I didn't mean to insult you," Leonardo turned defensive. "Well, one of us has to keep their head screwed on."

He felt like he was sinking himself deeper and deeper. They had this kind of conversation hundreds of times before but maybe he had gone a little too far. His friend looked like she was getting really angry; her fists were clenched as if she was about to push him into the river.

All of a sudden her hands flew up to her mouth like she was holding back vomit. Cagliostro's ring had a gloomy glow. And just then the bells struck midnight.

"He's here! He's here!" the magician muttered. "I feel a kind of rage taking hold of my belly and it burns."

"Where is he?" Leonardo shouted.

Sibilla's extreme reaction made him forget his skepticism. He looked to the right and left, examining all the people going by. Everyone looked harmless, glancing back curiously at the two investigators who were glaring at them. Then in the distance they heard a howl full of so much rage that it was barely human.

Sibilla pointed to the Ponte Vecchi, "*He* fooled us!"

The two journalists stared deep into the shadows of the old bridge. Leonardo saw something moving on the north bank under the ancient deck of the historical monument. Onlookers were already gathering and calls for help broke out. Francesco had also seen the tumult and was running over there.

"We didn't figure that the phenomenon would change directions. Shit, we failed."

"Stop bellyaching," Sibilla shot back, "and follow me."

Without waiting another second she ran across the Pont alle Grazie. In her haste she almost ran over Dalia who had stepped in front of her to ask what was happening. Francesco grabbed his girlfriend by the arm and dragged her along. Leonardo kept up as best he could, trying not to lose sight of the magician's flaming red hair. He had seen her like this before when Graham Carter hypnotized her in Paris to make her believe that Cagliostro's spirit possessed her. He clenched his fists at this memory and sped up despite the shooting pain in his wounded knee.

The screaming got louder the closer they got. The journalist cursed. The Pont Vecchi looked so close from the other bridge but he realized that he was not even halfway there when he passed by the Galileo Museum with its weird columns crowned with blue spheres near the entrance. And far in front of him Sibilla's red hair was reflecting the streetlights.

The beautiful magician felt like she had wings… of anger. Cagliostro's ring was pulsing, communicating to her all the negative energy that was attacking the victim in the night. She wanted to hit all the idiots on the riverbank doing nothing to help the poor thing but just standing there babbling. She pushed her way through ignoring the insults. There were still a lot of people here in one of the most touristic spots of the city just behind the Uffizi Gallery. Hard to believe that such a horrible tragedy could happen here.

And yet.

As she was passing under the vaults along Anna Maria de Medici Street, she saw the man clearly on the Ponte Vecchi near the bank. He was struggling with all his strength in a sticky, muddy quagmire like a seagull caught in an oil slick. He was screaming in rage and trying to strangle one of the three women who were having fun pushing him down in the swamp and pulling him back up by his coat collar. Thin black veils, like sooty smoke, covered their tall, thin bodies and their hair was blown by an invisible wind. Sibilla knew what she was dealing with… Demons!

The man threw a punch at the closest one but the dreadful woman laughed at his uppercut. Her icy smile split her face open like a carnivorous plant and she buried her prey's head in the mud. His enraged screams turned to gurgling.

So, this is it, Sibilla told herself, *this is how the murderous forces look!*

She scrambled over the low, stone wall and jumped. She landed in a tangle of bushes and rolled out with her red hair adorned by nature. After a few scratches she reached the riverbank where it was covered with damp grass. The man was getting tired and moved in slow motion. His nose and mouth were sticking out of the mud now. The demon furies were letting him get one last gasp before burying him in the noxious mud for good.

Sibilla raised her fist. The jade stone in her ring flashed, which put a stop to the creatures' celebration. "By the power of Cagliostro, whose heir I am, I order you to leave this dimension…"

Something huge drove into her so hard that she lost her breath. The magician rolled on the ground with her attacker. He was bigger and heavier than her and picked her up like a ragdoll, then throwing her into the water. The young woman struggled with her big coat as she sank in the Arno, pulled by the current. In a panic she flailed her arms and legs and gasped for air.

She managed to yell out "Francesco!" when she saw the coroner following her into the bushes. Then she calmed down enough to swim and crawled onto the shore. Dalia's boyfriend was there to pick her up.

"Quick!" she panted, "Maybe it's not too late to…"

She pointed to the place where the victim had disappeared. Francesco ran along the shore to the patch of mud but only a few bubbles were floating on the surface. Nevertheless, he threw off his coat and stepped carefully into the mud, which was turning less solid as the current reached it. Other people had started coming down from all sides to help but it was too late, Sibilla knew: the three furies were nowhere to be seen. They were done with their work and their victim and had gone back to hell where they had been summoned from. She was thinking of the man who had attacked her, trying to remember what he looked like. The surprise made her miss a lot but she remembered a black hoodie and a round face half-hidden inside it. She felt bad—why couldn't she recall more? Of course there was that anger infesting her, which was gone now.

"Sibilla!"

Dalia and Leonardo came running up. The magician frowned on seeing her friend limping again.

"There was nothing I could do," she wrung out her long hair. "We're facing a very powerful sorcerer or necromancer. He summoned demons to commit the murders. I saw three creatures… I tried to drive them away but someone attacked me, a real person."

"Whoever initiated the murders, no doubt," said a voice that Sibilla recognized.

"Carter?"

It was indeed the English Interpol agent who was walking up to them casually with a cigarette in his mouth. Leonardo sunk into a bad mood right away. He remembered the Brit's little tricks and still had a slight burn mark on his right wrist to remind him how twisted the guy was.

"Mademoiselle Sibilla, Monsieur Verga," Graham Carter spoke as if they were meeting at a garden party, "and you must be Dalia Barbieri from the *Courier de Toscane*. And splashing around over there I suppose is your boyfriend, Dr. Francesco Taddio. As you can see, we got here too late."

Immediately after throwing the woman into the water Guido ran away as fast as his chubbiness allowed. The scene of the new sacrifice was quickly full of curiosity seekers eager for a macabre spectacle, so it was easy for him to squeeze his way out of sight of suspicious eyes. But fear was wringing his guts. He had been standing under the Ponte Vecchio, waiting for the new victim to meet the three Furies. He had felt the presence of the patron. He did not dare turn around, afraid of being greeted with a cavernous, scornful smile out of nowhere. Except when the pretty redhead in the big, black, leather coat came running to the aid of their offering he had very clearly heard a voice:

"Hell! That bitch is going to ruin everything! Quick, Guido, go stop her!"

Without thinking twice the young man had charged. When he had the girl on the ground the voice of the Other had screamed hysterically, "Kill her! Kill her! Kill her!"

He could easily have wrapped his fat fingers around her throat and squeezed, but the idea of fouling his hands directly was repulsive. Therefore, he had decided to throw the redhead into the river in the vague hope that she would drown.

When he got to his scooter parked two blocks away he heard his patron pacing nearby, swearing up a storm, "Her again! That vile descendant of Dragut! I thought I'd killed all of them but they escaped! Curses on them!"

His eyes blazed when he saw Guido creeping up.

"Why didn't you kill her like I told you to, you stupid, fat maggot? That girl is onto us. She's going to stop our Great Work! There's so much left for us to do and everything's going to fall apart because of your cowardice!"

Guido wanted to melt into the sidewalk and disappear from the world.

But someone coughed behind them. He swung around so fast that his hood flew off and he stood facing a short girl with big breasts and a big smile on her face. He would have found her pretty except for those damned pointy incisors.

"Please, would the murderer who's terrorizing Florence grant me an exclusive interview?" Sandra asked.

Guido's haughty nature stretched his face into a shark's smile.

7.

They had not arrested them, officially, but the small room where they stuck the four of them was pretty severe. Only the steaming cups of coffee on the metal table lifted the impression of being there for interrogation. There did not seem to be a microphone and there was no one-way mirror on the wall like you see in the movies.

And it was in this unwelcome environment that Graham Carter gave them a briefing. "The man you couldn't save despite your speed at diving into the Arno was Fabio Argenti, a national champion of Tae Kwon Do and Aikido."

Sibilla was still shivering under the towel she was wrapped in. She frowned, "I told you I was pushed, Carter, and the person was our murderer."

The Englishman opened the one narrow window cut into the concrete wall and lit a cigarette before responding. "A pudgy guy in a black hoodie just like poor Giorgio Malatesta also described. I agree that he's our man. Even if it doesn't exactly explain how he got away with it."

"And we don't know how *you* figured that all these unconnected deaths was worthy of an investigation by the Cagliostro Section," Leonardo said.

Carter turned calmly to the journalist. He knew that the young man was suspicious of him and maybe he was right. The Interpol agent gave him a sarcastic smile before blowing out a cloud of smoke. "We all have our little secrets. I'll close my eyes to the illegal collaboration of your coroner friend if you stop asking about my methods."

Francesco and Dalia curled up in their corner. Leonardo gritted his teeth. This guy had them and they would have to cooperate if they did not want Francesco to get into serious trouble for divulging confidential information.

Sibilla was barely paying attention. She got lost deep in thought when Carter mentioned the sporting feats of the last victim. "A martial arts champion... maybe he was using it to blow off his anger. I felt his anger just like I felt the sorrow of the three homeless and the passion of the two lovers. And the guy eaten by his dog loved good meat. A glutton, lustful lovers..." She jumped up, her face suddenly lit up. "Can anyone give me paper and pen... and a map of the city?"

Dalia fumbled through her bag and put the first two objects on the table. Then she pulled up a map on her cell phone.

The cold eyes of the Englishman stared at Sibilla; "You're onto something, aren't you?"

"Maybe."

On the bottom of the paper she wrote the name of Father Celestino and next to it "stung to death by insects".

"What was the priest really like?" she asked Dalia.

"Uh, my aunt said he was nice but a little apathetic. He did charity work around the city but without ever getting too emotionally involved."

Sibilla wrote the word *apathy* next to the first victim's name. The pieces of the puzzle seemed to all be there but she had to dig deeper.

"Click on the crime scenes, Dalia, and let's go over all of them up to Santa Elisabetta."

In the small, bare room, there was no sound except the pen scratching on paper and Dalia clicking on her phone.

For the second crime Sibilla did not write the names of the three homeless men, she just noted *three philosophers* and the how they died, *sorrow*, as well as their moral characteristics: wisdom, big speeches. Above this she wrote Piero and Francesca, died in a lustful embrace in a whirlwind and next to them: young, lovers.

"If you write the words Francesca Malatesta, brother, spouse and lust on your search engine, what do you get?"

"The first link is the Wikipedia page of Francesca da Rimini," Dalia checked. "Young noble girl whose tragic love was immortalized by Dante Alighieri in *The Divine Comedy*. And there's a painting from 1855 titled Paolo and Francesca in hell."

"The poet Dante described them in the shadows, right?" Sibilla said.

The young apprentice nodded. "His verses are even cited in the article."

"Oh, I feel better already," Leonardo said. "For a minute I thought the investigation was going to turn rational and we were going to find out that Dante's ghost was behind all this."

"Dante's ghost or one of his fanatical followers," Sibilla replied. "The Divine Comedy is not too fresh in my mind but I remember very well the two cursed lovers condemned in the circle of lust to be tossed around by an eternal storm. Doesn't that remind you of the third victims?"

"It's true," Carter admitted. "At least as Giorgio Malatesta reported it."

Sibilla's eyes were sparkling with excitement. She finally had the connection between the deaths.

"Go and see if you can find other similarities between our deaths and description of the damned in The Divine Comedy."

She took a cup of hot coffee and leaned against the wall.

"And if my deduction is right we'll know the identity of the next victim."

"Everyone has dreams that can't come true. You understand, don't you, Sandra?"

The aspiring journalist, DJ and stripper (among other things) nodded her head and closed her eyes to keep the tears from falling. The interview with the mysterious killer had not exactly gone as planned. Sure the chubby guy named Guido was shy but he was very cooperative. He had answered her questions directly. However, Sandra quickly saw that the real brains was this man who had just materialized out of nowhere in Guido's room. She had jumped up, frightened by his sudden appearance, but the newcomer reassured her with a wave of his hand and soothing words.

"Don't be afraid, young lady, we won't hurt you. Just the opposite! I came here for you to find your joy."

Sandra could not help blushing because nobody had called her young lady since she had rounded thirty long enough ago to leave its marks. The stranger had straightaway launched into a long speech that Sandra did not really understand since it was about her life. Her vain attempts to get into show business, her failure on the radio that closed its doors on her, her amateur plays that were funny but total crap, her castings without callbacks, the work as an extra for TV shows, her stint with the local newspaper that slowly relegated her to useless items. And then the stream of cheating, violent boyfriends who did not want to share their life with a woman-child who refused to grow up. And the family who looked on her like a strange animal and finally cut off financing her artistic projects.

The voice of the mysterious man was gentle and compassionate but the words hurt because they told the truth. Before

99

he had finished the summary of her failed life Sandra was sobbing.

"I know life can be cruel and unjust, especially towards souls as sensitive and noble as yours," the patron continued after Sandra had dried her tears. "I saw it right away. You were not made for a life like this. You deserve a destiny worthy of your talent and your personality. But this world is too petty to let you rise up. I'm here to change all that."

And he unveiled his plan to her.

8.

Sibilla and her friends spent the night in a comfortable hotel room but under close surveillance by the police. The next morning they got an excellent breakfast through room service, thank you very much, and they allowed Francesco to go to work but with an escort who looked like a chicken. The others stayed inside.

Dalia spent the morning whining, "Sandra is all alone in the apartment. She's going to burn my pots and pans and get fingernail polish all over the table."

Graham Carter made his entrance carrying a pile of files and a laptop. He had searched for documentation about Dante Alighieri. Despite the somewhat offhand manner he treated them with, Sibilla was thankful that he took her theory seriously. Together they went through the passages in the long poem that dealt with hell and just as the magician feared everything matched.

In the vestibule of hell went running around *the miserable souls of humans who lived with neither infamy nor praise, who were concerned only with themselves*, the crowd of apathetic humanity being relentlessly chased by swarms of wasps and hornets. Father Celestino, the indifferent priest, had been stung to death by wasps at one of the entrances to the city.

In the First Circle of hell was limbo where all the just but unbaptized souls were confined for eternity. *For such crime and for no other guilt we were lost and our only punishment is that in desire we live without hope.* And among the damned were the Wise men of Antiquity who waited in vain to be saved.

The Second Circle was the final "resting place" of those devoured by a blind passion that made them lose their mind. Among them, as Sibilla had already mentioned, was Francesca da Rimini and her brother in-law, but also Cleopatra, Dido and many other mythical beauties condemned to be buffeted by endless storms.

In the Third Circle you find the gluttons harassed by the monstrous Cerberus, the three-headed dog whose barks are deafening. Dante met one of his contemporaries named Ciacco, the same name as the food critic who was eaten by a dog.

As for the Fourth Circle, he gathered together the misers and spendthrifts in the same absurd punishment of pushing and rolling huge weights that represented misspent or too jealously guarded wealth.

Finally to get to the Fifth Circle he had to cross the muddy banks of the Styx in which the angry, wrathful and melancholic fight as their furious cries get mired in the swamp. This explained why the last murder happened on the banks of the Arno.

After reading about the damned in the Sixth Circle Sibilla turned to Leonardo and commanded, "You're staying here tonight."

"Huh? Are you mad?" the journalist blurted out. "No way I'm leaving you with that… that snake!" He pointed angrily at Graham Carter.

"Luckily we've already passed the circle of the wrathful," the Englishmen calmly blew out a cloud of smoke.

"We're dealing with the Heretics and Unbelievers this time," Sibilla replied, trying to stay as calm as possible herself. "If our killer manages to identify us, he might use our personalities to destroy us."

Somebody other than the too proud Leonardo would have accepted this argument. But our man refused to listen and could not believe that he himself was in any danger. After all, incredulity was one of his sins. Moreover, the damned met by Dante and Virgil in the *Divine Comedy* were not called Verga.

"None of this tells us where our murderer is going to strike tonight," Dalia jumped in to quiet the sparks starting to fly.

The silence that followed her remark made her point. Sibilla examined the map again and a spot not far from the Ponte Vecchio caught her attention. After a quick search of the building there she looked at the others.

"I think I've got it."

"Are you ready, my girl?"

"I was born ready."

Sandra giggled at this answer she always dreamed of giving, straight out of one of her favorite movies. Her little laugh got stuck in her throat when the mysterious man shot her a look that said he had no taste for jokes. Oh, how his cold eyes blazed! It was hard to doubt his insistence that he was a sorcerer.

"Feed on your ambition, child, on that and nothing else. You have to be concentrated for tonight's work or your soul will also become a plaything for those forces that will be used for our grandeur. Do you understand?"

Sandra swallowed hard and nodded, "Got it."

The blazing eyes simmered down. "From now on you're the centerpiece in this game. As for the coming sacrifice, try not to look away from the victim."

9.

The Santo Stefano Church was comforting shelter during the day with its soled-beamed roof and its splendid nave that was also used as a stage for classical orchestras. At night there was little to interest tourists. The piazza around it was tiny compared to the other places in the city and had only three points of access through three narrow streets. It was simple to post a few plain-clothes policemen who could sit on their scooters and flirt with girls who were also undercover.

Inspector Bonelli had requisitioned an apartment on the second floor of a building across from the church and was watching the place with Sibilla and Dalia. The owners were an old couple who did not seem to mind the presence of a police officer, a beautiful redhead and a pretty brunette in their home. They just went to bed after making the three of them promise not to slam the door or stomp down the stairs when they left.

Graham Carter was not with them. He was at the Italian headquarters of the Cagliostro Section to give them all the information gathered during the busy day at the hotel. Sibilla did not miss him. His attitude had changed since the first time they had met in the Cosimo Ruggieri case. He had become cold and haughty. The young woman did not understand why the agent was acting like this. Did he think they were in the way whereas in Paris he had needed them? The magician felt deeply disappointed.

Inspector Bonelli, on the other hand, was great company. He promised the two girls that the young murderer would not escape. While waiting for the fateful hour he asked Dalia about her journalism studies and seemed impressed by her anecdotes.

The clocks of Florence struck midnight. Sibilla and the others stared hard and held their breath.

Dalia suddenly covered her mouth to hold back a cry of excitement: a pudgy figure wearing a hoodie just showed up. Sibilla smiled. It was her attacker from the night before coming to prepare for the next tragedy. But the new victim, the heretic who would have to burn in a flaming tomb, had not yet arrived.

"Let's get him," Bonelli whispered.

The police officer disappeared into the kitchen so he would not be seen or heard from the outside when he contacted his men. Sibilla and Dalia stood closer to each other, panting, scrutinizing the chubby young man who was looking around cautiously. The magician furrowed her brow: this guy did not fit the profile of a sorcerer; he looked like a nobody. And yet he was the one who had thrown her into the Arno last night and the fact that he was here as expected proved his guilt. Anyway, the Arbini brothers did not look the part either...

All of a sudden a door creaked opened in the small square. Dalia grabbed Sibilla's arm. The gate of the church had opened by itself. The two women saw the chubby guy stiffen up, tremble, then head towards the historic building like he was sleepwalking.

"Bonelli," Sibilla shouted. "The crime's happening in the church! Bring in your men!"

And without waiting for him she left the apartment, followed by Dalia. They forgot their promise to the old couple when they ran down the stairs, their heels drumming up a hell of a racket. They were outside in seconds. The young man had disappeared.

A weird light inside Santo Stefano alerted them. Orange flickers danced on the pavement. Sibilla turned around at the sound of footsteps and waved to the police coming out of hiding to arrest the suspect.

"He's inside and doesn't looked armed. No trace of a potential victim. Let me go first and you rush him when you hear me yell."

Bonelli and Carter had been smart enough to introduce the magician as a specialist in dark cults, which was not far from the truth, so it was not hard for her to convince them to let her act alone.

As she got near the big door with a smaller door set in it, she got goose bumps. Black magic was already at work. She entered with no more protection than Cagliostro's ring held out in front of her.

The sight was petrifying.

A figure being eaten alive by tall flames was flailing in the middle of the choir. Something in Sibilla whispered to her that it was all an illusion.

This cannot be. You can't burn like that. Nothing is real.
You should've listened to Leonardo!

With teeth clenched she chased away these parasitical thoughts so common around manifestations of dark magic. If she listened to the devious ideas, who knew what might happen to her.

She raised the ring sparkling on her fist and shouted loudly and firmly, "By the power of the Twelve and Cagliostro whose heir I am, may these evil spells depart and may this place be peaceful again!"

The jade stone emitted a bright light, brighter than the diabolical fire, and it struck the inferno and its prey. Sibilla felt the evil influence breaking down while the man now freed of the fire collapsed to the ground, his skin all purple and sweaty, his clothes ruined.

The police who came in as Sibilla was finishing her exorcism were stunned by the horrifying spectacle. Dalia was the first to get hold of herself and run to the victim. She put two fingers to his swollen, red throat and jumped back in a panic, "Call an ambulance quick! He's still alive."

When Sibilla and the officers, including Bonelli, joined her, she was staring at the panting body that gave off the repugnant stench of grilled pork. Her eyes were wide with fear and disbelief when they met Sibilla's.

"It's... the guy with the hood..."

Startled by the brutal understanding of what that meant the magician thought her legs were going to give out under her. "He was just a decoy. Whoever's behind this got rid of him because we identified him."

10.

As planned Leonardo paid no attention to Sibilla's orders and slipped away from the police posted outside his room. For this he had to be an acrobat despite his ailing knee. He climbed from one balcony to another until he reached an open window where he snuck into a messy room. Bed sheets and sexy clothes were strewn across the soft carpet and quiet giggles came from the bathroom, barely audible over the sound of the shower.

Lucky I didn't break in here earlier...

Laughing to himself at the idea of the vaudevillian scene his intrusion would have caused, Leonardo tiptoed to the door and snuck out of the room, then of the hotel, without a hitch. He had decided not to join Sibilla and the others but to go to the scene of the crime that would take place the next day. The journalist still did not believe in all this nonsense about witchcraft and magic spells. For him the victims had been drugged in some way. Maybe two drugs, one a hallucinogen and the other a poison.

Leonardo walked fast through the busy streets until he reached the big square where the Palazzo Vecchio stood. It would soon be midnight and he imagined his friend ready to jump on her suspect screaming esoteric curses. But he still had to admit that the glowing light of Cagliostro's ring was impressive. Almost as much as the imposing secular fortress in the big square which the young man was staring at. The façade of the monument was lit up with a soft, golden light that mellowed its menacing look. The clock in the belfry showed three minutes to midnight. A lot of people were strolling around the Fountain of Neptune and the Loggia dei Lanzi.

Leonardo took out his tablet and reread the description of the Seventh Circle of the Inferno, that of Violence. That funny little Dante had spiced things up by dividing the region into three rings according to the type of violence the damned were guilty of. The poet Virgil, his guide, first met those who had been violent against others, then against themselves and finally against God. In the first section the damned were stuck in a ditch of boiling blood. And as if this punishment might seem too soft for the Prince of Darkness, there were also centaurs shooting arrows into them. These creatures represented the bestial part of man according to a commentary.

The journalist looked around. He thought he remembered that somewhere in this square was a statue of a half-man, half-horse creature. His face lit up when he finally found what he was looking for just under the Loggia dei Lanzi. The building was open day and night so he could get close to the big sculpture representing Hercules defeating the centaur Nessus. With one hand the hero was twisting back the chest of the fabulous creature enough to break its back. The centaur was struggling desperately but he was obviously a goner: the son of Zeus was about to swing his club with all his superhuman strength to finish off his adversary.

Leonardo walked around the base inspecting the two stone fighters. He did not know exactly what he was looking for. A secret compartment, maybe a trap that would spring on the designated victim.

Completely absorbed in his search he paid no attention to the strokes of midnight until the first screams echoed through the square. He was startled and rushed out from under the Loggia. On the other side of the square, near the equestrian statue of Cosimo of Tuscany, a man was backing up toward the Fountain of Neptune. Not just backing away but writhing around and grabbing his body as if being stung all over. Tall, brown-haired, with square shoulders and jaw, he was waving his arms around and screaming in fear like a child.

"Stop! Leave me alone!"

The man took one last step backward and fell, almost like he was pushed. He went over the low wall of the fountain, catching his shirt on one of the bronze statues before dunking into the water. This did nothing to calm his twitches. He kept on squirming and screaming.

Leonardo remembered what had happened the night before and snapped out of his trance. He ran as fast as his bum knee allowed and leaped over the edge of the fountain. The other was face down in the water and looked unable to get up. Leonardo got his arms around him and pulled as hard as he could. He managed to get the guy's head above water.

"You're going to drown, you idiot!" Leonardo shouted when the guy started fighting against him.

The man sucked in air and panted, "Help me! The blood... the blo..."

Something seemed to pull him under water and he splashed all over the journalist.

"Oh no!"

Leonardo tried to pick him up again but the man had become heavier than the statues standing on the edge of the fountain. The reporter planted his feet firmly on the bottom, his fingers gripped the shoulders of the poor guy and he pulled with all his strength. The muscles in his arms bulged and his teeth grinded. He felt like his eyes were going to pop out of the sockets and his veins explode. But nothing happened. The man's movements became heavier and heavier and Leonardo had to give up when the pain in his knee became unbearable.

"Someone help me!" he yelled at the top of his lungs. "The guy's dying!"

His eyes searched the onlookers who were gathering around the fountain but they were too astonished or scared to react. Finally some of them decided to act and he was joined by three men and a woman. All together they tried to lift the poor guy who had stopped moving. Just as Leonardo was about to cry out for more help he noticed one person whose expression was different from the rest of the crowd. It was a woman, maybe thirty years old, who was almost unnoticeable because she was so small. She was wearing a black sweatshirt with the hood pulled over her hair. But he saw clearly her big, blue eyes sparkling and a twisted smile on her face. Her teeth were abominable.

Leonardo came back to reality when the others pushed him to get the man out of the fountain. The weird force had finally let him go. The journalist helped them lay the victim on the ground. Someone ran up saying he knew first aid. With nothing more he could do Leonardo wiped the water off his face and turned to look at the crowd.

The little woman with crooked teeth had disappeared.

11.

The guy was still alive but his burns were so serious that they had to transfer him to a hospital with a severe burn center. The doctors put him into an artificial coma and confessed that there was nothing else to do but wait. The victim was a sorry sight to see, lying unconscious on a hospital bed whose whiteness made a stark and gruesome contrast to the raw, red skin oozing puss. Neither Dalia nor the police at the scene had seen the flames that had ravaged the body but the result was here in its outrageous horror. The clothes had also burned and they had found no identification on him, just a notebook full of talented drawings with no spark of genius.

"I think that's the only thing that will identify him to relatives," Inspector Bonelli said. "We'll also get impressions from his teeth to take around to local dentists but his fingerprints are shot."

"If you've got his teeth maybe we could keep the notebook," Sibilla suggested. "Who knows, he might've scratched some clues or made portraits of his accomplices. Even amateur artists tend to sketch everything."

"You're absolutely right. I'll make an exception for you this time but of course I'll put Agent Carter in charge of it. And I'll tell headquarters to start searching for his dentist, then we'll go back to your hotel."

"Maybe you can... use your ring to interrogate the guy," Dalia said to Sibilla when the inspector had left.

"The powers of the ring are enormous but I don't know if it can work on a coma," Sibilla answered. "I'll try."

The beautiful magician raised Cagliostro's ring, which glowed brightly right away. Dalia stood at the door and glanced into the corridor. She did not want to admit it but this demonstration of magic scared her. She had followed Sibilla's adventures assiduously and had wanted to help in her investigations, but now that her dream was coming true she realized how frightening the occult arts, not to mention the deaths that defied logic.

"By the power of Cagliostro whose heir I am," Sibilla murmured, "you who we know nothing about, you who were tricked by the evil force that is staining this city with blood, come out of your mortal coil and show yourself."

The light from the ring enveloped the patient stuck with tubes and wires. The machines measuring his heartbeat and brain waves suddenly changed their rhythm. The red body shuddered on the white sheets. Sibilla concentrated on what she could feel. The magic seemed to be reaching out. Sinking deeper into the numbed psyche of the wounded she felt like she was hitting a wall of ice. Someone had set up defenses. The pretty redhead shivered. A very powerful force was protecting the young man's soul. The real leader had taken precautions when he used his henchman like a puppet.

Sibilla looked for a crack where she could slip through. She felt cold needles digging into her forehead like prickly thorns guarding an enchanted garden. Beyond the impassable obstacle she felt, far, far away, the young man's subconscious flickering slowly like a candle flame.

"Please, fight. They manipulated you and we have to know who it is," the magician whispered.

"Sibilla..." Dalia's voice came from afar.

"Wait a second. I think I've got something."

She tried to focus on the faint glimmer of life. If only Dalia would stop calling her and those machines would stop their annoying clicking and beeping...

Sibilla was yanked back into reality: the EKG was going wild and the body was shaking with violent spasms. White foam was spewing from the cracked lips.

"Dalia, quick, go get a doctor!"

She ran out into the corridor while the magician lifted her ring again. Sweat beaded on her forehead but she had to try once and for all.

"By the power of the Twelve, leave him alone, demonic being! I, Sibilla, Cagliostro's heir, put this man under my protection!"

The jade light washed over the burn victim again but it was vibrating, trembling, like a flame in a strong wind. The magician heard bitter mumblings mocking her. Then the room suddenly got cold.

"There you are, monster," she hissed between her teeth.

She concentrated all her energy on the blurry figure that she could see now leaning over the poor guy, shadowy claws clamped down on the blistered throat.

"Enough!"

The stone in the ring shot out a bright ray of light that struck the thing full on. The specter disappeared with an angry yelp. The magician fell to her knees, exhausted by the psychic effort. The machines were starting to calm down little by little. The door swung open and the doctors and nurses poured into the room.

"Go, we'll take care of him!"

Dalia helped Sibilla to her feet. "What happened?"

"I've never felt such a force. Only a being with centuries of practice could harness such powerful magic."

The sorcerer threw his head back and howled in rage. Sandra was startled and almost went to help him in the chalk circle where he sat. But she remembered her mentor's orders not to touch him and stay quiet.

Still she whispered, "Are you okay?"

"Of course not!" he barked.

Sweat was running down his cheeks like tears and his nose was bleeding. He moved his trembling legs and left the circle made of weird signs that he had traced on the floor. Sandra would have to clean this all up before Dalia got back. She was living a secret life now but took comfort in imagining the amazing report she would get out of the experience. She already had the title: My Voyage to the Depths of Madness or In the Footsteps of Occult Terrorism. Of course there would be human sacrifices as the necromancer had warned her. But wasn't it an exhilarating sensation to be able to kill a man with only the power of your imagination? And the sorcerer had given her the instructions: concentrate on the man to be sacrificed, then think of centaurs attacking him with arrows before drowning him in the fountain transformed into a pool of boiling blood. See the most ghastly ideas in her mind materialize... It was... exhilarating and nightmarish! She was proud of holding her concentration almost the whole time in spite of the spasms of horror coupled with the little sparks of stronger and stronger excitement.

Then the handsome young man had looked at her and thrown everything off. He was cute, sure, but also somehow familiar.

"So go and get cold clean water instead of gaping like an idiot," her master ordered.

He no longer spoke nicely like before. What did she do wrong? Nevertheless she obeyed and came running back from the kitchen.

"You didn't manage to eliminate Guido, Sir?" she dared to ask after the sorcerer had drunk his water.

"Of course not, stupid girl! That damned woman got in the way! May all the descendants of Dragut curse her! She's a lot stronger than I thought. We have to get rid of her as soon as possible!"

"If it's that redhead dressed in leather I can ask Dalia about her. They know each other and..." She froze. Now she remembered where she had seen that tall, brown-haired cutie.

"What is it?" her master looked inquisitively at her.

"Oh, it's just that I remember seeing another friend of Dalia's. He was trying to save the guy we kill... sacrificed."

"What was he doing there? Did he see you?"

Sandra shrunk. The pretty boy had stared right at her and almost ruined her concentration. But she shuddered to think what the terrifying sorcerer would do if he knew the truth. He had eliminated Guido without blinking an eye.

"I was as cautious as a little mouse."

12.

Inspector Bonelli drove Sibilla and Dalia back to the hotel where they would have to be confined. It was already late and the streets were almost deserted. They drove in morose silence. Dalia fought against sleep. She was exhausted but she had been so terrorized that she was afraid of nightmares.

Sibilla, on the other hand, was thumbing through the notebook, her mind distracted by the relation between the Divine Comedy and the murders decimating the city. She sensed a link with the History of Florence and Dante's life. The city of the Medicis had seen periods of splendor interspersed with bloody episodes. One of the longest and most famous had pitted two parties against each other, the Guelphs and the Ghibellines, in the struggle for power. In Dante's time the latter had suffered great setbacks and therefore took advantage of the violent rivalry that tore apart the Guelphs, a rivalry between two families, the Vieiri dei Cerchi and the Donati, called respectively the Whites and the Blacks. Dante supported the Whites and like his coreligionists, he had been sentenced to exile. That's why he was not buried in Florence, the city that was so dear to his heart.

A drawing suddenly broke Sibilla's concentration. She squinted. The streetlights marched by, eerily illuminating a skillfully sketched face.

When they got to the hotel the magician was surprised to see Leonardo at the entrance, surrounded by Graham Carter and his three henchmen. Sibilla gently shook Dalia who had nodded off and climbed out of the car.

"What's happened to you?" she asked her friend. "I hope you didn't try to follow me."

"Not at all. I wanted to get a head start on the murderer by visiting the scene of the next crime. But the bastard had the same idea!"

"That was too risky, Leo," Sibilla scolded when the journalist had finished telling his story in their luxury jail cell.

"Risky but smart. For once your stubbornness will be useful to us."

"What a touching compliment. I have to admit that it's a little sadistic pleasure for me to see you not knowing whether to strangle me or hug me. But it's no comfort that I couldn't save that guy…"

Indeed, the stranger at the Neptune's Fountain died on the spot. Leonardo was there at the end, with his aching knee, exhausted and powerless, sitting on the edge of the monument where Graham Carter had found him.

Sibilla put a comforting hand on her friend, "There was nothing you could do. I understand how you feel. I felt the same thing tonight. And you, Carter, what led you to the Palazzo Vecchio? Intuition?"

"No, I just followed Verga who was leaving the hotel just as I was coming back. I knew he was onto something when he got to the Piazza."

He took a heavy package out of a leather satchel at his feet and slipped it into a plastic cover for extra protection.

"When you got the idea of a connection between the murders and the *Divine Comedy* I went to our headquarter at the Vatican."

Sibilla and Leonardo looked at each other with the same silent thought in their minds: the Vatican? This section of the international police certainly had a long reach into the secrets of power. Behind them Dalia did not stir. She had finally surrendered to sleep after trying in vain to get in touch with Francesco. She was snoring quietly on the big sofa near the door, still holding her phone.

"This is an original exemplar of the work illustrated by Botticelli and kept in the Apostolic Library," Carter was caressing the wrapped package. "Another manuscript is in Berlin. Both were studied carefully by our service because we believe this poem is, in fact, an incantation."

"And our murderers are killing all these people for… some kind of magic spell?" Leonardo asked. "Good God, these guys are more screwed up than all the wacky fans of Nostradamus and Cosimo Ruggieri put together. What do they think they'll get from all this?"

"Maybe chaos," Sibilla said. "Could I see the book, Graham?"

The British agent handed the package to her. Sibilla took the book gently out of the plastic and then unwrapped it. She stared at the ancient volume for a minute before carefully turning the pages. The stylized writing was hard to decipher and some of the magnificent illustrations had not been finished. Nevertheless, the document was priceless.

"This book was illuminated more than a century after Dante's death since Botticelli was born in the 15th century," the magician said. "But an old spell can be transmitted from the original to the copies. I feel it in the pages. Are there others like this?"

"Except for Berlin, not to our knowledge," Carter responded. "But maybe…"

"Maybe the murderer has a copy," Sibilla finished for him. "A book impregnated with powerful magic is in the hands of a dangerous sorcerer… whose picture I have here."

She took out the notebook with partly burned drawings and opened it directly onto the sketch that had attracted her. The face was handsome and harmonious, lined with thin wrinkles but firm and strong-willed. The mouth, on the other hand, was just a cruel line and the eyes behind the heavy lids drilled into your soul, even in the mere drawing.

"Let me introduce Maleficus," Sibilla said quietly. "One of the most evil beings the Earth has ever seen."

13.

Sandra was starting to regret her collaboration with the old man. Still, she had done everything he had told her to, getting a new victim off his hit list. But this was not enough for him! She also had to stay up all night searching the Internet to get information on the people hanging out with Dalia. She was not Lisbeth Salander and dawn was already rising when she finally found the cute guy.

"Leonardo Verga!"

The nodded. He was burning with an inner fire that seemed never to go out.

"And the woman? Did you find her first name? Her last name is Drago, that should be enough, right?"

"I have nothing on her," Sandra was on the verge of tears. "All I know is that Dalia calls her Sibilla when she talks about her. And no Sibilla Drago shows up on the search engine."

"Of course not, stupid girl! Because it's an alias!"

For his part Maleficus was scolding himself bitterly for having sacrificed Guido. It would have been much better to get rid of this whiney girl whose fussy behavior was getting on his nerves. And time was pressing. Sibilla would end up predicting his next moves. He had to checkmate her tomorrow night. And for that he had to strike hard, very hard.

He threw the small, black squares of paper on Sandra's desk along with tweezers, a bottle of silver ink and a list of names that had to be crossed out at the top. "Write instead of whining. Write down all the names on this list and add Leonardo Verga and your roommate. I'll make sure they get them."

"But I want to sleep…" Sandra grumbled.

"You sleep when the work is done or you'll be sorry."

He left the room and slammed the door. He was not sleeping either. He had a new employee to hire.

A little after 7 a.m. Sibilla left the hotel with Graham Carter. It was not hard to convince the Interpol agent when she explained that around 150 miles from the historic city they would find all the pieces needed to complete their investigation… at Dante's tomb in Ravenna.

"No sadder end than dying far from the city he loved," Graham remarked as the big, black sedan took off. "But do you think his remains are really there?"

"There's only one way to find out," Sibilla fiddled with Cagliostro's ring.

They left Florence to the east, drove along the Arno for a while, then passed a few towns that were just waking up. Sibilla wrote a text message for Leonardo, who would still be sleeping, to tell him where she was going and when she would be back.

As she was typing she had a sad and creepy feeling that she would never see her friend again. Maybe she should have asked him to come along. Maybe she had made a mistake…

You are very dear to me, she wrote, *and I count on finding you safe and sound when I get back. Be careful! The man we're looking for might know who you are.*

She sent the message and leaned back with a sigh.

"There's something that always surprises me," Carter said as he drove smoothly. "From the first time I met you, you and Verga, really… Why someone versed in magic would burden herself with a skeptic? He never stops contradicting you and doesn't help the investigation."

Sibilla looked at Carter. He had hammered out this tirade calmly and as the rising sun was bathing his hair in a golden halo she realized that she knew absolutely nothing about this man. On the surface he was pretty nice, seductive even, but wasn't that what they said about the devil?

"It's because of his incurable skepticism that I trust him," she finally answered.

In the quick glance he threw at her she saw his perplexity and she felt a tinge of satisfaction.

"Since I started investigating the supernatural I've seen lots of people who were seduced by the dark forces around us like the Arbini brothers or that poor kid lying in the hospital right now, even Cosimo Ruggieri. Magic is a force with no limits except those of the universe. It's so tempting in the power it can give you, don't you think, Carter?"

The agent remained silent. The Tuscan landscape paraded by them with its gentle hills and majestic cypress trees.

"So, my only trusted ally is an inveterate skeptic. Though I sometimes find his attitude annoying, I still think at least his pigheaded ideas won't be corrupted by all the attractions of occult powers. That, Carter, is why I burden myself with him. Does that answer your question?"

"Clear as a bell," the Interpol agent droned.

They hardly talked at all for the rest of the trip. Sibilla examined the old Vatican manuscript again and Carter focused on the winding road. Behind them thick, dark, menacing clouds gathered on the horizon.

Faint music woke up Leonardo. He stretched peacefully in the big hotel bed. They may have been under surveillance but being imprisoned in a palace was not a traumatic experience. He grimaced when his knee knotted up in pain.

Damn fracture. I bet they'll have to operate again...

This thought ruined the good mood that he had awoken with. He had gone through months of physical therapy after the accident caused by the Arbini brothers and he thought he was out of the woods. But the pain was coming back, worse and worse. He threw off the sheets and cursed Maria Carpi and her bright idea to send him hiking among the brigands in the Alps.

His cell phone started blinking on the night table. He read and reread the message on the screen. Especially these words: *You are very dear to me and I count on finding you safe and sound when I get back.*

Leonardo smiled. Sibilla would never hold it against him that he was hard on magic. She would always be there for him in the worst of times. With these few words she reminded him that he could count on their friendship. That might be all but it was more than enough...

"You too, pretty witch, are dear to me. Be careful." he sent back.

She had left with Graham Carter for the day. His breath stopped for a moment. Not from jealousy. She owed him nothing. No, it was just that he did not like the idea of her being alone with that guy. This famous Cagliostro section looked to him like a doomsday cult and not an official department of investigation.

Wearing his only pants Leonardo limped over to the window and opened the curtains. The night before the streets were washed with a sweet, orange glow. Now they were drowned in shadow. The journalist looked at the sky being invaded by leaden, menacing clouds, rolling and twisting like the damned being punished in hell. He shuddered. Dante's poem was starting to infect him with morbid thoughts.

When he shook off his gloomy reverie he noticed a small, dark object sitting on the windowsill. A piece of paper, black like a blade of night. A little rock lying on top to keep it from flying off in the wind. Leonardo opened the window. In some distant part of his mind he thought he heard Sibilla's voice: *Be careful.*

The words kept repeating, a warning sign too faint to be heeded. "After all, what danger could come from a piece of paper?" he wondered as he picked it up. When he saw his own name written in silver ink on the black background he remembered the bewitched letters sent to Sibilla by Araldo Arbini.

But it was too late.

A bright flash then a brutal headache bent him double and he felt nothing but debilitating pain. It was as if he was floating in a void, alone with just this agony drilling into his head. When the torture stopped after a brief, excruciating moment, he found himself sitting on his bed. The window was open and a cool breeze was moving the curtains. He did not remember opening it. He just remembered reading Sibilla's message... and he still had the phone in his hand.

The death last night is still disturbing me.

He forgot about everything and went into the bathroom to take a nice hot shower. He had a long day in front of him.

On the carpet, near the window, the breeze blew away some tiny, silvery confetti.

Gianni was walking lazily down the already bustling streets. Despite the blisters caused by his old shoes and the ulcerations of his armpits and legs and also the awful hunger gnawing away at this stomach, he had never felt so good. Life was finally showing promise. Hope was finally showing up at the end of a long life of wandering, rejection and hardship. Even in the enchanting museum city the lost souls drift around with no other goal but to find food and temporary shelter, no other purpose but to suffer as little as possible. And last night an angel alit near him. An angel taking the shape of a smiling old man whose words had comforted him. No one had ever spoken to him with so much kindness.

"This world has to change. And we're going to do it together. In the new world you will be a lord. In the new world others will love and respect you. In the new world you will no longer be hungry. All you have to do is listen to me and obey."

And to show him the extent of his power he had touched Gianni's forehead with the tip of his finger and, my God, the fantastic visions he had seen, the exquisite sensations he had felt! He saw himself enthroned in a plush armchair, rubbing his bare feet together, freed of blisters and fungus, soaked in a golden basin full of perfumed water. Tiny fish were swimming around his toenails and tickling him as they nibbled away. The room he rested in was small and cozy. A door opened onto a kitchen and he smelled the enticing odors. Tomatoes and garlic mixed with wine, dried fruit cakes baking in the oven. And he could see a young blonde girl wearing a thin dress, flitting around and smiling at him with a wooden spoon in her hand. He broke down in tears when the images of his simple happiness vanished.

"All this will be yours. Yes, you just have to follow my instructions."

The old man put his fingertip on Gianni's forehead again and a handsome young man whose face was twisted into a bestial grin filled up his vision. The intruder had pushed Gianni's comfortable armchair and toppled it over. Then he kicked away the golden basin with the little fish and brought out a

Molotov cocktail which he lit and threw into the kitchen. Pretty girl, tomato sauce and sweet-smelling fruitcake were pulverized in the explosion.

"No! No! Bastard!" Gianni had howled.

"You just saw what is in the way of your happiness," the man said. "Help me destroy this evil person and paradise will finally be yours."

The homeless man came back to the present when he saw that his feet had carried him to his destination. He had to wait for hours but at midnight everything would be done. He would make sure that Leonardo Verga could not hurt him.

14.

The clock on the dashboard read 9:45 when they reached the suburbs of Ravenna. They drove through a series of clean streets lined with modern housing lacking any real personality. They could have been in any suburb in Italy or even in France that sprang up around an old city. A strangely dull entrance for a city thousands of years old and founded by the Thessalians.

It became a lot more interesting to look at when they reached the historic center but except for the majestic basilica with its stone tower looming over the rows of cypress trees and some houses with bright walls, the rest of the freshly painted buildings lacked that stamp of originality that existed in Florence.

They found parking easily in a big lot near the basilica, so it was only a short walk to the square in front of it. The paving stones were smooth and regular. To the left was a park protected by metal grating that went all the way to the famous tomb of Dante standing next to the Franciscan cloister. The place was very quiet. There was only one couple of young tourists staring at the funerary monument, a neoclassical temple topped by a small dome and dating back to the 18th century. The door of the tomb was open and you could see the sarcophagus with a bronze wreath lying against it. A lamp burned from the ceiling so you could clearly make out the bas-relief over the poet's tomb.

The history of Dante's bones was an epic in itself because the remains lying in the beautiful sarcophagus from the start had been moved across the city to hide it from the Florentines who wanted to take their prestigious fellow citizen back home, then from Napoleon Bonaparte and then it was lost before being found again by chance on his 500-year anniversary. All the moving around worried Sibilla that the remains in the small building might not be Dante's. Only Cagliostro's ring could verify whether the dead was famous or not.

The two detectives had to wait another ten minutes for the French tourists to finish arguing about whether the poet should be sent back to Florence or not. The skies were clear and the sunlight filtered through the leaves and danced on the small, green mound where Dante had been buried before they built the mausoleum. When the couple finally left, still in heated discussion, Sibilla raised the ring. Carter stepped back quickly as his typically British stiff upper lip suddenly vanished.

"By the power of the Twelve and Cagliostro, my mentor, I demand you who once animated this desiccated corpse to show yourself and speak to me."

The jade sparkled and a ray shot out and enveloped the tomb. A green light glowed around the mausoleum and then seemed to be sucked inside. The birds stopped singing and the wind died down, freezing the branches in eerie stillness. The air around them darkened like a storm was coming. The oil lamp burning in the vault went out. The silence was as heavy as a block of marble before a loud, cavernous scraping sound broke it. It came from inside the mausoleum. A long shadow, thin and draped from head to toe in a tattered shroud, stumbled to the door. It stopped at the threshold, slowly lifted its right arm and pulled off the sheet that was covering its head. Sibilla recognized him right away. There were plenty of paintings and sculptures but she never would have guessed that his eyes had such an icy glare of raging desperation. His long nose bent down over his lips making his face look like a sinister mask. The face of a fasting saint, Leonardo would say.

Sibilla called him by name, "Durante degli Alighieri?"

The specter turned slowly towards her. The magician thought of the Statue of the Commander in *Don Juan* by Molière. She thought she heard stone scraping when the austere head pivoted on the slender neck.

"Who dares trouble my eternal rest? With what impious magic have you come to torture me again?"

"*Again?* Someone came to wake you up before me, Signor Alighieri? Was it an old man? A sorcerer?"

The air got gradually darker. Carter was just a silent shadow next to her.

The apparition nodded, "Oui-da, a demon of olden times. He invoked me with his foul magic and forced me to give him what I had been guarding for centuries. He is going to open the Gate of Shadows and all my sacrifices and all my efforts will have been for nothing. Commend your soul to God, magician."

So that was it! The Gate of Shadows was an old legend making the esoteric rounds. It was a passage into a frightening dimension that the Christian leaders wove into the myth of Hell, which facilitated the conversion of thousands of fearful, naïve souls. Sibilla knew nothing about the creatures that haunted this territory. If Maleficus had managed to get his hands on one of the keys to this gate, the situation had gone from bad to worse.

"Signor Alighieri, how can we keep Maleficus from opening the gate?"

"Alas! That demonic man also took the antidote to the forces of Evil. The part of my poem about Paradise has lines that could protect the world. What a useless guardian of humanity I am."

Sibilla was now completely surrounded by darkness and she shivered violently. The air was frozen into frost and her breath was thickened by the cold that half hid the grieving ghost of Dante. Spirits can corrupt their environment and put the living in jeopardy. The dead poet was a prime example of a dangerous invocation. His distress oozed out of his and wrapped Sibilla in an ectoplasmic envelope. She could not speak out of her numb lips. Dante held out his hand. He did not mean to hurt her and she knew it, but he was jeopardizing her by plunging her into his own limbo.

"It's not too late for you, magician, servant of pagan forces," the ghost whispered. "Come with me to the other side and you can watch the world safely in the Circle of Philosophers. I'll be your Virgil because you look so much like the vision I have of my Beatrice."

It was very flattering but not very alluring, she wanted to reply. Her teeth chattered so hard she could only spit out, "C-C-Carter!"

He finally reacted and stepped forward. "That's enough, Dante Alighieri, my heir is not another muse for you to use as you want."

The poet stepped back, his head bowed, like a child caught being naughty. Sibilla knew that voice. The surprise broke her numbness like icy glass suddenly heated up. It was still Carter's body standing next to her and when he put his gloved hand on her shoulder she felt the ancient power of the Twelve, the formidable magic of Cagliostro, a strong soul that had never surrendered to the lure of evil no matter how powerful.

"Master," she mumbled, relieved.

Carter nodded and smiled but it was not his voice or his gaze. "I was waiting for you in this ethereal sphere beyond death, my girl. It was impossible for me to contact you because Maleficus' presence ruined all my attempts. I'm glad you thought of coming here so I can tell you how to fight this evil sorcerer. Dante didn't lie when he said everything was stolen but I've been ready for this for a long time."

Turning to the phantom of the Florentine bard he spoke gently, "I know you were a good man, Dante Alighieri, but your great weakness is to have always given in to despair. You were a good guardian but these feelings of grief and failure and abandon attracted the dark designs of Maleficus."

The specter fell to his knees and frosty tears sparkled down his gaunt cheeks. "I saw the forces of darkness triumph. I saw myself abandoned by my people and become guardian of knowledge that was too heavy to carry. O wise spirit, how can I find peace after enduring so many ordeals?"

"Stop lamenting because from now on we are taking on this labor. Go in peace."

Obeying a nod from her mentor, Sibilla pointed the ring at the dead poet. Without needing to invoke her power the green light lit up the darkness, revealing the trees around them and the heat of the sun on the golden stones. Dante's ghost gradually faded away as it backed into the crypt. When the oil lamp overhead lit up he disappeared completely.

Sibilla, however, was not yet fully back in the world of the living. Everything was bathed in golden light and fluttering like reflections in a pool of liquid gold. The birds in the trees were frozen in the amber sun, with spread wings and open beaks. Cagliostro was there in his real form. The magician waved his hand and there appeared a grimoire, bound in white leather with pure a silver spine. He held it out to her. It was as light as a swan's feather.

"Here is Dante's treasure, his magic version of Paradise. Time is pressing, my heir. Maleficus has raised an army of pariahs who have nothing to lose and have no riches in your world. Thanks to my blessing you will know what to do. If you keep a loving heart, if you stay just, everything will work out."

He gave her a kiss on the forehead. The light suddenly came back and Sibilla hid her eyes from the blinding flash. The rustling of trees and the songs of birds, all the peaceful sounds were so suddenly brought back that it was almost painful. The beautiful magician slowly got her footing in the reality she knew. Everything was as before. Except for Graham Carter who was sitting on the ground, obviously groggy. Sibilla squatted next to him.

"Nothing broken?"

"Bloody hell," he muttered, "I saw that ghost appear and then a nasty cold spell hit me and I must have passed out. I do have some powers but I'm not as used to the occult forces as you are."

Sibilla smiled. She would not tell the Interpol agent that he had been possessed by spirit of Cagliostro. Even she would take some time to get over a possession like that.

"I got what I came for, Carter. Let's get back to Florence. I can drive if you want."

With the pentacles drawn in red chalk, the walls covered in esoteric designs and the smell of incense and sulfur choking the air, Sandra's room was more like a devil's altar. She had not even had time to complain. Maleficus had sent her out into the city to make sure the dropouts he had recruited were all ready in their strategic locations where the human sacrifices were going to take place. The idiot girl was still oblivious but he would kill her with his own hands once the great, dark work was accomplished. He had made up his mind to see her die a horrible death just because she annoyed him so much.

Maleficus was in the middle of a drawing of a big, scarlet eye with an oblong pupil. He closed his eyes and in a loud, clear voice intoned, "I want to see Leonardo Verga."

Right away the scenery around him changed. Even with his eyes closed he saw the busy street, the cars and scooters speeding by. The houses marched by and wobbled a little with the limp.

"You should get that knee looked at."

His vision turned to the left and Maleficus saw the pretty, worried face of Dalia Barbieri, Sandra's roommate.

"Won't matter," a deep voice echoed inside the old man's head. "It hurts sometimes. The doctor already told me it's normal."

He's lying but he won't have time to regret it, the sorcerer snickered.

"When Sibilla gets back from Ravenna, everything will be over," Leonardo went on. "She contacted me to say she's bringing something back that can stop the murderer. One of those magic things connected to Cagliostro."

Maleficus snapped out of his trance. The Drago woman was confronting him again! He thought he was protected from all counter-spells after stealing the grimoire that was guarded by Dante's ghost, but this damned woman apparently found a way to block him. How could he stop her when she was out of his reach? He had to keep her from reaching Florence. He paced Sandra's room searching for a plan. His gaze fell upon different objects decorating the room, stupid stuffed animals, drawings and those idiotic fairies. Then he looked toward the window and stopped pacing. He opened the curtains and watched the menacing clouds that had been gathering in the sky since morning. A wicked grin made his face even less appealing than usual.

15.

Early in the afternoon the temperature in Florence plummeted. At the same time, the sunlight faded away as if someone had blown out the sun. The thick layer of clouds over the rooftops rumbled cavernously, shaking the walls. People rushed home to get warm and escape the coming rain. The wind blowing through the streets was cold enough to freeze your bones. Fretful gossip sprang up because nobody had ever seen such a phenomenon in this season.

Leonardo and Dalia were authorized to go out so they joined Francesco in their favorite café and watched the brutal change in weather. The apprentice journalist cuddled up to her friend, for warmth as well as for comfort. The manager of the small restaurant lit the fireplace that was once used as a bread oven. The dark, heavy clouds quieted down and a hard rain started beating against the windows. Heavier blows announced that grail had joined the dismal party. Water ran down the walls and across the streets, paving a burbling path through the uneven pavement.

Leonardo heard Dalia and Francesco talk about the old sorcerer who could be blamed for the murders and perhaps for the unseasonal weather. Maleficus… He must have been really crazy to call himself this. No doubt a big fan of Professor Moriarty or some other super-villain. He probably used hypnosis and sleight-of-hand like Dr. Mabuse. But to go so far as to believe that he could control the weather…

"Maybe we should go back to my place," Dalia suggested.

Leonardo and Francesco agreed. A soaking wet man entered the restaurant just then. The three of them recognized Inspector Bonelli. He accepted a cup of hot coffee with pleasure.

"Sorry but I have orders to bring you back to the hotel in case of any problems. Straight from Agent Carter."

"But he left Florence with Sibilla," Leonardo said. "Do we really have to go with you?"

"You do. I have to keep you safe. The roads are cut off and the network's down. I'd feel better keeping my eye on you."

Dalia's protest did not change his mind and they all had to follow the officer begrudgingly, with no idea that around the corner in Dalia's apartment the cause of the problem was summoning dark forces.

They were less than six miles from Florence. Sibilla had driven half the way, then she let Carter take the wheel after a quick stop for a snack. The sun was high in the sky and sparkling on the Arno that flowed to their left. There was no warning sign for the army of dark clouds that suddenly rose up in front of them, a huge, flashing wall whose swirling was lit up by bright lightening strikes. Just seeing this formidable cloud was enough to amaze anyone. But Sibilla and Carter knew it was nefarious when they saw that it was gathered directly over

Florence, leaving the rest of the sky around the suburbs clear and blue.

Carter pulled over on the shoulder of the road. The magician and the agent stared in mutual bewilderment at the weird meteorological phenomenon. Except for the distant rumbling of thunder, everything around them seemed to share in their dazed silence.

"Magic?" Carter finally asked.

"Without a shadow of a doubt," Sibilla said. "Maleficus must know that we left the city and want to stop him when we get back."

Carter drove off again. With his foot to the floor he swallowed up the miles between them and Florence, which was now invisible behind the dark wall. When they got closer they ran into a huge traffic jam. The honking horns were just a faint whisper compared to incessant roar of thunder that had moved closer. Now Sibilla and Carter saw the obstacle better—a diabolical storm whose shadowy tentacles reached from the wet ground up to vertiginous heights and then curved into a dome of bad weather. The police were trying to get the cars to turn around. It proved problematic for the semis and people were cursing and waving their arms around.

When a police officer came up to the sedan Carter rolled down the window and showed his Interpol ID.

"I can't let you through, Sir," the officer said. "Even if you were the Queen of England. The Arno is flooded and dragging cars away and the wind in there is really strong."

"That," Sibilla explained patiently, "is exactly why we're here. They sent us here to figure out what it is. It'd be really hard for us to work if you keep us out of there. No blame on you if anything happens to us. It's the dangers of our job."

The officer looked at Carter's ID, then at the storm, then at the pretty redhead. He gulped hard before waving them through. They slowly passed all the vehicles heading in the opposite direction.

After a few miles they entered the maelstrom. Stronger and stronger gusts of wind shook the car and the windshield wipers were useless in the downpour. Sibilla was amazed by the storm. Maleficus must have called up some special power but did he have enough energy to keep it up for long?

A bushy object suddenly flew at them. Carter swerved to avoid the uprooted cypress that had come at them like the lance of a galloping knight. The tires spun on the wet asphalt. Sibilla screamed when the road vanished and the car tilted down directly at the Arno swirling and crashing like a water-fall. Carter tried to get control but the sedan was sliding to the left. Sibilla wrapped her fingers around Cagliostro's ring in a vain hope for protection.

Then a green light suddenly glowed inside the car.

After a violent shock the car stopped moving. Sibilla flew back against the seat. Her heart was beating so fast it made her ears hum. The car had hit something that kept it from diving into the raging river.

Carter put his hand on her shoulder, "Are you hurt?"

"I'm okay but you…"

There was an ugly bruise on the left side of his face and his lip was bleeding. Apparently his head had hit the door.

"Still better than drowning," he said. "If it weren't for this tree…"

Despite his injuries the Englishman was still cool-headed but Sibilla thought she could see worry and confusion in his eyes. She shared the feelings. The tree that had broken their fall had come out of nowhere. But this was no time for won-der.

Sibilla put the grimoire she got from Cagliostro inside her coat to protect it from the rain and asked, "Can you walk?"

"I can run if I have to. Do you think the old sorcerer can keep this storm going until midnight?"

Sibilla shook her head, "I don't have his knowledge of magic but I know enough to say that this spell requires a lot of…"

She could not finish. She had just seen the dashboard clock.

"Carter, is it just me or are the minutes ticking away at breakneck speed?"

The agent looked at his watch, "It's not just you."

"Oh no." Sibilla turned pale. Her hands were sweating as they gripped the *Paradise*. "Maleficus didn't create a dome of bad weather but rather a temporal vortex. From now on time is running faster in Florence."

16.

The storm continued and all the telephone lines were down. The electricity, however, was holding out bravely even if the lights were blinking off and on. Back in their hotel Leonardo and Dalia had nothing to do but wait for Sibilla and Carter to get back. As the hours flew by so their anguish grew. For the journalist his guilt for letting the magician leave was fighting with the now painful memory of the morning text message... *Be careful!*

If only she took her own advice! He hoped she did not get back on the road.

Out of the corner of his eye he saw Dalia cross herself quickly, her eyes riveted on the leaden clouds pouring out rain and lightning. Francesco had left with the firefighters to help the victims on the outskirts of the city and the young woman was hoping he would be back by nightfall. When he saw her discreetly invoking God, Leonardo almost regretted being an atheist. But the Christian God hated magicians and sorcerers and would not have protected Sibilla.

His ears were starting to buzz. Leonardo shook his head and then rubbed his right ear, knowing it would do nothing. Louder than the drumming rain and chaotic weather, he thought he heard a constant murmur like a human voice whispering through the walls of his consciousness, tapping against his eardrums, gently pinching his brain cells to be heard. And although at first he could not make out a single word no matter how hard he tried, little by little, words formed, then images and a weird impulse in his legs joined the mumbling in his mind. He started feeling cooped up, suffocating, he had to get out, go and rescue Sibilla. He could save her!

There is no God or magic or chance, the voice whispered clearly now. *You can only count on yourself. Only you can save her life.*

At first Leonardo pushed it out of his mind. He had promised not to take any unnecessary risks like Sibilla had said in her message. But this feeling of urgency, of claustrophobia, it was all becoming too much so he finally jumped up, which caused a shooting pain in his knee.

"I have to leave, Dalia. I have to get out of here."

"Me too," the apprentice journalist moaned. "I'm worried about Francesco and I can't just sit here with my arms crossed."

Obsessed by his own thoughts Leonardo did not see that Dalia was suffering from the same fever.

With no further ado the two of them put on their coats, ridiculous shields against the furies outside, and tiptoed into the hallway. Leonardo looked both ways for an officer on duty who could arrest them but the place was deserted. Except for the roaring wind the hotel was as silent as a tomb. Even Leonardo's inner voice was quiet, but he still felt pricked by an urgent sensation of great danger.

They walked cautiously on the soft carpet and down the grand staircase. The receptionist in the lobby was not at the desk. An open newspaper had been left on one of the armchairs and a cigarette was burning in an ashtray, lifting its smoky spirit in a long, lazy ribbon that reached all the way to the decorative ceiling.

The two journalists hesitated a moment in front of the watery curtain outside the big, glass front doors and the shadows shaken by the gales. But the same manipulating force wiped away all their fears by substituting alarming images of their loved ones in the storm.

Leonardo opened the door and marched into the street with Dalia right behind him. They both disappeared in the rain.

In the hotel lobby the old enamel clock decorated with cherubs showed twenty minutes to midnight.

She slipped again and Sibilla dropped into a slimy layer of mud that was getting bigger and deeper in the deluge. Carter helped her up. He had to stick his mouth to her ear to be heard over the incessant din.

"We're going too slow! We'll never make it to the city in time!"

Sibilla felt despair weighing down her footsteps more heavily than the mud sticking to her boots. Maleficus knew what he was doing; his mastery of magic was centuries-old.

Carter slipped then and Sibilla went down with him as she tried to hold him up. The grimoire she was guarding under her coat splashed to the ground. She swept it up immediately but her heart skipped a beat. When she saw the rain evaporate on the white velum cover she knew that Cagliostro was still with her in the old book.

"Shame on me for not thinking of that," Sibilla mumbled. "I deserve this little mud bath." She hugged the book close to her and with her eyes closed she murmured, "Master, come to our help."

Her ring sparkled and the light reflected off the drops of water like countless tiny, fragile prisms. Carter watched on fascinated. Iridescent beams shot out, forming a wall that surrounded the two detectives. The drumming of the rain and the roaring of the tempest gradually faded away.

"My master, Cagliostro, your servant still needs you," Sibilla gripped the grimoire harder. "Get us out of this trap, help us."

The ring kept making a protective barrier that rose up to form a dome over their heads. At their feet the slimy ground slowly hardened. Then small channels appeared, crisscrossing the ground like a net what had been a brown quagmire of mud and trampled grass turned into smooth, gray pavement. Cagliostro's ring lost its glow and the prismatic dome protecting them from the elements vanished.

Sibilla opened her eyes when she felt the rain falling on her again. Carter helped her up and together they marveled at their new environment. The lightning revealed the low, yellow and white buildings with brown shutters, but especially the huge building of white, green and red marble whose façade was pierced with stylized niches, each with a statue that looked out upon the torments of the world with impassive eyes. To the right of this monument a square tower rose up defiantly into the furious sky.

Carter turned around and saw another building, cruder and squatter, but whose golden door surmounted by three sculptures was a wonder: the Baptistery of Saint John.

"Cathedral Square," he said. "Our protector likes to go sightseeing."

Sibilla did not answer. Her gaze was lost toward the top of the Campanile di Giotto where the view of Florence could hush the complaints of the most reluctant tourist who has to climb up the stairs. And ringing as if in thanks for her admiration, the bronze bells in the tower drowned out the rumblings of the storm.

The first strokes of midnight.

Sibilla grabbed Carter's arm, "Cagliostro brought us here because I have to cast the spell of protection from the top of the Campanile."

Without wasting any time talking about it, the pair went around the boxy tower to the entrance. Carter took off a glove and revealed his tattooed hand.

"I'm going to melt the lock. We only have a second."

He grabbed the door handle and his fingers turned red as an acrid smoke rose up. But when the twelfth stroke of midnight rang out and was carried away on a noisy gust of wind, Carter froze and squinted.

"Oh no…"

Sibilla turned around and felt her blood rushing to her heart. He was coming at them from the Via dell'Oriuollo. Soaking wet and disheveled, he limped as fast as his bum knee allowed. His face was tense and twitching as if he was deeply troubled.

"Leonardo!" the magician shouted.

The young man passed right by without seeing them. He turned sharply to the right of the cathedral before Sibilla and Carter could react. As soon as he was in front of the monument he stopped and looked around, completely disoriented. Suddenly he flinched like he had been stung and he grabbed his arm. The sleeve was crackling and fuming. He screamed and then a bruise appeared on his right cheek.

Sibilla knew exactly what was happening. She shrieked, "No! Not him!"

She started to run to help him but Carter grabbed her arm. He put his glowing hand back on the lock and burned it off.

"Hurry up and do what Cagliostro wants. It's the only way to save Verga."

Despite the anguish wringing her guts and bringing tears to her eyes, Sibilla listened to the voice of reason. Choking back sobs she dove into the tower with the horrible feeling of abandoning Leonardo in his hour of need.

17.

Maleficus opened his eyes and howled in rage. In the vision of the puppet who was supposed to sacrifice Verga he had just seen Sibilla. Despite all his efforts the descendant of Dragut managed to get into the city. This woman had formidable power. But she was too late, far too late: the sacrificial hour had sounded with the strokes of midnight. The old sorcerer stood up and stretched his arms out toward the window. The inside panels flew open and ripped the thin, purple curtain covering them. The wind rushed into Sandra's room. Posters were torn off the wall and flew around the circle of candles. The flames shot up and burned the paper, creating a whirlwind of fire around Maleficus.

"Open your eyes, my puppets, and through your vision let's watch our victims perish! Through your vision let the infernal torments of the Lower World appear! Tonight the Gate of Shadows will open and I, Maleficus, will be master of the demons! And of the Earth!"

The flames carried on the wings of the wind rushed out the window and defied the pouring rain, spreading out across the city like so many witches flying off to the Sabbath.

The people of Florence thought that the worst had come upon them with the incessant rain and raging wind that emptied the streets of the historic city. But things took an even more tragic turn when some inhabitants ignored the safety warnings and left their houses, urged on by some strange, insistent impulse. Thus, in the huge square before the Basilica Santa di Novella, there were no less than ten people standing under the wild skies. They did not know each other but they all took their place at different points of the site like actors in a carefully prepared play.

Carlo Venedico was one of them. He stood at the farthest point of the piazza and looked around, lost. He knew the place well from hanging out here after work because there were plenty of girls and pretty tourists needing a guide. His little role as good Samaritan was always good for a hook-up. He just had to win their trust, get them to drink more than usual... Tonight, though, in the middle of this storm, what was he doing here?

He thought about finding someplace warm to hide but a sharp pain lashed his back. He fell to his knees, out of breath from the horrible shock. A sinister laugh answered his groans and another burning lash cut deeply into the skin between his shoulder blades. Venedico screamed in pain and jumped up. He turned around and thought he had gone mad on seeing the gigantic creature who was grinning and showing its teeth blackened by cinders and curdy blood. The monster was completely nude and covered with an anarchy of black tufts of bristling hair on scarlet skin. Its eyes were blacker than a bottomless pit and squinted in bestial joy. Once again it raised the burning whip that had flayed Venedico two times already. He screamed again but he could not dodge the scorching lash that bit deeply across his face from one cheek to the other, slashing his nose in the process. Blinded by terror and unbearable pain, he ran to an alley to escape the living nightmare but the whip cracked in front of him, forcing him to change direction. He ran all over the place, not even thinking about stopping, with the demon behind him guiding him at will like a giant cat waiting for its prey to tire out so it could finish him off with the whip.

The other people in the square were experiencing a fate as lethal and gruesome as this. Their screams were lost in the tumult of the storm.

Leonardo understood nothing. A second earlier he was in front of the marvelous façade of the marble Cathedral and now he was standing in an arid landscape amidst pale yellow ruins that stuck out of the sand like ogre's teeth. Lumpy, purple clouds cluttered the sky like smoke from a fire.

There was a brief flash of orange light and a burning streak lashed his right arm. His wet coat sizzled and prevented further damage but when a second ember hit him in the face the pain snapped him awake to the danger of his situation. He looked around for shelter. An old shack nearby would do the job. He ran for it.

The sky suddenly looked like it was on fire and a rain of burning coals fell on the young man. He missed the wet rain from earlier when the small, fiery darts pelted his skin. The dilapidated shack before him was getting no closer despite his all out sprint. His heart was racing and his skin quivered at every scorching caress of the embers. Leonardo tried to keep calm as his feet crunched the sand.

I've been drugged too and all this is a hallucination. The pain isn't real. I'm not burned. I'm not in danger. This isn't real!

If he started to panic he would end up like the guy in Neptune's Fountain. He had to stay calm and focus. But how could he stop these visions? He was not about to spend eternity in a rain of fire. One of the melting drops burned his neck and he fell to his knees, protecting his head with his arms, which were assailed by sparks.

"Help! Someone stop this nightmare!"

"Verga, I'm here! Look at me!"

Leonardo heard the voice coming from the other side of the world, weak but urgent. He tried to recognize it, this anchor in reality, despite the scorching arrows piercing his arms and legs and back.

"Carter? Is that you Carter?"

"Yes, Verga, I'm right next to you."

An ember dropped on his temple, almost in his right eye. The journalist wiped it off in a panic. His skin was on fire.

"I see a huge desert and fire… fire falling on me! They drugged me, Carter! Take me to the hospital!"

He heard a grumbling noise in the distant and caught this: "Ah, the rain of fire falling on the blasphemers… Logical enough."

"Carter!"

His hair was sizzling with a nauseating smell. He rolled in the sand to put out the flames. He felt some kind of a wave tickling him, rubbing him.

"Stop moving, you big idiot, I'm trying to take care of your burns. My power can do it."

"Sibilla!" Leonardo groaned. "Where's Sibilla?"

He wanted to talk to her one last time… before these damn hallucinations killed him…

"She's close, Verga. She's doing what she can to save you."

Dalia was also counting on Sibilla's speed. She got separated from Leonardo without realizing it. The journalist had continued west toward Cathedral Square. The apprentice had split off to the south. Her feet seemed to be carrying her of

138

their own free will and she felt neither wind nor rain. All that mattered was to find Francesco, to save him from whatever danger he was in. When she got down Via Proconsolo, the looming presence of the Bargello Museum made a shelter from the rain. She stopped in front of the building that bore a certain resemblance to the Palazzo Vecchio. A small voice whispered that Francesco had taken refuge inside the museum. But the monument was closed at night, so how could he get in?

There!

The door on the corner was wide open. Dalia felt like she was swallowed by the darkness when she entered. And right away she felt anxious. What if a guard caught her? She also thought of the ghost of the fanatic priest Savonarola who had been imprisoned and tortured in this fortress. Now it was just the statues of the great Renaissance artists that stood guard in the shadows. Why be afraid of human genius?

She wandered at random. She did not dare call out his name but she was on the watch for any sign of him. The place was completely unfamiliar to her. She had visited the museum with her class in elementary school but never had the chance to come back and marvel at the splendors of Donatello, Verrocchio and Michelangelo. She was, therefore, quite lucky to be standing in the inner courtyard being pelted with rain.

The majestic stairs leading to the loggia had turned into a waterfall and the coats of arms on the streaming walls looked more alive at every lightning flash. The statues in the lower gallery and the ones in the loggia were gone, no doubt taken to the exhibition room where they would be protected from the elements. Dalia noticed these details distractedly. Just like she vaguely thought of taking shelter under one of the arches but she was too obsessed with Francesco's fate to worry about the storm.

A little laugh that she recognized poured down from the loggia. She looked up.

Sandra.

Her roommate was grinning from ear to ear, baring her crooked teeth. Her big eyes sparkled as she stared at her with sinister joy. Dalia thought of one of Tim Burton's poems called "The Staring Girl". But here was no pleasantly strange child. Just a kind of crazy girl whom she thought was her friend.

Dalia knew right away that she had fallen into a trap and Sandra was not on her side. "Oh no…"

"Heeheeheehee!" The little laugh whirled down on her.

Then the nightmare began.

While she was running up the marble tower with her lungs on fire and tears rolling down her cheeks, Sibilla felt like she was abandoning her friend and letting him die alone.

Hold on, Leo, don't die! I'm going to break the spell!

Through the thick walls she very clearly heard the painful screams and calls for help.

The magician got to the first landing. Wet gusts of wind swooped up her red hair. Her legs were already moving on. How many stairs to go? Better not to ask that question. And especially don't waste time looking out one of the big, ogive windows with grills over it.

She flew up the flight of stone steps with Cagliostro's ring lighting her way in the dark and her fingers gripping the grimoire. Above her, getting slowly, stressfully closer, the bells vibrated lightly in the heavy winds.

When she got to the second landing she heard Carter call out for help with a fear in his voice that she thought he was immune to. The situation must be getting really desperate. Then Leonardo yelled for her with his pain-laden cry. She gathered all her strength to keep going up.

The highest point to have the whole city at my feet. I will see all of Florence at one glance in order to save it, to save Leonardo! With a few words!

When she reached the third landing where even stranger winds were blowing through the tall windows, she got scared: Leonardo was not yelling anymore.

Carter did not know where to put his hands. The blisters and burn marks were popping up all over Verga's body. He was suffering the rain of fire for the Blasphemers, the Violent against God, as described by Dante in canto XIV. If only this idiot of a journalist would believe in the reality of his wounds he could get healed more easily instead of rolling around on the wet ground without even listening to the Interpol agent. Out of frustration the Englishman grabbed the young man under his arms and tried to drag him to shelter under the gallery of the building on the edge of the square.

And if the square itself is affecting the spell? He suddenly thought. *If I get him out of the area, then his torments will stop.*

But Verga was so heavy… The Englishman could only drag him for a few feet. It was like dragging the whole world in his hands. The incident at Neptune's Fountain that Leonardo talked about just crossed his mind—how the victim became so heavy that the journalist could not pull him out of the water. Maleficus had taken all precautions to keep his victims in a specific place. Blood had to be spilled in occult locations for the ritual to succeed. Even more reason to get him out of here. If only he could get a grip on reality for a few seconds and follow Carter under the arches.

The agent saw someone watching them from a gallery. It was a man whose age-ravaged face made it impossible to tell how old he was. His tattered clothes were little protection against the cold but he just stood there without moving, staring at them ghoulishly.

"Help! Come help me!" Carter shouted.

But the other did not seem to hear. He watched them without even blinking his eyes, obviously reveling in the sight of Verga's suffering as he turned into an open wound weakened more and more by the pain.

Carter's anger got the better of him. He dropped the journalist and ran at the man who finally blinked his eyes in surprise.

141

Carter grabbed the collar of his wet coat and shook him. The guy started swearing at him and tried to run away in a panic. But all his energy was focused on one goal: watch Leonardo's agony.

The Interpol agent suddenly thought of the kid lying in the hospital and realized he was one of Maleficus' minions.

He pushed the ragged man against a door. "The show's over, bastard! Where's the man who asked you to be here?"

The guy rolled his sleep-deprived, bloodshot eyes. Terror floored him and he collapsed, trembling as if he were freezing cold.

Verga screamed at the same time. Carter swung around. The journalist was slowly getting up, looking groggy.

"Good lord..."

The Englishman knocked out the vagrant with a right hook before running to his partner. One by one his burns were fading away in the rain.

"Carter," Verga's hoarse voice shouted. "The hallucinations stopped. That's what killed all those people. They're so real that made the people believe in their injuries."

The Interpol agent laughed out loud and slapped the young man's on the back. "You're an inveterate skeptic, Verga, and it'll be your undoing one day. For now let's go into the campanile and hide ourselves from malevolent eyes."

A violent clap of thunder froze them in place. The windows in the city rattled so hard they almost broke. A bright flash of lightning struck the square and shattered the pavement. Carter and Leonardo shielded their eyes. When they looked again, there was an old man, tall and thin, standing in the middle of a circle of blackened, steaming cobblestones.

"As usual," Maleficus growled, "I have to do everything myself."

18.

Dalia could not move. Her feet were rooted to the ground. Literally. A monstrous transformation had taken place as Sandra watched on, still smiling. Roots had broken through her leather boots and pierced the paving stones, nailing her in place. She was panicking and defenseless. Twigs and leaves had sprung out of her aching skull to cover her hair. Among the long list of torments described by Dante in *The Divine Comedy* one of them she remembered most.

I'm suffering the punishment of those who committed violence against themselves—the suicides!

She remembered what happened in the second ring of the Circle of the Violent because she had carried the burden of attempted suicide. Slashed arms and wrists; high ledges she sat on but never did more than contemplate the inviting void; medications swallowed with a bottle of whiskey that she eventually vomited on her parents carpet, followed by stomach pumps and emergency psychiatric help.

She had thought all this was behind her, especially when she got her first tattoos to cover the scars on her arms. Now all of a sudden, as she was slowly changing into a tree inside this historic fortress, everything came rushing back, slapping her with shame and hatred of herself. She had told nobody about it. Not even Francesco. And she had cut ties with everyone who had witnessed her depression, including her parents.

Now she was bitterly regretting not being more honest with the man she loved and whom she would probably never see again.

Francesco! Help me!

"Heeheehee," Sandra snickered. "They're coming to get you, Dalia."

No! She had almost forgotten about the horrid creatures who tore the leaves and branches off the tortured souls in Dante's poem.

Hateful shrieks rattled her eardrums. She tried to raise her head but the branches coming out of her neck made the simple movement extremely painful.

Overhead flew creatures with their broad wings spread out, laughing at the storm and diving at her. Then, in a flash of lightning, she clearly saw the hideous faces of her executioners with the bodies of huge vultures: ivory fangs glistening behind puffy lips like a bunch of scars, hooked nose, black, pearly eyes popping out, waxy skin, all framed by black hair as slimy as leeches.

Dalia howled in terror when the harpies attacked her with their claws.

Carter raised his glowing hands that steamed and crackled in the rain. It made no impression on Maleficus who came striding toward them, his white hair flying around his gaunt face like a weird halo crowning the Devil.

"Run away, Verga! I'm going to try to hold him off," the Englishman said.

"Run away? Hold me back?" the old man cackled. "That is not in your power."

Then he stared hard at Leonardo who found himself back in the desert. This time he could not move or scream when the first flames hit him.

Jets of fire shot out of Carter's fingers straight at Maleficus, who fended them off with a simple wave of his hand.

"Die, you stupid Englishman."

A powerful gust of wind threw the Interpol agent against the marble wall of the campanile. He cried out in pain when he felt his ribs break but the wind did not let up, it was crushing him against the wall.

"Maleficus!"

A voice came down from the top of the tower. The old sorcerer looked up and bared his teeth in a vicious grin.

"Finally you show yourself, little pawn of Cagliostro."

Freed from the hypnotic gaze Leonardo snapped back into cold reality. The wind stopped crushing Carter with its lethal power. The agent slid to the ground, groaning and nauseous with pain.

Sibilla had reached the top of the campanile. At the railing she could see the whole city lit up in flashes of lightning. She leaned over the piazza. Despite the distance she had no trouble seeing the nefarious energy of the old sorcerer whose eyes were glittering like fire on ice. When the evil man smiled up at her victoriously, her guts felt ripped open by fear, hatred and despair.

"Descendant of Dragut!" the sorcerer shouted. "I have already finished off several of your ancestors. Despite the teachings of your master, I will break you too! It's too late to stop me! The blood of human sacrifice is running through the streets of Florence!"

Then he looked down at Leonardo who was starting to twitch with pain again.

"I only need to sacrifice *him* and the Ones at the Gate of Shadows will become my army. Even the Twelve cannot stop me."

Leonardo's cries of pain drilled into Sibilla's ears.

No, he's going to kill him! The monster! The monster!

Calm down. Another voice whispered to her. It was a blend of Carter's authority and Cagliostro's gentleness. *Remember what your master told you. Don't let hatred get the better of you. The words of the manuscript must be recited with a calm, just and loving heart.*

Sibilla took a deep breath and thought about Leonardo, about her mother, about Maria Carpi, about Cagliostro, about her friends, about Phenix whose courage always amazed her, about Dalia and Francesco, about all these good people who were reason enough for saving the world.

When she felt ready she opened the white leather cover of the grimoire. The pages were made of vellum so smooth that the rain slid off them without damaging the colored ink that was still remarkably bright. And there on one page the benevolent beauty of Beatrice drawn by Botticelli swelled Sibilla's heart with the love needed for the power of the words that she read aloud. Everything was written in old Italian, which was hard to understand, but the grace of these forgotten words did the rest:

La Gloria di colui che tutto move
Per l'universo penetra e risplende
In una parte più e meno altro ve.

The wind carried the words of the poet right through the clouds, all over the city, sweetly caressing the ears of those who could hear the distant voice. They reached Leonardo in his bizarre prison and he started coming back to reality, out of the burning world, back to the slippery pavement of the piazza. He believed, however, that he was still stuck in the vision when he saw the golden door of the Saint Jean Baptistery across from the cathedral glowing like molten metal.

Maleficus, unaware of the phenomenon, raised his hands to the sky. A mass of black clouds gathered over the campanile. The billowing lumps crackled with lightning. Blue sparks rose from the ground and static electricity made even wet hair stand on end. The charge of electric energy was going to destroy everything in its way, Leonardo realized in a panic. And Sibilla was keeping her eyes focused on the book. She kept chanting the magic words that had saved her friend.

"No!"

Leonardo wanted to rush at the old sorcerer but a surrealist vision stopped him: sparkling forms detaching themselves, one by one, from the Baptistery door. He saw men with long togas, women with braided hair, even angels dressed as warriors, their wings spread wide—living statues sculpted out of pure gold. And when a hand fell upon Maleficus' shoulder, his anger swelled like the clouds on seeing the guardians of Florence awakened by the sacred incantation.

"No! No! Curse you all!" He pointed at the top of the campanile. "My vengeance will…"

A golden hand closed over his mouth. He was swiftly surrounded by the sparkling beings who grabbed him and dragged him kicking and flailing to glowing door. Just when he was about to be swallowed by the rippling surface, Maleficus managed to shake his face free of the implacable grip and he howled one last word full of hatred:

"SIBILLAAAA!!!!"

The cry was cut off when the guardians threw him through the golden door. A blazing eruption and a distant rumbling like an avalanche scared Leonardo who threw himself to the ground and covered his head. When he dared to look up the door looked normal, the clouds had cleared off and the rain had stopped. He went to the Baptistery and cautiously examined the sculpted doors. The angelic beings were exactly like the ones he had seen take Maleficus. And now, imprisoned between two of figures with folded wings, there was a figure who looked strange because he seemed violently angry.

He jumped when he felt a hand on his shoulder. It was Sibilla, exhausted but smiling.

"I'm curious to hear one of your logical explanations;"

In the courtyard of the Bargello museum, a Dalia in rags, bleeding from dozens of claw marks, heard the angelic voice. Without understanding the words she knew that they were for her. She yelled and shoved one of the harpies with all her strength. Surprised by the reaction, her torturers were about to double their ferocity but they, too, heard the voice and immediately shot up into the sky with fear stamped on their faces.

Dalia groaned in pain as she tore herself off the pavement and out of the hallucination that had almost killed her. She put one foot slowly in front of the other and was glad to feel the familiar, reassuring solidity. Even the rain had stopped.

Sandra did not appreciate her return to normality. She stepped back when the harpies abandoned their prey. And when her roommate shook off the waking nightmare, she panicked.

"But... die! Die, bitch! The old man said you would die!"

A cold rage jolted Dalia. While the lashes started closing up, she ran up the stairs to get to Sandra who was slow to realize that it was time to get out of there. Too late. The other caught up to her before she could reach the gallery. The young

147

journalist grabbed her ex-friend by the hair and threw her hard against the base of a statue. Then she straddled the small woman and started pummeling her until her knuckles hurt. Only then did she manage to calm down a little.

Squatting now, with a bloody nose and a loose tooth, Sandra was sobbing and blabbering tearful excuses. Dalia just sneered at her and went back down the slippery steps.

The sky was clearing and one by one the stars came out. The young woman took time to contemplate them before leaving the museum, still shaken up. She called Francesco on her cell, which was miraculously untouched, and broke down in tears when he answered.

19.

Three days later...

When she opened the door of the small restaurant, Sibilla saw who she was supposed to meet sitting in the rear with his back to the wall.

"Good evening, Mr. Carter."

The Englishman looked up from the file and smiled. Sibilla's punctuality was always appreciated. He wanted to stand up but the magician waved her hand for him to stay seated. The brief encounter between Carter and Maleficus ended with a few broken ribs and a dislocated shoulder that he kept in a sling. Moreover, the agent's face still showed marks from their car accident.

A thin, dutiful waiter handed them menus and in perfect English with a heavy Brooklyn accent he asked if they wanted a drink. He frowned when Sibilla answered in Italian, disappointed that he could not show off his mastery of foreign languages, but he came back quickly with the two glasses of Vino Nobile she had ordered.

"I think you really avoided a global disaster," Carter said after a sip of wine. "My superiors sent me some new documents that shed some light on the infernal world that Maleficus was trying to invoke."

He showed her the documents he was examining. They had been sent by the Cagliostro section via courier specialized in sensitive deliveries. Sibilla looked through the file and a shiver ran down her spine. She found ancient engravings of an infernal world, gruesome photos and she noticed that some statements and reports were signed by Jean Sten, a man whose credibility on the subject was beyond reproach.

She closed the file and gave it back to Carter. "Maleficus must have signed a pact with evil forces coming from another universe. His goal was to open the doors for the arrival of beings who have been threatening our world for centuries. If it wasn't for exceptional people like Cagliostro and the Comte de Saint-Germain who stopped them, they would already have pillaged the Earth."

"And we can count you in on that too, my dear. Cagliostro chose wisely when he made you his heir."

A joyless smile appeared on Sibilla's pretty face. "This secret war has lasted a long time… I hope I'm not just postponing the inevitable."

The waiter came back to take their order. Carter chose the same as Sibilla, trusting her taste and wanting to keep talking out of earshot.

"Many forces of good are at work in Earth," he said. "Think of the genius involved in writing the magic grimoire and sculpting the inter-dimensional door that sent Maleficus into the void. And all that before the discoveries of Copernicus and Galileo."

"Yes, I felt the power of the good magic that night. I have to admit, however, that I doubted we'd win, even with the help of the grimoire."

She paused when the waiter came back with two big plates of steaming hot pasta with hare sauce. Carter took a bite and was a convert.

"Speaking of the grimoire," he said after swallowing his delicious mouthful, "What did you do with it?"

"That's funny, I was going to ask you pretty much the same question about Guido Scottatore, Sandra Ventre and all the dropouts Maleficus used."

Carter's forkful of pasta froze in mid-air as he stared across the table at her.

She pretended like it was nothing. "Guido, the guy with the hoodie. His brother finally came to the hospital and identified him. Strangely, his burns had disappeared. When his brother came back to see Guido the next day the room was empty. According to the nurses and police they took him away to be interrogated. Inspector Bonelli, who was guarding Sandra in a cell, told me the same thing: Interpol agents came and snatched her up. They had all the papers. What do you figure on doing with them, Carter?"

The Englishman put down his fork and sighed. His meal seemed less appetizing all of a sudden. "It wasn't my decision, Sibilla. Some bigwigs in the Cagliostro Section figured they would be better off under our surveillance. These people were confronted with evil forces and accepted to help these forces of their own free will. The Section believed that the simple fact of siding with Maleficus makes them too dangerous for society."

"An overweight, aspiring artist, an immature, little woman and a bunch of homeless… enemies of the society, certainly," Sibilla said softly. Her eyes were gleaming with suppressed anger. "You know, Carter, I believe you're hiding something and I'm going to lay it out: I doubt that the Cagliostro Section took them away for the good of society. Maybe they were ready to participate in a horrible crime but they were lost souls. I don't like this secret detention. I don't think you're just locking up dangerous citizens. You want to get something from them. The fact that they experienced magic makes them very interesting, right?"

Carter's face looked hard. He took a deep breath and shook his head when Sibilla finished her statement. "I feel like the trust we established during our first encounter in Paris has just been shattered. No need to tell you that it makes me sad."

The agent's cell phone shrieked and put an end to the tortuous tension. Carter answered it and Sibilla breathed calmly. She, too, felt deeply disappointed. Finding out that a new official agency was going to deal with paranormal cases had been reassuring but that this same agency was secretly playing with people's lives with impunity... Maybe once they got what they wanted the Section would let Guido, Sandra and the others go. The forces of Evil are most perverse in seducing weak spirits. And weak these poor people were, in different ways.

Carter snapped her out of her thoughts. "We have to get back to the hotel. It concerns you. You know a journalist called Dave Kaplan, don't you?"

A cold shackle tightened around Sibilla's throat. "Something happened..."

This was not a question.

"I'd rather talk about it at the hotel. All I can tell you is that if you're not familiar with Thailand, you're going to be very soon."

20.

He felt like he was drowning in sunlight. The gentle warmth enveloping him slipped into his mouth, his nostrils, infiltrated his lungs. The old man screamed to chase away the suffocating sensation. The golden beings let him go when he shouted out the curses in the ancient language of the forces of darkness. Their beautiful faces twisted with unspeakable suffering and they pushed him away to escape his impious mouth. At first laughing at their defeat the old man quickly changed his tune because he was surrounded by nothing but light whose gold and amber hues mingled in dazzling harmony but no trace of a door that would lead him to the world of mortals.

Maleficus was furious. Sibilla would pay for this. He hated her with all the depth of his dark soul and he despised himself for not knowing how to render her harmless, for underestimating her. Then he calmed down. Rage was a bad counselor and would not get him out of this trap.

151

He closed his eyes and concentrated. Could he use the eyes of his acolytes to see the plane of reality from which he had been snatched away? He thought of everyone he had involved in his diabolical plan but unsurprisingly he could not reach anyone because his contact had been too brief with most of them. And Guido, pathetic Guido, Maleficus concentrated as hard as he could but the fat kid remained out of touch. As if his old ally were rejecting him. Could he be holding a grudge against the old sorcerer for trying to kill him? In that case, he would have to focus on the less pleasant option.

Maleficus concentrated on his last hope. He gritted his teeth as he visualized the bright eyes devoid of intelligence, those hideous, crooked teeth and the drooling, mushy voice. The old sorcerer's face twitched with disgust but he had no choice. He emptied his mind, disconnected from his body, leaped into the luminous currents like a cork on a river, and remembered how he could control the hallucinations of his victims through the eyes of this little woman.

He felt his environment change. The gentle lapping of the golden waves turned into a muffled rumbling. Maleficus recognized the ordinary sound of air conditioning. He concentrated on the physical body and could feel long hair sticking to wet cheeks. Tears. By reflex he lifted his hands to wipe away the tears and he smiled. A weird feeling in his mouth. He ran his tongue over his teeth and found he was missing an incisor. They had left cigarettes for him. No, not him. Sandra.

He brushed away some strands of hair and studied his surroundings. He was in a small room whose main colors, gray and white, reminded him of hospitals. He was sitting on a rough blanket covering a small bed. He noticed the simple furniture: table, chair, sink glistening in the bright, fluorescent light. A big mirror across from him was the only luxury but he was not fooled—they were watching him. He saw a door on his right, perpendicular to the mirror. It had no handle.

Maleficus sighed. He had escaped his prison only to find himself in another. But at least this kind of environment was more familiar.

The door opened and a man came in. He was around 50 years old with a kind, round face, wearing tortoise-shell glasses and a suit that was a little too tight. He put his hand on Maleficus' shoulder.

"I see we're cheering up. That's good."

He spoke in excellent Italian but with a smooth, German accent. His fatherly tone of voice irritated the old sorcerer but he knew this was his chance. The man still saw a whiney woman. Maleficus tried the rest of his tears and pretended to sniffle pathetically.

"Yeah, better," he responded imitating Sandra's pretentious voice.

"That's good," the man repeated.

He sat next to her on the bed. The sorcerer saw the badge on the guy's chest. His name was Schiller. Next to his name was a green symbol that he knew only too well: a snake pierced by an arrow. The emblem of one of his oldest enemies. This idiot Sandra, then, had got herself caught by the agents of the Cagliostro Section.

Interesting.

"Now, Sandra, we're going to start at the beginning. You're going to explain how you met this man and what you did for him step by step. Don't worry, nobody is here to judge you. You're just a witness in an investigation. If you cooperate, we'll let you go without a problem. Okay, feel better?"

Schiller's words rippled with sincerity. Maleficus knew this guy had a gift of persuasion. More and more interesting. He smiled back, showing all his crooked teeth like Sandra always did.

"Sure, better." He stared hard into Schiller's eyes. "Much better."

The German froze and turned pale. For a few long minutes the middle-aged man and the little woman stared at each other without moving. Then Schiller blinked and color came back into his cheeks.

"Much better," he whispered while the Sandra's body suddenly fell to the side and lay motionless on the bed.

Schiller/Maleficus stood up and straightened his tie. He would have to buy a suit that fit him better. It was going to be fun to leave his mark on this organization.

A Thai Ghost Story

1.

December 26, 2004. Khao Lak, Thailand.

"I'm going back to get a real breakfast," Christophe shouted as he turned around on his surfboard. "I'm starting to get tired. You want to come with me?"

His friend Mitchell, an Australian with brown hair the color of caramel candy and just as square, laughed, "Just say you've got a hell of a hangover from our Christmas party, mate! But sure, why not. Maybe pretty Liza will be at the restaurant."

Christophe felt himself blushing. How did this brute of a kangaroo know? Ah, who cares, the wonderful prospect of sharing an iced tea with pretty Liza gave him plenty of energy to paddle quickly back to shore. The small hotel snuggled between the white sand beach and the lush forest was slowly waking up. Except for the mosquito bites and sore muscles from surfing this vacation in Asia was turning out to be quite memorable. And if he and Liza could...

Mitchell caught up to him. He was paddling smoothly but his muscular arms swallowed up the distance like it was nothing. The two young men eyed each other with a little smile and started a race, an unfair race since it took no time for the Australian to leave the Frenchman in his wake. They reached the shore panting and laughing.

At this very moment the sea decided to pull back fast, swirling water around the tourists' ankles and dragging sand back into the open sea. Surprised by the phenomenon, the surfers turned around to look. In the distance, the white, foamy horizon looked as if a bar of ivory had just risen out of the water.

"That's weird," Christophe said.

Mitchell patted him on the shoulder, "Let's go get a closer look."

The Frenchman nodded and noticed that other people around had the same idea: a bunch of them were curious and heading down to the sea, which had flowed far back. Cameras were out. The phenomenon amazed everyone. Tourists turned into fishermen and went scrambling over the algae-covered rocks.

Mitchell and Christophe walked forward, shielding their eyes with one hand and carrying their surfboard with the other. Far off in the distance they heard a rumbling sound like a waterfall.

The Australian was first to understand what it was when he saw a foamy wave overturn a small sailboat. "It's a tsunami, mate! Run!"

Christophe watched the advancing swell with his jaw hanging down. Mitchell had to give him a shove to snap him out of his stupor. Both of them gripped their boards and sprinted over the sand toward the hotel. The guests were catching some morning sun on the terrace. Among them were Christophe's friends. And Liza was eating fruit with her sister.

"Hey, Totophe!" his buddy Sebastian called out. "Why are you running so fast? Did you get a look at that sea?"

"It looks like a tidal wave," Liza's sister said.

"Oh shit…"

"Quick! Get out of here!" Christophe yelled at them.

He dropped his surfboard without thinking of the 500 euros he had paid for it, grabbed Liza's hand and ran for the green shade of the forest.

"Hold on!" Liza screamed. "I'm barefoot! I've got to…"

Her voice was drowned out by a loud roar as the ground shook. Christophe turned around and his scream was stuck in his throat. A foaming torrent, bearing all of Nature's fury, crashed on the beach. The tourists and the hotel employees took off but they were not fast enough and were snatched up by the tsunami. The two young French people turned back and ran. Mitchell was already ahead of them at the edge of the forest.

When they finally reached the trees Christophe felt himself being lifted off the ground.

While trying to keep hold of Liza's hand, he made vain attempts at grabbing the branches or trunks of the trees. He ripped off a fingernail on the bark but he did not feel a thing because he was so focused on his terror. He saw himself dying, swallowed up, drowned and pulverized.

Something sliced his wrist and he let go of Liza. He thought he heard her scream in the roar of rushing water.

A huge tree stopped his delirious tumbling and he held on to it while the waves surged around him, over him, choking him. If he stayed here he would never make it out. Fear injected just enough energy to help him climb. The thick branches were godsends for gripping.

Christophe yelled in victory when he rose completely above the watery trap, but he did not stop climbing. The water under his feet was rising and roaring like a hungry dragon. The current was sweeping away debris and he thought he saw a human arm sticking out of a raft of broken branches. He continued his desperate climb with renewed energy. The giant tree was shaking in the sea's assault but nothing could uproot it.

When he figured he was safe Christophe let out a long sigh of relief, then leaned his head against the tree trunk and wept. He was an atheist but right now he prayed fervently. He prayed for his friends and for Liza. He swore that he would give anything to see them alive.

He did not know how long he stayed up in the tree. He apparently passed out a few times. His injuries hurt and he had to slap the mosquitoes that landed on the streams of blood dripping over his skin.

The sea below him was drawing back. He could not hear anything. He climbed down slowly, wincing at every movement. When he put his foot on the wet ground his legs wobbled. He leaned on the tree trunk so he would not collapse. When he finally felt steady enough to walk he took one step forward but immediately fell to his knees. The silence around him only made things worse.

"Help!" he croaked.

He cleared his throat and called out again. Not a sound. Even the birds were quiet. They should have been singing again by now...

Christophe dried the tears running down his dirty cheeks and sat back against the tree that had saved his life. He felt dizzy and exhausted, not only by the physical effort it took not to die but also by the sudden drop in adrenaline. All he wanted now was to rest and stay still.

Something silky slid around his wrist. He yelped and rolled over to escape what he thought was a snake. He got up on his bruised knees and looked at the roots of the tree, which had been laid bare by the tsunami. Something was moving in the tangled mess, moving smoothly, trying to give him a sign. It was too regular to be a reptile. Christophe leaned forward slowly, holding his breath. He saw something black and oblong among the roots. It was a weird stone statue, as big as a funerary urn, representing a face sculpted with clean, balanced lines. It was covered with mud in places but still perfectly intact. It must have been buried at the foot of the tree and dug up by the water.

I think I just made a nice archeological find, he thought and forgot about his precarious situation.

But the statue could not have been moving. As the young man wondered what he had seen, the silky brush was felt again on his torn off fingernail.

Christophe jumped and tried to get away but a kind of black, shiny scarf coming out of the statue had wrapped around his wrist.

A voice suddenly rang out in his head. It spoke in a language that he had never heard before but the words made sense and managed to excite him.

Help me! Please, help me! I'm hungry and cold and it's so dark...

An intelligent being was imprisoned in the statue. Whatever it was Christophe had to help it. Running away would be a crime. The silky tentacle gently unwound and left him free. The being trusted him.

"I'm here," the young man whispered as he crawled to the relic. "What should I do?"

Kiss me. Put your lips to mine. Warm me up. I am yours and you are mine. Forever.

How could he do otherwise when the mental voice was moaning such sensual promises that it made him quiver? He had no idea what the statue was hiding, what creature had been unearthed by the waves, but what he did know was that he was going to do something crazy. And intense.

He laid his lips on the smooth, cold statue.

Hundreds of thin ribbons; silky and black, sprang out of the stone and wrapped around his head, holding him still. Christophe struggled against them. His screams were muffled by the stone plastered to his face. Something cold and sticky unrolled, like the proboscis of a butterfly, and slipped between his teeth. He thought he would die of pain when it pierced the roof of his mouth to enter his brain.

He did not suffer long. All the contents of his skull were sucked out by the proboscis with a slurping noise that annoyed the young man for the few seconds he had left to live. His bruised feet stamped the wet ground of the forest as he convulsed, more and more slowly. Once he was dead for good the black ribbons let him go and the proboscis slid out of his pale lips.

When they found Christophe's body weeks later, partially devoured by bugs, they added him to the frightening number of tsunami victims.

But under the roots of the tree that had served as a gravestone for the young Frenchman, nobody noticed the small statue.

2.

Ten years later

Magnificent trees surrounded him, rising up to the vaulted canopy of leaves. A little sunlight managed to sneak through the leafy dome and mingle with the vines that dragged on the mossy ground. He reached out for one ray of golden light and felt gentle warmth on his fingers. That was where the dream got really interesting, incredibly realistic and intriguing.

All of a sudden he heard a call. He held his breath. His heart beat harder in his chest. A voice, a feminine voice had darted between the mossy trunks and supple vines and was now circling him with a whirlwind of sound. He knew he was being called. The cry was, in fact, a nuptial song that was meant for him.

He started walking again, faster, impatient to find *her*, to see *her*, to touch *her*. After a bit he started running. He did not feel the dead leaves or grass or wet earth that his bare feet trampled, nor the branches that sometimes scratched him. She was the only thing that counted in his life from now on.

His heartbeat drummed in his ears like a primitive melody. The melody became a plea, then a promise and finally a command.

Come to me. Come to me.

And at last he found *her*.

She was standing in the middle of a clearing, so beautiful in her simple garb. The golden light enveloping her, brushing her dark skin with precious hues. Her long, dark hair covered her body but did not hide her round breasts or curvy hips. She was an Eve from ancient times, attractive and sensual, but also a broken statue of jasper: one of her feet was just a stump that she hid under the moss.

Her magnificent eyes, those sparkling and toxic yellow eyes, hypnotized him. He felt himself leaving his body and plunging into the dark pupils. He wanted to speak. All that came out was a kind of soft, deep growl, bestial and languid.

Waves of warmth washed over him. He wanted her here and now. He took her in his arms almost brutally. She did not complain. She smiled and hugged him just as forcefully. Then she looked up at him and kissed him passionately.

Things suddenly turned weird when he felt silky vines shoot out of the woman's hair and wrap around his arms and legs to squeeze him more tightly in her amorous embrace. The dream Eve smiled, satisfied with her work. She put her lips on the pulsing jugular of her betrothed.

He felt his body burning when she bit him on the neck and licked the first drops of blood.

He shot up in bed.

For a moment Leonardo did not know where he was. Then the constant hum of the engines reminded him that he was in a plane heading for Bangkok. He turned to the right to see Sibilla studying a file, furrowing her brow and pursing her lips.

Then Leonardo remembered their last investigation in Florence and the call sent to them by Graham Carter right after. He knew the journalist Dave Kaplan by sight and had read a few of his photo essays. He was hard-working and meticulous and like Leonardo not given to belief in the supernatural. However, he was a good friend of Sibilla and she was upset to learn that he was now in a coma. The alarm was sent in by a young photographer accompanying him, an English woman named Cookie MacFerrin. Two nights ago she had to break into Kaplan's hotel room and she found him lying in bed, almost totally drained of blood. Her explanations were so confused that the Thai police thought it best to hold her for interrogation. As for Dave, he was hospitalized but his vital functions were so low that there was little hope for recovery.

Leonardo wanted to look at his watch to know how long it would be until they arrived in Bangkok but he remembered that he had forgotten it in Florence. The final images of his dream were dissipating like the clouds they were flying through at the moment. But the reporter felt both frustrated and lethargic, like a teenager with raging hormones.

He stretched.

"Sleep well?" his companion asked.

"I had a lucid dream for the first time in my life. I have to say it was pretty nice. And I didn't even ruin my neck in this ridiculous seat."

"Well, I moved you a little when you started leaning over and drooling on my shoulder."

Leonardo glared, "I don't drool when I sleep."

"You think so because you drool on other people and not yourself," Sibilla said distractedly as she leafed through the file, which had a smiling, professional picture of Dave Kaplan at the head.

"How long till we get to Bangkok? Leonardo asked.

"Soon."

"How soon?" the journalist pressed.

"Soon within the hour," Sibilla replied. "We'll stop at the police station where an agent from the local Cagliostro Section is expecting us, an inspector Pongwilaï. He has authorization to let the English photographer go. She's the only one who knows what happened to Dave."

"I don't mean to rub it in and I know you're worried about Kaplan but I also read the file and that girl was drunk when she messed up the hotel."

Sibilla just sighed. Leonardo put a sympathetic hand on her shoulder. He had almost forgotten his dream.

The small room where they kept Cookie MacFerrin looked like a tiny classroom for unruly children. A blackboard covered with white scribbles was the only decoration. With her dirty elbows on the table and her face buried in her hands, all they could see was short, orange hair sticking out at the police officer across from her. Her shoulders were trembling under a ripped t-shirt and the wound under the bandage peaking out was obviously hurting. Her voice was stuck in her throat and if she tried to speak she would probably just sob. Terrible memories were constantly replaying disturbing images. She was hoping it was all just a dream. A bad dream, for pity's sake.

She was tired and broken and to top it off she reeked of cheap booze and rotten meat: she had fallen into the dumpsters from the restaurant under Dave's window and passed out in the filth.

She had been worried sick about Dave and was ready to convert to every religion in the world if it would do any good.

The door opened. The cop guarding her said something in Thai and then he left. The Englishwoman heard clothes rustling and more footsteps. She did not move.

"Miss MacFerrin," a gentle voice said.

Finally she looked up and jumped when she saw the three newcomers. A man with brown hair, a redheaded woman, both Europeans, and a short Thai policeman smiling kindly and holding out a Kleenex.

"Wipe your face, Miss MacFerrin, your tears are leaving white streaks in all that dirt."

This was said with no mockery at all but with great consideration. The girl just looked at them without understanding. The Thai officer in his forties with a round face and bushy moustache over an ever-present smile in total contrast to the other man, tall, thin and kind of cute but with a sour face. The redhead was really pretty and had a perfect body molded by her black suit. In other circumstances Cookie would have hated her because she always felt too small and skinny.

"Thanks," she finally stuttered and took the tissue from the cop.

She did her best to clean her poor face. The tissue did not stay white for long.

Sibilla was also examining her. She noticed that the Englishwoman was a little older than she looked in her rebel teenager getup. Despite the t-shirt with the logo from the band PIL, her ripped jeans and ratty sneakers, she must have been around twenty-six. Her big, hazel eyes glistened with tears.

"I'm Inspector Pongwilaï," the small officer introduced himself. "And this is Sibilla and Leonardo Verga, Italian journalists working for *Flash* in Milan."

Cookie MacFerrin sniffled and dried her nose. Then she muttered, "*Flash*, I know, we have the same boss."

"Miss MacFerrin, Dave Kaplan is a dear friend of mine," Sibilla said. "So, I, too, am very worried about him and I only want one thing—to know what happened to him."

"As you can see," the Inspector said, "we're here to help you."

"And Dave? Do you have any news?" Cookie's voice trembled.

Pongwilaï put his hand lightly on her shoulder. Sibilla admired the gesture. The officer seemed endowed with great empathy and his voice was soothing. He had made a good impression on her when he met them at the station. Her heart skipped a beat when he repeated the news he had given them a minutes ago:

"The doctors at the hospital don't know if he'll pull through, frankly. His EEG seems to indicate that he's brain dead. He also lost a lot of blood. He's being well cared for but we can't be sure of anything. Be strong, Miss MacFerrin."

Tears poured down the young photographer's cheeks. She made no attempt to wipe them away. Sibilla felt a deep sadness wash over her. She had taken the shock of the news rather calmly but seeing the anguish of another person close to Dave made her drop her brave face.

"I don't want him to die," Cookie spluttered. "I... If I could ... could have known earlier what was happening..."

Pongwilaï took a pack of tissues out of his khaki shirt and started drying the young woman's eyes, which was no small task considering the salty river running down her cheeks.

"If it's any consolation, Miss MacFerrin, he isn't in any pain. But I think you could see him."

She opened her eyes wide with hope, "Really?"

"Really," the short officer's eyes sparkled. "But on one condition: You tell us everything from the day you first set foot in Thailand until the minute you got her to the police station. I want to know every detail."

The Englishwoman hid her face in her hands again, "Bloody hell! I've told everything I know three times already!"

"Well, this'll make it four," Leonardo grumbled in Italian.

Cookie MacFerrin shot him a suspicious look, easily guessing that he was feeling bored. Sibilla pinched his arm. He jumped but held his voice.

With tactful kindness Pongwilaï defused the situation, "You can tell it however you want to make it less painful and tedious. And do it on the way to the hospital. Yes, Miss MacFerrin, I'm letting you out of this cramped, little room."

"Cookie," she mumbled.

"Excuse me?" the Inspector replied.

"Everyone calls me Cookie. The Miss MacFerrin kind of gets on my nerves. My old college professors used to say it all the time. I got sick of it."

"Cookie it is," the officer said. "We're wasting time. I imagine you're eager to see Dave Kaplan."

"I want to see him again but I want to see him alive," the photographer sighed. "And Kasemchaï?"

"Your guide?"

"Yeah, they arrested him because he broke down Dave's door. The hotel security was taking too long."

"He was let go after an hour or so. He's the one who contacted me."

Cookie's face brightened, "Oh, that's one less thing to worry about."

Without further discussion she stood up. Pongwilaï opened the door and led the three others down the long corridors.

"Is this Kasemchaï a friend of yours?" Sibilla asked.

Pongwilaï smiled and winked at the magician. "A useful acquaintance. I helped him get on his feet after a rough childhood. In exchange he makes sure our foreign visitors stay safe."

Cookie followed them silently. She did not hear a word of the conversation between the pretty Italian and the short Thai cop. She was lost in thought and confused. How was she going to tell them about everything that happened after she and Dave landed in Thailand?

3.

Two days earlier the only thing that worried Cookie was knowing if they were going to get their story in Bangkok without a civil war breaking out. And she was especially hoping she could tolerate the spicy Thai food. She and Dave had taken their baggage through customs without a problem. Being journalists made things easier. The *New York Examiner* and the *Daily Digest*, American publications from the Wilson group that they worked for, were known all over the world. They came to investigate the lives of the Thai after the tsunami that ravaged part of Asia ten years ago. They were supposed to meet survivors, mostly orphans, and see how the country was slowly rebuilding. A passionate subject that could link the disaster to current tensions. However, the young photographer had misgivings: the airport was crawling with soldiers in bulletproof vests holding machine guns.

"Oh no, they're going to search me," she squawked when she saw a uniform waving them over.

"Stop being paranoid, it's the same for everyone." Dave tousled her hair.

"Yeah, but you're a respectable, middle-aged westerner and me, a punk. People like me have a bad reputation. And did you notice the fuss they're making now. Maybe reporters aren't so welcome here after all."

The Englishwoman got worked up for nothing. After a quick passport check, they took their bags and headed for the main terminal. Dave carried a heavy, red duffle bag over his shoulder and was already sweating in the humidity. As for Cookie, her feet were starting to swell up in the leather oven of her Doc Martens.

"Do you know where to meet the guide the boss contacted?" she asked while wriggling her bloated toes inside the boots.

Dave checked out the people waiting for the travelers. When he finally saw the guy who must have been their guide and interpreter, he rubbed his eyes.

"What the hell?" he mumbled.

Cookie saw the guy too and could not help spitting out, "*Holymotherfucking crap!*"

The native was a giant Thai, at least six and a half feet tall. He was as impressive as a Buddha statue and in one huge, strangler's paw he held a sign with red capital letters: Mr. and Mrs. Kaplan. His dark, deep-set eyes glistened in the middle of his round, emotionless face, a rare expression among the Thai who always smiled to be polite. The giant's long, well-groomed hair made him look like Attila after devouring Genghis Khan.

"Holy shit, that big bastard there," Cookie whistled.

"Don't talk so loud, Cookie-girl," Kaplan whispered. "If King Kong hears you, he's going to squish your head between two fat fingers."

Cookie almost broke out laughing when they went over to King Kong aka their guide.

"Hello," Dave said, "I'm the Mr. Kaplan on your sign. And there is no Mrs. Kaplan but this is Cookie MacFerrin."

"Hewwo," Cookie was biting her lip to keep from giggling.

"Hello, I'm Kasemchaï," the giant said in English with an accent you could cut with a knife.

He imprisoned one of Kaplan's hands in his fist. Cookie was afraid for a second that their guide did not know his own strength and would crush her friend's bones like stale crackers. Kasemchaï repeated the meeting ritual with the girl. Her small, thin hand completely disappeared for a brief, terrifying moment.

"I'll drive you to your hotel," the Thai giant said. "Let me carry your bags."

Kasemchaï's car was a museum piece. The great grandmother of all cars. It was impossible to tell the make or the color, somewhere in the range between dirty white and droppings from a bird infected with the avian flu. Dave and Cookie looked at each other without saying a word. Words were pointless.

After a minute Dave commented, "Uh… this should be interesting."

"In my neighborhood nice cars are always stolen," their guide explained. "This hunk of junk drives nice and will never be stolen."

He tossed their bags in the trunk and without further ado Dave and Cookie climbed in. The American journalist sat next to the little punk in the backseat. She yelped when she felt something pointy on her butt.

For about an hour the guide drove with amazing calmness and confidence through the disastrous traffic of Bangkok. The streets of the big city suffered a constant onslaught of cars, bikes, motorcycles, buses, trucks… Everything in total chaos. The use of turn signals was apparently never taught to them. The accelerator, on the other hand, was clearly their favorite part.

Dave took a few pictures with his Canon with scant attention to the pandemonium and accidents that their car regularly avoided. Cookie covered her eyes a dozen times, praying that they would escape an inglorious death in this pile of junk.

Kasemchaï finally entered a more peaceful part of the city. The brakes grinded to a halt in front of a three-storey white building standing in the middle of a garden of palm trees. Cookie was relieved to see that it was not some huge hotel that the architects in Bangkok were so fond of.

While Kasemchaï helped them with their bags the girl rubbed her belly and tried to look unhappy. "I'm starving."

"You're a walking stomach," Dave laughed. "You already ate two apples, a bag of disgusting chips and a whole box of brownies before we landed."

"I have a special metabolism, kind of like a mutant."

"I don't mean to interrupt you," Kasemchaï cut in, "but I know the perfect place for a good meal."

"Thanks Kasemchaï," Dave said. "I'm counting on you to show us the best restaurants around. How about we meet in an hour? Come on, Glutton Girl."

"After you, Slick Town."

They took time to set up and clean up a little in their room. The Englishwoman changed her t-shirt and thought it wise to switch her hot Doc Martens for a pair of black canvas sneakers with white stars on them. Then she went and knocked on Dave's door next to her own. No answer.

He must have gone down already.

Cookie ran down the stairs into the lobby. Except for a couple of old American tourists with the same love of baseball caps with bent visors, no Dave. The receptionist had not seen the journalist.

Cookie lumbered back up the stairs grumbling righteously against lazy men and knocked harder on Dave's door. With still no answer and a little more worry than she wanted to admit, she went back to her own room and headed for the window behind the thin white curtain, which looked a lot like the mosquito netting around her four-poster bed.

She stepped out on the wooden balcony and realized she had a beautiful view of this part of the city. Across from the hotel, in the middle of the small park, was a house on stilts. Cookie leaned out to get a better view of the charming building with red walls and brightly painted beams. Children were climbing in the trees or playing with sailboats in the bamboo fountain. Others were sitting at the feet of an old, bearded man in a wicker chair. The elder seemed to be reading a story from a big book open on his knees.

Cookie smiled at the tenderness of this peaceful scene. The old man looked up at her and waved. His long white beard looked like a trail of fresh snow sparkling in the sunlight. Cookie was a little taken aback by the gesture from a complete stranger, but she waved back nonetheless.

The wonderful odor of curry suddenly tickled her nose and her belly growled. She had to wake up Dave or else her stomach would start eating itself. Looking over at Dave's balcony next to hers she saw that the glass door was ajar. The breeze was blowing the curtains. It should not be too hard to get over there. Spiderman could do it.

Hoping that the nice, bearded pappy would not call the police, Cookie climbed onto the railing with both hands against the wall. She had to avoid looking down. Her goal was five feet away. Without a second thought the little punk girl jumped as far as she could. Her foot landed on the other railing and she grabbed on, hopped over and made a perfect landing.

"Yeehaw!"

She gently pushed open the glass door and slipped through the curtains. Dave's motionless body lay on the bed. Were there moving shadows behind the folds of the mosquito netting? Cookie really believed she saw a misty figure floating above the journalist, who suddenly shook in his sleep and uttered a muffled cry.

Cookie ran to the bed, parted the netting and jumped on the mattress to chase away the *horla*. She thought she heard fabric rustling and aggravated panting.

But there was no one in the room except for Dave.

The American was not even awake. He was wearing only his black pants and was covered in sweat. He seemed to be having trouble breathing.

"Hey, Dave, wake up you big baby." Cookie's stomach knotted up as she shook his shoulders. ""Wake up, Dave! Wake up! Hey, Kaplan!"

Not knowing what to do, she started jumping on the bed and singing at the top of her voice the first song that popped into her head: "Wake me up! Before you go-go!"

Dave jumped up, completely disoriented and rattled by the earthquake in his bed. "Cookie! What the f…" he started to say.

"Up and at 'em! I'm starved." Her heart was pounding. She would never admit it but she had been on the verge of panic.

"How'd you get in here, you wicked pixie?" Dave sounded annoyed.

"The window was open, so I hopped over the balcony like Spiderman. I'm hungry!"

While talking, Cookie kept jumping on the bed like a punk grasshopper. One leap that was a little too enthusiastic launched her into the mosquito netting that tore off the ceiling. The little punk got all tangled up in the white veil.

"Help!"

"Cookie," Dave sighed and picked out a shirt from his bag, "You're so immature."

They ended up finding Kasemchaï in the lobby. He was waiting for them, his round face still stuck on neutral.

"You took your time," he said.

"It's Dave's fault," Cookie defended herself.

"The girl's right," Dave admitted. "I couldn't get her untangled from the netting she got stuck in."

To their great surprise Kasemchaï cracked a big, friendly smile, unveiling a chipped incisor and one gold canine. "It was an emergency, then," he said. "Follow me and I'll take you to the place I was talking about."

"We're not taking your piece of ju… your car?" Dave asked.

"No need. It's just around the corner."

And how! The place in question was the charming house Cookie had admired from the balcony. She smelled the delicious scent of spicy cooking. And she totally forgot about the weird thing floating over Dave in bed.

"I'd never guess this house was a restaurant," Dave remarked.

"You're right, Mr. Kaplan. In fact, it's not, it's an orphanage. I lived here when I was a kid."

Cookie scrutinized the Thai giant. Imagining him as a child was beyond her.

They entered the beautiful garden shaded by tall trees. The guide called over three children who were playing chase around the bamboo fountain and spoke to them in Thai. The kids looked at the two foreigners and held back laughter with their hands clasped over their mouths, then disappeared into the big, red house, leaving echoing traces of their giggles to drift through the trees.

"Mama Boon-Mi and Papa Boon-Nam will be pleased to offer their hospitality," Kasemchaï said.

The old man with the snowy beard who had waved to Cookie showed up after a couple of minutes. "Welcome to my humble abode," he spoke perfect English. "I'm Papa Boon-Nam."

Dave greeted him by bringing his hands together in front of his nose and bowing slightly. This was how you did the *wai* in greeting elders. "Sawatdi krap, Sir. 'I'm Dave Kaplan and this is Cookie MacFerrin. Thanks for welcoming us to your home."

"We hope we're not too late for lunch," his colleague added discreetly.

"Please no 'Sir'," the old man smiled, slightly embarrassed. "The pleasure's all mine."

Papa Boon-Nam invited them to take off their shoes and follow him. They could her the constant babbling of children and the smell of the cooking was making Cookie near hysterical.

The veranda was used as a dining room. They had laid out tablecloths and cushions on the deck. Twenty kids from two to fifteen years old were ready to eat. The least timid of them smiled at the newcomers.

"Kasemchaï!" a few of the kids shouted and waved their arms.

The guide joined them and sat on a cushion that completely vanished under his huge butt. He patted some of the happy little heads and shook a few small hands with his huge paws. Papa Boon-Nam took the two westerners to the railing. There he laid down a red cloth edged with colored threads and some multicolored cushions.

A lady almost the same age as the old man, Mama Boon-Mi, brought the food on a rickety cart. Her smooth, swift movements clashed with her white hair and wrinkled face. She was helped by three adolescent girls who flitted about filling the bowls. With her famished eyes Cookie inventoried what the old lady put down on the cloth: a kind of yellow rice, scented soup, fish, prawns, fried vegetables. And next to the bottles of fresh water she was ecstatic to see beer!

Once everyone was served the old lady and the three girls sat around the scarlet cloth with Papa Boon-Nam, Dave and Cookie.

"Help yourselves, my friends, and bon appétit," Papa Boon-Nam said before serving a modest portion of rice and fish along with a bowl of soup.

Cookie quickly tasted everything that was edible. She tried soup, found it very tasty and took another big gulp. Then she stuffed herself with different vegetables before realizing that something was wrong inside her mouth.

"Watch out," the old man warned too late, "we like our food very spicy."

"I thought I knew," she tried to say but her mouth was literally on fire and her eyes and nose were turning red.

Except for this slight inconvenience, the rest of the meal was wonderful. With his camera always at hand Dave took a few shots of their hosts and the kids after getting their assent.

"Kasemchaï explained to me why you came to Bang-kok," Papa Boon-Nam said as he put down his bowl. "Your guide was working for Phang Nga when the wave destroyed everything. The same for the oldest of these children who were living in Phuket, Ranong and Satun, the worst hit parts of the country."

"And you welcomed all of them?" Dave asked. "From what I could gather in my reporting, not too many people were so generous."

"But there were some. And I had set up this shelter in the '70s at the start of the conflict with the separatists of Pattani. I took in orphans whose Muslim parents were killed to settle scores. See, I'm not originally Thai. I was born in Japan in 1934, in the province of Hiroshima. My father died on Iwo Jima and my mother in the bombings. I went through a lot of really hard times known only to children who were literally left to die by adults. So, I know what suffering is, Mr. Kaplan."

The rest of the day was spent like this in lively conversation and wild tales of poverty and survival. The kids and Kasemchaï answered Cookie's questions while Dave took their picture. Everyone gave a detailed story of their tragic history. The Thai giant told how he had escaped the tsunami that had killed his parents and friends. Kasemchaï pointed to a 10-year old boy and a girl around twelve. The two children were his cousins and the last of the family. He had crossed most of the country on foot with the infant boy in his arms and the baby girl on his shoulders. He was young but luckily already a force of nature at the time and he earned enough for them to survive by working hard jobs. He had even taken part in a few illegal *muai thai* matches. He pulled up his shirt and showed a jagged scar on his hip.

"They sometimes fought old style," he explained. "We stuck broken glass on leather straps and like that there was more blood and guts. For that kind of spectacle we were paid well."

Kasemchaï recounted his story casually but the world in which the tsunami had thrown him was terrifying!

It had been dark for more than an hour when the interviews ended. They had a frugal dinner before saying good night. As he was leaving Papa Boon-Nam held out two small packages wrapped in orange tissue with golden threads.

"Before we say goodbye, I'd like to offer you these talismans of protection. Most Thai people wear them."

Dave smiled with a little embarrassment, "I appreciate the gesture but you know, I'm not…"

"I insist," the old man's face suddenly turned serious. "We didn't have time to talk about it but a lot more than human life was ravaged by the tsunami. There are forces that were sleeping in their dark, underground nests and the big wave woke them up. Since then they have been roaming among men. Be very careful."

Cookie felt her hair stand on end. Kaplan's face was firm, letting no emotion show, but he accepted the old man's gift and thanked him with a curt *wai* before turning to go.

Papa Boon-Nam looked at the Englishwoman, took her hand and put the package with the amulet in her palm. "You still doubt there are spirits around you but I don't think it would take much to convince you. Watch over your friend. I have a bad feeling."

Cookie caught up to Dave who had already put on his shoes and was in a hurry to get back to the hotel.

"What's got into you?" the photographer asked, tying her shoes as fast as she could. "After four trips to Thailand you're only now finding out about their beliefs?"

"No, that's not it. But when the supernatural gets mixed up in things, trouble's never far behind. There you go," he laughed bitterly, "I'm becoming superstitious!"

Cookie put Papa Boon-Nam's talisman in the back pocket of her holey jeans and took Kaplan's hand. The rustling of trees accompanied them on their way back to the hotel.

"We've got a nice article here and this talk about ghosts can provide ambiance. No one's going to start calling you 'ghost hunter' for it—they've got enough of that in Italy."

Dave relaxed and smiled, "You're right and it's special enough to deserve attention. I'm just tired. I'm going straight to bed."

Cookie sneered, "To hell with being special."

The two journalists got their keys at the front desk and Kaplan said good night to his friend.

The Englishwoman hesitated in the lobby, not sure what to do. She really wanted a nice cold beer on this warm evening but at the same time she was worried about Dave. Like Papa-Boon Nam she, too, had a bad feeling. But with her mouth feeling dry her decision was made.

She went into the hotel restaurant. Except for a few guests scattered around the place was dead. The punk girl ordered a Singha and went onto the terrace. From there she could hear the lapping water of the Chao Phraya River and the buzzing of water taxis. Near the railing they had lit some candles and incense sticks around a tiny red house with a pointed roof. It reminded her of the amulet, so she took it out of her pocket. While sipping her beer she turned the object over in her hands. It looked a little like a pocket watch attached to a red ribbon. The edge of the object was silver and in the center was a flat jade stone engrave with Thai writing that Cookie could not decipher. She put the ribbon around her neck.

"It's a pretty gift, you know."

Startled, she almost spit out her beer. An employee of the hotel was smoking a cigarette near the red house. She spoke in almost perfect English and was looking over the trees as she blew out long clouds of smoke. Cookie thought she was a little sickly-looking but her melancholy face was kind.

"The old man who runs the orphanage gave it to me," she said. "Maybe you could tell me what it protects against?"

The employee stepped over. She was so thin that she made no sound on the lacquered wood floor. Without even trying to touch the medallion she examined it carefully and smiled.

"It protects against evil spirits and all attempts of murder. You just have to activate it with the prayer inscribed in the jade."

She pronounced a few words. Cookie was mystified and looked back and forth between her gift and the skinny woman.

"So now it's activated?"

The woman smiled, which only made her look more tragic.

"Every amulet is unique and this one will only protect you. I'll say it aloud and you repeat after me."

Cookie obeyed, feeling a little stupid. After she had pronounced the final, incomprehensible words, loud voices shattered the silence and English tourists spilled out onto the terrace. One of them was wearing a cap with bells hanging off it and the others were slapping him on the back.

Cookie turned back to thank the employee but the woman was gone.

One of the partiers, a guy who looked Indian and whose big, black eyes glistened with drunkenness, came over to hand the punk a beer.

"Hello! If you're still thirsty, it's our friend Harold who's paying tonight."

Cookie raised the beer toward the jingling cap, "Well, thank you Haorld."

"Hey, you're English too!" someone else shouted. "Stick around and have a drink with us!"

The invitation was too tempting. After two hours of drinking with them she finally decided she had reached her limit. She had to lean hard on the table to stand up. Then she saw the employee wandering through the lobby and she waved.

"Hey! Yoohoo! Are we making too much noise?"

The only answer she got was the woman waving her over anxiously. And the journalist felt her good mood suddenly darken. She stumbled over to the woman.

"Where you going?" her new friends brayed.

"I'll be back!" Cookie shouted as she approached the employee.

The woman whispered, "Your friend's in danger. You have to go to him right away."

Fear took hold of her instinctively as if some forgotten predator was nearby. Staggering with the alcohol, Cookie did her best to follow the woman who scooted soundlessly to the stairs and darted up so fast that the Englishwoman thought her feet did not even touch the ground.

"Hey, wait up!" She stumbled on the first step and fell over, almost smashing her nose.

The receptionist on duty stood up. "Everything okay, Miss?"

"Yeah, sure... no... My friend's sick... Got to call an ambol... ambul... ah shit!

Cookie paid no attention to the stupefied look on the receptionist's face but ran up the stairs. The employee was standing in front of Dave's room. She was wringing her hands, obviously feeling nervous and scared.

"Quick! It might be too late!"

Cookie leaned against the door and tried to turn the handle. Then she knocked, louder and louder, not caring about the other guest.

"Dave! Open up!"

"Quick, Miss," the skinny woman groaned. "No time! He's going to die!"

"But 'aven't you a... key?" Cookie asked and shook the handle.

The Thai woman shook her head, "I can't get you in."

Then Cookie remembered her acrobatic stunt from earlier. She went to her own room and ran to the glass door. She acted on instinct more than any other of her senses, which were numbed by alcohol. She had to fight the lock to be able to get out into the night air. Noises from the party on the other side of the building and the hum of distant traffic managed to penetrate her drunken fog.

No lights were on in Papa Boon-Nam's house. Everyone must have been asleep. Just seeing this made her feel completely alone and helpless.

"Hurry up, Miss!"

Cookie swung around at the voice and had to grab the railing to steady her dizziness. "How'd you get over there?"

The hotel employee was now on Dave's balcony. Cookie's vision was blurry but she thought she saw the woman's cheeks start to glow.

"Miss!" the Thai woman urged her again.

Dave Kaplan's balcony door was cracked open and a weird sound was coming out of it. It was soft and wet, followed by a sickly groan that ended in a gasp of agony.

"Dave!" Cookie shouted.

The gasp and the rustling sounds were suddenly cut off. Without a second thought the punk girl climbed over the railing and jumped. For a moment she felt like she was drifting in mid-air between the two balconies. She knew that she made it when she stumbled into the employee who did not even try to get out of the way. But instead of crashing into the frail body, she fell on her knees directly on the wooden planks. Her jaws snapped shut painfully and she scraped her hands and knees. She had no time to realize that she had gone right through the woman because her eyes went straight into Dave's room.

What she saw made her jump to her feet and stand petrified with fear.

Dave was stretched out on the bed in the middle of the mosquito netting. He lay there as pale as a marble statue in the darkness. A black, deformed figure was leaning over his body. Moist tumors were rubbing against each other making a soft, slimy, swishing sound. Grafted into the center of the dark swellings a porcelain face was parting its lips that looked like poisonous cherries and revealing sharp, white teeth covered with fresh blood. Red, shiny trickles ran down its delicate chin and dripped onto the crumpled sheets.

Cookie screamed. The thing was eating Dave! She ran to help her friend. But the creature was already on the move.

"Watch out, Miss!" the employee yelled. "It's a *phi*!"

The monstrosity rammed into Cookie and sent her flying back against the railing. A shrill, vibrating whistle reminiscent of a rattlesnake's tail pierced the girl's ears. In an attempt to push away her ghastly attacker she threw her hands out but they just sank into a spongy mass. She screamed again in disgust and turned her head as the thing tried to suffocate her with its tumors.

"Kasemchaï!" she shouted desperately in the hope of waking up the house below. "Papa Boon-Nam!"

The porcelain face clicked its pointy teeth an inch away from Cookie's cheek. Out of the corner of her eye she saw the employee wringing her hands and looking lost. "Miss! Your amulet!"

Cookie spent two precious seconds remembering the necklace whose cold metal was stuck to her chest. The monster suddenly planted its fangs in her left shoulder. The young Englishwoman howled in pain and almost tore off her t-shirt when she grabbed the amulet. Without even thinking she stuck the artifact against the creature's face. The porcelain skin sizzled and turned black, giving off a suffocating stench. The monster let go of her shoulder but the shrill cry coming out between the ivory fangs kept piercing her eardrums like a red-hot needle.

The thing backed away and the journalist thought she was free but the filthy creature jumped at her again and knocked her off her feet. Cookie fell over the railing. She had just enough time to see Papa Boon-Nam's house upside down before she crashed on a soft, stinking surface.

4.

The police car finally managed to break free of the Bangkok traffic jams and enter the underground parking lot of the hospital where Dave Kaplan was being treated. Pongwilaï had driven with exemplary calm in spite of the heat and the gridlock. He had listened attentively to Cookie's story while keeping one eye on the road.

Sitting next to the small cop, Leonardo looked tense. The English girl's story was bizarre. Just the kind of story that would pique Sibilla's interest. The magician drank in every word of the girl sitting next to her. The worry showing on her delicate features reminded Leonardo that it concerned her close friend's tragic fate and he scolded himself for his skepticism.

While Pongwilaï maneuvered the car into a parking space, the punk girl finished relating the nightmarish tale, staring at her interlaced fingers. "The restaurant bins saved my life. I don't know if it was all the noise I was making that woke up Kasemchaï, who was sleeping at Papa Boon-Nam's, but he came running over to the hotel and found me stuck head first in the garbage. He could not have understood what I was saying. It was all gibberish. But he went to ring the receptionist. Seeing no one coming and me in a state of panic, he broke down the door."

Cookie was sniffling again. She brought her hands up to her trembling lips as if trying to help the words come out.

"It was… it was awful," she moaned. "Dave was white and the sheets had soaked up his blood. It looked like his throat had been cut in his sleep and… and yet… yet…"

She could hold out no longer and she broke down in tears. Sibilla handed her a tissue.

"You don't know the weirdest part, Miss… Cookie," Pongwilaï said. "Except for a tiny wound on his neck your friend had no injuries to explain all the blood loss. It was his blood but we don't know how it got there."

"The hotel employee talked about a *phi*," Sibilla said.

"That's what they call ghosts here in Thailand," the officer explained.

"The employee who knows all about amulets and ghosts?" Leonardo asked. "Did you question her?"

Pongwilaï shook his head, "Nobody at the hotel fits the description."

Dave was still horribly pale. Sibilla's heart skipped a beat when she saw her old friend hooked up to all those tubes and wires like a bunch of umbilical cords. It was being fed intravenously. The Italian noticed a blood bag hanging over the bed.

"Does he still need more?"

The doctor in charge of the American nodded and looked embarrassed, "For some unknown reason his circulatory system is drying up and we have to keep transfusing. But I don't know how long we can keep it up. We don't have an infinite supply of blood."

"He's not the first, is he?" Pongwilaï said.

The doctor switched suddenly from embarrassment to anxiety, "That's right. It started a few years ago. I've heard from other hospitals. All my colleagues are baffled, totally clueless about the cases, which always end in fatality. It might be a new virus causing a kind of anemia."

"Oh Dave…" Cookie knelt by the bed and held one of his needle-infested hands. "He's so cold," she said and started crying.

Sibilla wanted to do the same but that was not going to save Kaplan. She choked back her tears and announced, "I'd like to be alone with the patient for a few minutes, please."

When everyone had left she distractedly caressed the jade stone that was sparkling on her finger.

"Dave, if you can hear me, I hope you won't get mad at me for practicing one of my magic tricks on you, but there's only one way to found out what's happening to you."

She pointed the ring at the livid, listless body.

"By the power of Cagliostro whose heir I am, I beg you, spirit enclosed in this mortal coil, appear to me and answer my questions. Trust me, my friend."

A ray of light shot out of the ring and enveloped the body in a bright green halo.

Sibilla examined Dave.

Nothing happened.

Stunned, the magician lowered her ring.

They had stolen Dave's soul.

Night was falling when they got to the hotel, the scene of Cookie's disturbing tale. Kasemchaï was waiting for them at the entrance, his face like stone.

"Kaz!"

The little punk jumped out of the car and ran into the arms of the giant Thai. Surprised and a little embarrassed, he tapped her gently on the shoulders as she buried her warm tears in his shirt.

"He's not... not awake," she stuttered. "The doctors don't know if... if he'll ever wake up."

"Oh," he was sincerely worried. "I'm sorry, Miss Cookie. I would've come earlier if I'd known..."

Sibilla joined the pair and patted the young Englishwoman on the back, "I'll do everything I can to help him. I'm going to spend the night in this hotel and wait for any signs of the supernatural."

"I can't come back here," Cookie muttered while drying her tears, looking like a lost, little girl. "I'm too scared."

"You can sleep at Papa Boon-Nam's, Miss Cookie," Kasemchaï said. "The kids will be happy to see you."

"I don't know if I can go with you on this bogeyman hunt," Leonardo yawned. "I don't think I've fully recovered from my expedition in the Alps and that bad trip in Florence. Besides, the jet lag is killing me."

"Arrangements have been made for you to stay in the rooms next to Mr. Kaplan and Miss McFerrin," Pongwilaï said. "I'd love to stay and help in the investigation, but you must have noticed the soldiers all over the streets. It's an old Thai habit: a coup d'état is in the works. Even if General Prayut says he's all for peace, I have to go back to the station to prepare for any eventuality. But here's my number. If you need any help, I'll do what I can."

The officer said goodbye. Kasemchaï and Cookie went to Papa Boon-Nam's.

"Leo, I'd rather you stayed with me," Sibilla told her friend after they got the keys from the front desk. "You heard the doctor. Who knows if the thing that attacked Dave isn't already looking for new prey?"

"Don't worry about it. I'm going to take a nice shower and I'll be rearing to go. Promise!"

"I'll drop off my things and go down to the terrace. If you're not there in half an hour…" With that she disappeared into her room.

Leonardo smiled. A real mother hen. But it's to be expected after what happened to Kaplan.

He went into his temporary abode. The room was in good taste, soberly decorated but comfortable. The city lights studded the wooden floor with shifting shadows. The thick windows muffled the traffic noise. Leonardo put his suitcase on the bed, took out a change of clothes, then headed to the bathroom. The mirror looked back at him with baggy eyes set in a tired, unshaven face.

While undressing he tried not to look too closely at the scar across his knee. He was not at all pleased with the way it was healing. He still had bad pain. The doctors tried to look positive with their diagnosis of a recurring shooting pain in the ligaments. Leonardo's personal diagnosis was much more pessimistic. He chased away these depressing thoughts by turning on the water and climbing into the bathtub. The jet from the showerhead hammered his skin and splashed the bathroom. He soaped up vigorously, then rinsed off.

Then he felt a hand on his chest.

Leonardo yelped in surprise and swallowed some water. The palm on his torso was soft, strangely cold and pressed against his racing heart. He did not know how to react. His brain was bogged down by a weird sensation that reminded him of his dream on the airplane. A soft, supple body, whose shape he felt precisely, pressed against his back and another hand was placed on his cheek. It forced him to turn his head and then soft lips met his. The kiss seemed to last an eternity.

He saw nothing but the steam from the bath clouding the mirror and a hazy, harmoniously oval face.

Sibilla was ready quickly and went downstairs to the terrace. A few tourists were sipping cocktails at the railing and looking at the moon slip between buildings while the lights of the city flickered on. The Italian woman did not admire the sight. She was staring at the tiny house that had fascinated the Englishwoman. The magician had heard of animist practices that built miniature dwellings for spirits. She squatted down to get a closer look at the figures representing the *chao thi*, the lords of the place, that were put in different rooms of the model. The role of these good genies, these guardian angels so to speak, was to protect against the *phi*, the dangerous ghosts that were legion in Asia.

"Doesn't appear to be working," Sibilla sighed.

She glanced behind her. The tourists were drinking at the other end of the terrace paying no attention to her. She pointed Cagliostro's ring at the small house.

"By the power of the Twelve, o wandering spirit watching over this place, show yourself and speak to me," she whispered.

A green halo enshrouded the house, then a human form materialized next to it. Sibilla was surprised to see that the phantom wore the uniform of a hotel employee with a few differences in the collar and length of the skirt that made it look like an older uniform. The woman's face was pale, sickly. Sibilla had no trouble recognizing Cookie's mysterious helper.

"Good evening, Miss," the pale woman said. "What can I do for you?"

"First of all, I'd like to know your name and how you died."

"Oh…" The ghost's eyes glimmered briefly. "I'm Saraï and I died soon after the tsunami. I escaped the wave but I was caught under rubble with the corpse of my younger brother. I came to Bangkok to work and forget but you can never forget. Never. So, I tried to join my little brother."

She showed her neck: the rope had left a pink scar on her pale skin.

"Unfortunately I was stuck here. And not a second goes by that I don't think about my little brother. I miss him and he misses me. The pain and grief of his absence gnaws away at me but I'm a prisoner. He has to wait. Maybe it makes him suffer to see me bound to this place?"

"I promise you that your torments will soon come to an end," Sibilla said with pity. "I can help you but I'll need your help first."

At these words the pale face literally lit up. A soft, pearly glow infused her hollow cheeks and a semblance of life emanated from her frail body.

"Really? You'll help me to cross over into the other world? What do I have to do? Tell me quickly and I'll do whatever it takes to help you."

"I'm sure you will. What do you know about the creature that stole the soul of my friend, the American Dave Kaplan?"

Saraï's ghost suddenly shrank away. Sibilla stepped forward and held out a reassuring hand but her fingers passed right through the transparent body.

"No, please, don't be scared. If I want to fight this thing, I need to know more."

"It's like no other phi," Saraï finally decided to speak. "It was already haunting the city before I died. A streak of red light like blood on fire, that's how I saw it for the first time when my soul left my body. Follow the trail of blood. It weaves its web and it prefers foreigners who don't know how to protect themselves. I think it has a particular fondness for westerners."

"Where is it right now? Do you see it?"

Saraï nodded and her whole body quivered. Sibilla thought of the dying flame of a wood fire in the open steppes.

"It's here, isn't it?"

"Yes! Yes!" the ghost stammered. "Up in your friend's room."

He felt a little prick at the base of his neck but the pain quickly gave way to a delightfully warm feeling that clouded his senses like the hot steam on the mirror. The journalist thought distantly that he should turn off the water before he passed out in the bathtub but two fresh hands were pressing on his shoulders so hard that he could not move. While the drop ran down his chest and face, he was only aware of the ivory face hovering over him. Then he recognized the two golden eyes that glimmered like sparks in a fire.

He had found the woman of his dream.

She brought her red lips up his ear and whispered words in an unknown language that he nevertheless understood.

"Dokmaï. I've finally found you. We're together again. Forever."

Leonardo did not know what to say. His mouth was dry in spite of the water splashing his lips. A vague fear knotted his belly, the last vestiges of his survival instinct.

"Who are you?" he stammered.

"It's me, your beloved, Mekhala. I thought you were lost but here you are, my love…"

"I'm not… I… Please…"

He could no longer control his words or his emotions. He felt hot, burning up, with a delightful fever. The woman smiled on him like cold marble in moonlight.

"I'm sorry, Dokmaï. We'll never part again. Oh, how I missed your kisses."

The creature leaned over and kissed the journalist with greedy passion. Plunged in a voluptuous abyss of luxurious sensations, Leonardo did not think of pulling his mouth away, even when he felt his tongue tasting the ice-cold, sooty tentacle.

The bathroom door flew open and banged against the wall. Sibilla was there with Cagliostro's ring glowing on her finger.

Seeing the creature looming over her friend Sibilla immediately thought of the deep-water anglerfish that lure their prey with a light growing out of its hideous head. The gaunt, perfectly oval face was just the end of an extension from a lumpy, gooey mass that looked like a bunch of guts spilling tar. In the middle of this foul blob there was a huge, milky, open eye, edged with long eyelashes that moved like tentacles. These were holding Leonardo by the shoulders right now.

The eye blinked and stared at Sibilla. The face-bait emitted a shrill, angry whistle.

"By the power of the Twelve," Sibilla shouted, "foul creature, I order you to go back to the hell that created you!"

Cagliostro's ring shot a ray of light that hit the thing head-on. It howled in pain and rage and let go of Leonardo, who slumped over, groaning. The magician stepped forward to finish it off but the phi, in a furious reaction, knocked her off her feet with one of its tentacles. Sibilla fell into the bathtub, right on top of Leonardo who grabbed her, thinking she was the creature, before passing out.

Sibilla pushed off of him but then slipped on the wet enamel. The absurdity of the situation struck her: here she was fighting with her best friend who was naked as a newborn babe.

The phi used this to its advantage. It shriveled up and sank into the tile floor with a sucking sound. In a few seconds there was nothing left of the evil presence.

5.

"He's not out of the woods."

Kasemchaï had been informed by Sibilla and taken Leonardo to Papa Boon-Nam's. They put him to bed and the old man, after a quick examination, found a mark on his jugular. The edges bore traces of a corrosive lipstick and were still leaking blood. In the soft glow of the lamp it was clearly, obscenely visible.

In spite of the warm room Leonardo shook with intermittent fevers. A sickly sweat covered his pale cheeks and his blue veins shone through his filmy skin.

Sibilla stood up with her fists balled before her trembling lips. "But I asked you to stay with me. I knew you weren't safe."

Leonardo tried to speak but he was too weak. An irresistible urge to sleep weighed on his eyelids and limbs and clouded his mind.

"Keep your cool, Miss Sibilla," Kasemchaï advised. "We got some precious clues from the ghost of that woman."

"And you freed her?" Papa Boon-Nam asked.

"I kept my promise, yes," Sibilla whispered.

The old man nodded and stroked his white beard, "Your action saved a poor soul. Astonishing, really astonishing."

"But, Papa Boon-Nam, you, too, believe in magic since you gave that amulet to save Cookie," Sibilla said. "Saraï's ghost talked about a bloody web being woven by this phi. It has to be hiding somewhere around here like a spider awaiting its prey."

"We find the center of the web and we find the lair," Kasemchaï said.

Sibilla smiled at the giant. With the support of the two men she started to feel a little better. The creatures from beyond who were haunting this country were not very familiar to her, so without the invaluable aide of insiders she could easily have surrendered to panic.

Leonardo moaned and put his hand on his throat. His friend thought of the frightening scene in *Dracula* when Lucy Westenra, under the influence of the vampire, was suffocating in her sleep. The creature that had attacked the journalist was no less horrific than the famous Count.

"The phi stole his blood," Papa Boon-Nam said. "It didn't have time to take his soul but it's going to suck up his life."

Tears welled up in Sibilla's eyes. She raised her hand toward the shivering body of her friend and her ring sparkled. The jade glow enveloped the young man's body and gradually a thin, red line that looked stuck to the patient's jugular came into view, inch by inch, then disappeared when it reached the edge of the light from the magic ring. Sibilla had to move the beam to follow the bloody string that passed right through the wooden wall.

"Well," the magician sighed, "there's our trail. I'm going to follow it. Papa Boon-Nam, could you call Inspector Pongwilaï? I've tried to contact him but I can't get through. And I can't wait here."

Kasemchaï sidled up beside her. "I'm going with you. You're obviously able to fight against spirits and demons, but against humans you need Kasemchaï. And the streets aren't so safe now. The military has imposed a curfew and anyone caught outside is arrested on the spot."

"I'm coming too," a tiny, slurred voice said. Cookie was standing in the doorway holding a bottle of beer. Her red eyes implied that it was not her first. Before Sibilla could deny her, she spit out, "I see them. When I'm drunk, I see the wires and I don't need the Green Lantern ring."

She stretched out her thumb and index finger and plucked an invisible harp. When Sibilla pointed the ring at the Englishwoman, it revealed a blood-red string exactly like the one coming out of Leonardo's neck. Cookie's fingers were right on top of it.

The little punk shuddered and stumbled back. "It's super creepy. Looks like a vein. Course I never, uh, touched a vein before."

"It's a dangerous mission," Sibilla said.

"She has my amulet just like me," Kasemchaï said. "And think of the curfew. Your glowing ring will get us spotted. We need her."

Sibilla glanced worriedly at Cookie who had to lean against the wall to stand up straight. The big Thai was right, however, about Cagliostro's ring, but this other alternative seemed just as risky.

Leonardo groaned again and scratched at his throat, "I'm choking. I don't need to know… what attacked me but… hurry up… save me… again," he finished with a nervous smile.

The magician went to the bedside and kissed his fore-head. "You're right. No more wasting time. We'll follow Cookie. You hang in there."

Leonardo took her hand and pressed his lips to her palm. She felt him as cold as ice despite the fever in his eyes. He let go unwillingly and whispered, "I'm counting on you."

"Be very careful," Papa Boon-Nam warned. "The phi are lost souls but their ruling passion is anger and that's what controls their actions."

"We'll be careful," Sibilla promised.

One last look of encouragement for Leonardo and she left. Kasemchaï took Cookie by the arm and they followed the pretty Italian through the house and into the garden.

When they reached the road the Thai guide led them into the shadow of a lemongrass bush. A jeep drove past the property with four soldiers inside who were holding rifles and watching the sidewalks and houses. The military was not taking the curfew lightly.

Once the sound of the engine had faded, the giant and the two women crept out of the darkness. They were barely on the street when Cookie covered her mouth to stifle a cry:

"Fuck! There's a bunch of them!"

"A bunch of what?" Sibilla whispered. "Red strings?"

The punk nodded vigorously. "Yeah, I see dozens of 'em." She squinted and looked around. "They're coming from all over but I think they're all leading…"

She pointed her finger at an eerily deserted road that crossed a canal. The buildings and shops with their awnings provided enough protection for them. The three of them hurried over the bridge. The view was clear and they could see headlights in the distance but they, too, were open targets.

Once they were on the other side Cookie stopped. "The strings are a little higher, like they're being raised up… So, if we're in the middle of the road…"

Her eyes followed the invisible red wires until she almost fell backwards. Kasemchaï had to catch her.

"They all converge at the huge thing over there!"

The giant Thai saw the dark, formidable mass that a spotlight lit up briefly.

"The Ghost Tower," he gasped.

6.

The Sathorn Unique was a symbol of the economic disaster that hit Thailand. The 50-storey tower was supposed to have luxury apartments and shops but work was finally abandoned after the 1997 financial crisis, leaving the building almost finished but totally uninhabitable. Even though it is a favorite destination for urban explorers the world over, most of the Thai try to avoid it. Disturbing legends are whispered about this concrete block: the ghosts of Bangkok are supposed to reside there. And there are plenty of stories about visitors and guards finding victims of suicide.

Kasemchaï told all this in a whisper, in the shadows behind a restaurant next to an empty lot. The tower's imposing mass loomed over them and they had to twist their necks to see the rounded balconies at the top. Sibilla thought of a huge wasp's nest. Cookie saw the sick, venous heart of some Lovecraftian creature. The red strings all met at the top and were slowly starting to fade. The long, vigilant walk and three good heaves had lowered her alcohol level. She fished out another bottle of beer from her backpack and opened it discreetly.

"I'm sobering up."

Sibilla took the beer gently out of her hand. "I'll take over with my ring. You two, stay here."

"No!" Cookie and Kasemchaï protested in unison.

A moment of silence but nothing seemed to have been alerted by the voices.

"We've got our amulets," the Thai said more softly.

"The hotel girl told me it was enough protection," Cookie added. "Better to be three against that nasty thing."

Sibilla looked at them and shook her head, "Well, time's pressing so I won't argue."

She stepped out of hiding and crossed the street. Life seemed to have deserted the city despite the patches of light on the sidewalk.

"We can get in to the tower by that little alley over there," Kasemchaï said, dragging Cookie along.

They entered the dark alley between humid walls. The electrical cables over their heads, bleak twins of the lines of blood, formed a network that slashed across the night sky. Kasemchaï took out a flashlight and lit the way forward, chasing off some scurrying rats. As they passed by a twisted, rusted fence overgrown with plants they saw the gaunt face of a homeless man who blinked his sleepy eyes.

The three of them tramped over another fence that weeds were taking back to nature. Vines had invaded the first two floors of the tall tower. They had to squeeze through a thick curtain of plants to enter by a broken glass door. The concrete floor was strewn with rubble and debris.

The noxious odor made them stop for a moment in a nauseous stupor as if the stench was solidifying around them into a putrid shell. It was like a demented chef had been stewing dead rats in urine and blood for centuries. Cookie bent over to vomit. Sibilla and Kasemchaï plugged their noses and wondered how they were going to climb up 50 flights in this suffocating atmosphere.

The giant pointed the flashlight at the floor and hid part of it with his hand so they would not be seen from the outside. Sibilla helped Cookie straighten up. The Englishwoman wiped her mouth and pulled her t-shirt up over her nose to filter out the pestilence.

"It must be one really angry phi to stink so bad," Kasemchaï said.

Sibilla's cell phone started vibrating. She was startled but did not jump. Hoping it was Pongwilaï, she answered.

"Miss Sibilla?" the officer's voice murmured in her ear. "I'm sorry I didn't call earlier but I was negotiating with a lieutenant of the junta. As you can imagine, it was not a pleasant conversation. Papa Boon-Nam told me everything. Where are you?"

"I'm in the creature's lair with Cookie and Kasemchaï. The phi made its nest at the top of Sathorn Unique."

Pongwilaï swore at the other end of the line. "I called an exorcist but helping a grandma almost 100 years old to get to the top of that monster is not going to be a walk in the park."

"You know how vicious this ghost is," Sibilla said. "Find a strong cop to carry her. But do it fast because we're not waiting around. My friends are dying."

She hung up before the officer had time to answer, then she turned to her companions. "Let's go."

Kasemchaï spotted an access ramp and they were soon on a dilapidated balcony choked by a big tarp. Despite the windows being wide open the abominable odor persisted. And yet, when they were prowling around outside the tower, they had smelled nothing. The giant Thai imitated Cookie by pulling his t-shirt over his nose and the three of them went looking for a way to get upstairs other than the two rusted escalators that had never worked. They ended up climbing it anyway for lack of an alternative. The next floor was huge, planned for shops. This tower was a ghost before it had ever been occupied.

They climbed another dead escalator that creaked under their weight. Kasemchaï tiptoed with his arms outstretched.

It was waiting for them on the landing.

Cookie stifled a cry and hid behind the comforting belly of their giant guide. Sibilla lit up the scene with her ring. With a black shirt clinging to its body and a badge on its chest the corpse sitting in the old wheelchair next to the escalators must have been a security guard. Dried blood speckled its chin and neck. It could not have been there for a long time because it showed no sign of decomposition.

Looking at the jagged wound on the jugular Sibilla was surprised that there was not more blood. Then she remembered what the phi liked to feed on.

194

"Now I understand why it was so easy to get in," Kasemchaï said as he grasped his amulet.

Sibilla studied the corpse for a moment. The same fate awaited Leonardo and Dave. She walked around the macabre welcoming committee and swept the ray of light around her.

"There," Cookie whispered.

Sibilla pointed up and they saw all the red lines woven together and disappear into the high ceiling. Some of them were moving, rippling, like arteries pulsing from an invisible heart. The Italian imagined the blood of her friends flowing through these strands. She gestured to the others to move on.

They explored a whole section of the floor before finding a stairway hidden between two empty stores. They started climbing up, trying to save their breath as much as possible. Sibilla was first, followed by Cookie while Kasemchaï brought up the rear. Numbers were painted in red on every floor, simple but reassuring markers in the darkness of the dusty, narrow stairwell.

Between the ninth and tenth floor Sibilla motioned to stop. Two red strings were vibrating lightly in front of them. They were a little thicker than the one connected to Leonardo's throat. One of the veins was stretched out at knee level; the other was higher, leaving just enough room to bend over and step through. They all had no doubt that touching the strings would alert the evil entity.

The two women had no problem getting through but Kasemchaï had to contort his huge body. When his foot slipped on a broken piece of concrete he almost fell but the two girls held him steady, one around his waist and the other grabbing his shirt. They stood frozen in this uncomfortable position with the giant Thai leaning over like the tower of Pisa, his nose only inches from the red wire. Kasemchaï was horrified to smell the sweet, metallic odor of fresh blood coming to him over the ambient stench.

Once the colossus was out of danger they resumed their ascent, whispering words of encouragement to each other. From time to time they crossed blood wires that they had to step over. Sibilla felt like she was Sam in Lord of the Rings sneaking through Shelob's lair to help Frodo. Cagliostro's ring was her Phial of Galadriel.

They found their second corpse on the 30th floor. They were so winded that the new abomination totally wiped them out. A string thinner than the others, a curdy, sickly brown color, was stuck in the dead man's grayish throat. Putrefaction was hard at work: the swollen belly stretched tight a t-shirt with a picture of the Ramones.

A black cap lay next to the curly haired head while the blue lips formed a macabre smile. Sibilla realized that the victim was around the same age as Leonardo and for an awful second she saw her friend lying on the stairs, the same morbid grin on his bloodless face.

"We have to keep going. There are only twenty floors left."

Kasemchaï grunted his agreement. Cookie moaned at the announcement of the number. But the three of them got to their feet and slid along the wall to avoid touching the rotting form.

The final floors were like climbing Everest in the dark. When shadows from the city finally danced along the walls they almost ran forward in triumph and relief.

But first they had to get through a net woven of bloody wires.

7.

The red lines went right though the steps, covering a whole part of the stairs. They were so close to their goal…

Sibilla and company went down to the lower landing.

"Looks like we lost the element of surprise," she whispered.

"Maybe those red things don't detect anything," Cookie suggested.

"No, I think our intuition was right from the start."

Sibilla's cell phone vibrated again. She answered it right away.

"Pongwilaï?"

"Yes. Where are you?"

"We're at the top of the tower and we're going to attack the phi any minute now. We found two dead bodies."

"That doesn't surprise me," the officer said. "For certain tourists the tower is a jewel in the explorer's crown. But before doing anything, listen carefully: I'm downstairs with the old exorcist and some other police… and soldiers."

From the hesitant tone of his voice this was not good news.

"I had to explain that some tourist had broken the curfew. A contingent was at the station and didn't want me to come and help. They want to arrest you and kick you out of the country when you get down here."

"If we get down alive," Sibilla said. "What about Kasemchaï?"

"We had to explain the witch's presence by saying that a native was your guide and was refusing to come down because of the ghosts. Some soldiers don't believe in spirit and had a good laugh. Maybe that'll make them more lenient toward him. He might go to jail."

Sibilla looked at Kasemchaï and frowned. "I hope not. Listen, we can't wait for you."

"No, indeed and I have a plan: the old witch is going to recite her exorcism through a megaphone. That should distract the phi long enough for you to do what you need to do."

"So we should wait till we hear the ritual?"

"Exactly. Good luck to all of you."

Pongwilaï hung up and Sibilla turned to her companions.

Cookie asked, "We're in trouble, aren't we?"

Sibilla shrugged her shoulders, "Aren't we already?"

A droning voice, muffled by the thick wall, came mumbling through a poorly adjusted megaphone. The red lines flapped and fluttered.

"That's the signal," Sibilla said. "Don't let go of your amulets and stay behind me!"

She jumped up the stairs. Cagliostro's ring was warm on her finger and seemed to be vibrating with a life of its own. She plowed through the purple barrier and felt a current of hot air, pulsing with life. Another leap and she was in the open air. The stars had deserted the deep-blue sky but shined over the neighboring towers, giving a dim glow to the graffiti on the big terrace.

The panorama was breathtaking but the ugliness of the thing in front of Sibilla ruined the view: the phi in its lair, much more daunting than the monster she had seen in the hotel bathroom.

A gigantic mass of black organs that bristled with long, bright red veins, the ghost was almost ten feet tall. Several delicately oval heads bobbed at the end of willowy tentacles, lures for careless men. One of them had a burn mark on its alabaster cheek. A single, enormous, milky eye blinked in the middle of the blob.

The phi whistled, obviously disturbed, and sucked its network of bloody strings back into its flabby bulk. The old exorcist was still chanting the ritual in her hoarse voice. Along with the magic from Cagliostro's ring it should be enough to destroy the ghost.

Sibilla pointed her ring. A bright light engulfed the entity, which howled in pain. Behind the magician, Kasemchaï and Cookie held their talismans up high. The three of them marched slowly toward the abomination.

"By the power of the Twelve and in the name of Cagliostro whose heir I am, I order you to free the souls! Free Dave Kaplan and free all your victims!"

"Yeah, leave Dave alone, you bastard!" Cookie yelled.

The phi whistled again from all its red mouths and shot a tentacle at Sibilla. She dodged it and the gooey arm crashed into concrete. The pretty Italian responded by calling upon all the energy in the ring and the jade light got brighter around the deformed specter. The smell of burned flesh started emanating from the open wounds. Down below the old priestess' voice reached shrill heights that seemed to be achieving its punishing goal.

Made more confident by the entity's plight, Cookie and Kasemchaï stepped closer, amulets held tight. The thing tried to strike with one of its slimy tentacles but the Thai giant blocked it with his arm, a swift reflex from his years of practicing muay-thai and then he stuck his amulet on the black flesh.

Another howl from beyond. The phantom struggled and managed to knock him over but he was back on his feet in no time.

"Free all those who you have captured!" Sibilla shouted.

A cry of rage shook the walls and the phi moved off toward the rusted frame on the edge of the terrace. At the same time the long, gooey threads like hair dipped in molasses, flew out into the sky, stretching toward the horizon as the body seemed to slowly deflate.

"It's escaping!" Cookie warned. The Englishwoman was brave enough to run at the phi and grab a flabby bulge with her bare hands.

"No, Cookie, get away!" Sibilla cried out."

A tentacle hit the punk girl in the chest and sent her flying over the edge. Kasemchaï, however, dove just in time to grab her by the arm before she fell. The phi had time to complete its weird transformation, stretch out, thin out, until the body was no bigger than a fat newborn baby.

Sibilla grabbed a handful of threads. "I'm not going to let you get away like this!"

Another weird transformation took place: the magician's hands blended with the ghost. She had the awful feeling of being stuck into ice-cold mud. Then she was pulled off her feet.

It's taking me with it!

She did not have time to be scared of the empty space opening up under her feet because she was drowned in the gelatinous blob that was squeezing her in its disgusting clutches. She struggled against it as the ectoplasmic rolls stuffed into

199

her mouth. She snapped her jaws shut, bit hard on the foul gag.

"Help, master!" she gargled, "Ca… Cagliostro!"

The gentle warmth from the ring immediately filled the darkness around her mouth and cheeks. Groaning she managed to free her hands and bring them together in front of her face.

Cagliostro, my master, protect me!

The filthy flesh that was trying to crush her released its hold but Sibilla still felt herself flying through the dark. She was inside the phi and since it could not kill her it was going to spit her out, twisting its body like a boa regurgitating an indigestible porcupine. The ring gradually spread its light around the magician like a protective cocoon and the phi body around her sizzled and stuck together.

The magician heard a terrifying howl of pain and everything seemed to go faster. She felt the speed increasing inside the ghost dragging her along. The thing was running back to its den like a wounded animal. The top of Sathorn Unique was, in fact, just a hunting ground.

Bolstered by the power of the ring and with her curiosity piqued Sibilla concentrated all her thoughts on the entity. She felt waves of intense emotion pass through her without really touching her.

By the power of the Twelve, creature of the dark, who are you really? Where do you come from?

She asked the question again and again but only got curses in response. So, holding out her hands together, Sibilla decided to find the truth for herself. She crawled forward in that space outside of reality. In a strange language that she could nonetheless understand the ghost begged her to leave it alone, not to go any farther.

Have pity, I'll give back the souls of my lovers, have pity…

Deaf to its pleas Sibilla kept wriggling forward until her hands felt a weird, warm organ in the middle of the jelly flesh.

She pulled herself up to what seemed to be a giant heart beating fast, then she put her arms around the thing.

"I don't hate you for what you did but you can't keep killing all these men," she murmured.

She had kept her eyes closed during her slow exploration and when she opened them, she was looking into the transparent brightness of a veined heart. Thus conquered, the phi opened its soul and Sibilla learned the story of Mekhala.

8.

A little girl.

A little girl with a shriveled right foot, deformed. A little girl who loves her father with that desperate tenderness of lonely children. A father, a fisherman, a widower, who swallows his bitter grief every morning in order to feed his daughter. The elders of the remote village say: she's crippled and cursed, abandon her in the forest. A father who refuses because she looks so much like his poor Mekhala. That's why he gave her her name. A little girl who plays alone with the wooden doll her father made for her, dresses it with leaves and flowers. A little girl who swims alone in the sea because the other children run away when they see her. Children who run away whenever she comes near because they think they will wake up one morning with a twisted foot like hers if she touches them.

A girl.

A girl whose father disappeared at sea. A girl chased from the village. A girl who finds refuge among the roots of the biggest tree in the forest. A girl who lives by hunting and gathering, who retreats into bitterness. A girl who crawls like a snake through the ferns to spy on the villagers. A girl who steals. A girl who is caught by Dokmaï the stranger. Dokmaï and his pale blue eyes, his thin face, his nice smell. Dokmaï who looks at her without fear, without disgust and lets her leave with the knife she wanted.

A young woman.

A young woman who loves Dokmaï. Dokmaï hugs the young woman in his arms, mingles his breath with hers. A young woman's skin against Dokmaï's. The big tree where she lives, a shelter for their embraces. A young woman loves Dokmaï. A young woman's belly grows big and round. Dokmaï goes away, hides behind a lie, never comes back. A young woman cries, weeps, sways holding her swollen belly. A young woman spawns a baby at her feet and anger in her heart. A young woman sneaks into the village in the middle of the night. A young woman looks for Dokmaï's hut. She finds Dokmaï sleeping on a mat with the chief's daughter held so tightly in his arms. Their nudity illuminated by the moon. Her heart burns with anger. A young woman wielding a knife. Dokmaï's knife. Blood and screams. Blood on a young woman's hands. Blood on her thighs. A young woman caught by the villagers. A young woman hit in the face and belly. A young woman taken into the forest, thrown into a ditch at the foot of the big tree. A young woman who begs them to spare her newborn baby. A young woman buried alive. A young woman chokes on clumps of earth. A young woman dies whispering one final curse.

A dead girl.

A dead girl who remembers and waits. A dead girl whose bones lie under the tree that grows slowly over her remains. A dead girl waiting and remembering. A dead girl feeling hunger burrow through the ruins of her soul. A dead girl waiting. A dead girl feeling trapped under the earth by its immense weight. A dead girl feeling the wave come. A dead girl feeling nourishment come. A dead girl feeling freedom come. A dead girl is free to feed, free to get revenge.

Sibilla awoke with a start. She was lying face down on mossy ground. She got up, disoriented, lost in a dark forest, the silence of trees.

She was not in Bangkok anymore.

The pretty Italian wiped the dirt and debris from her cheek and clothes. She had expected to be covered in some kind of mucus after her long trip in the guts of the phi but this humiliation had been spared.

A movement to her right.

Sibilla turned, Cagliostro's ring held out.

"Mekhala!"

A rustling sound behind her. She swung around.

"This can't go on, Mekhala!"

Something brushed her cheek. Sibilla yelped and tripped on a root that immediately wrapped around her ankle and lifted her up. Her ring freed her and she plopped on the ground.

"You can't eat souls forever!"

Yes!

A coil of hair slapped her hard. Another whacked her head. Another whipped her back and shoulders.

"Stop! I want to free you! I've seen everything, Mekhala, the story of your life, your loneliness, your anger!"

Sibilla pointed her ring at an unbelievably long lock of hair that was retreating under a huge tree.

"And I saw your father," the magician went on. "He loved you. He loved you unconditionally. There are men who are not traitors."

Yes! He left without me! He died!

"And your baby, Mekhala? Don't you want to put it to rest? It has lain in you for so long and it shares your rage and curses."

Sibilla searched around the trunk of the tree with the light from her ring. She had seen it in the phi's memories. The roots and the leaves quivered but nothing attacked.

She's starting to listen to reason, Sibilla thought.

Then she came face to face with a little statue on a bed of moss. The villagers had put it on the ditch where Mekhala's remains lay buried to prevent her from finding rest, to punish her for the murder of Dokmaï and the chief's daughter. But there had been so many dead since then, so many…

Sibilla lifted the statuette and threw it as far as she could. Her action was answered with a heart-wrenching wail.

"You hear? That's your baby, who was also a prisoner!"

She knelt down and put her hands flat on the moss.

"By the power of the Twelve, be free, Mekhala, and join the afterlife with your child. Rest in peace."

Cagliostro's ring glimmered and enveloped the giant tree. The deep roots and massive trunk, all the way to the smallest twig and tiniest leaf, lit up from the inside by its sap turned phosphorescent. Then the wood cracked and new leaves, bigger and greener, blossomed.

The ground on which Sibilla was standing rose up and she stumbled back when a bright ectoplasm sprang out, almost throwing her to the ground. It climbed up from branch to branch and stopped at the top of the tree. A newborn babe was cuddled against the chest of the apparition that was clothed in nothing but hair like a gossamer veil. Despite its right foot that was horribly deformed and atrophied, the specter stood gracefully on the top of the tree that had sheltered its remains for centuries. The baby whimpered, burped and Mekhala's ghost rocked it gently. Sibilla guessed that the child was a boy.

Slowly she lifted Cagliostro's ring. "Go in peace, both of you."

The jade flashed. The late Mekhala and her baby dissipated in the light, leaving nothing behind but some sparks that were carried away by the wind, into the sky, to mingle with the stars.

Sibilla backed away. The leaves of the big tree murmured softly in the breeze and the moon lit the darkness with its opal glow. Everything finally looked at peace.

The magician suddenly felt exhausted. She dropped down on the wet ground and stayed there looking up into the sky. She searched the stars for the sparks that had been a terribly lonely young woman. She wished her a pleasant journey to the afterlife and to finally feel all the love that had been denied her. Then she looked at the moon and shuddered. The pale star made her think of Leonardo lying drained of blood at Papa Boon-Nam's.

Despite all the damage from the supernatural voyage, her cell phone vibrated and snapped her out of her reveries.

"Sibilla? Where are you?" Pongwilaï's voice sounded worried.

"Far away, I'm afraid, but safe and sound."

The pretty Italian struggled to her feet and started down a gentle slope.

"I freed the ghost," she said as she stepped carefully around the trees. "It brought me to its grave and I freed it. It was only fair... a very unhappy, young woman."

"That's where most of the phi come from," Pongwilaï said. "Congratulations, you saved many lives. I will call on you right away if anything like this happens again."

"Speaking of lives, any news about Leonardo and Dave?"

The young woman stopped and leaned against a tree trunk streaked with vines to brace herself for the bad news.

"They're fine," the officer answered gladly. "Papa Boon-Nam told me Leonardo is speaking. He's weak but lucid. As for Kaplan..."

Sibilla tried not to cry from relief when she heard about the doctors' surprise on seeing the American wake up not knowing why he was hooked up to all those machines. When the policeman paused, Sibilla thought she heard the sound of waves in the distance. She started walking again.

"Cookie and Kasemchaï are with me at the station. They're relieved to hear you're safe and sound. I had to arrest them myself to save them from the soldiers. Unfortunately Miss MacFerrin will be kicked out of the country in two days for breaking the curfew. You'd do best to leave with her until our new government gets settled."

"I have to be found first," Sibilla said. "I'll call you back when I know where I am."

She hung up. A path wound between the trees and beyond was the shimmering sea. Despite her stiff and tired legs the magician managed to make it to the beach. 20 or so young Westerners were on the sand lighting paper lanterns that they put into miniature boats. Sibilla's arrival surprised them. She invented a story of a creepy taxi abandoning her here after robbing her.

"That happens sometimes," a tall, blond guy with an Australian accent said. "But you're in luck. You're in Khao Lak and there are some nice hotels around. Like ours! I'll give you my room and sleep on the beach." He held out his hand. "My name's Mitchell by the way."

"Sibilla. Thanks a lot for the offer, Mitchell. Are you commemorating something?"

"Yeah, every year we celebrate the birthday of our friend Christophe. He died here in the tsunami."

Sibilla followed her generous benefactor down to the gently lapping water. Everyone put their flickering boats down and pushed them out to sea. The water accepted their offering and rocked the little, seafaring fireflies under the starry heavens.

Lucia

"Ah, Verga, you're back! None too soon. I thought you were still lying in the hospital or maybe decided to just stay in Thailand."

"Good to see you too, Maria." Leonardo closed the door to his editor-in-chief's office. He was still having trouble getting over his encounter with the phi. The bruise on his neck and the bags under his eyes proved it. He sat across from his boss.

"What do you want?" the *Flash* editor got right to the point. "Don't tell me it's for a raise."

"Now that you mention it…"

Leonardo dropped the joke when Maria trained a menacing eye on him through the veil of smoke from her eternal cigarette.

"In truth, I have some questions to ask you. About Sibilla. The thing with the Arbini brothers showed me the importance for her anonymity at *Flash*. Unless there's a traitor in our ranks, of course."

"The personal data of every employee is now in a safe," Maria crushed out her half-smoked cigarette in the ashtray. "I don't trust computers anymore, not since that monster Zeno hacked mine."

"And papa Arbini?"

"He's still at it. Now he's trying to get us charged with homicide. Luckily Patricia Hope, Sibilla's friend, and Sir Wilson have hired good lawyers."

"I do feel a little sad about the two buffoons…"

"We're not responsible for their tragedies. They dove headfirst into a dangerous world where they couldn't get out alive. Don't forget what they did…"

The young man nodded. Despite his shattered knee he did not hate the two brothers who had paid dearly for their stupidity. Impatience and lack of empathy, two evils that consume the youth all over the world...

Feeling another wave of gloom creeping up on him he got straight to the point, "When I first started collaborating with Sibilla I remember that you insisted on her anonymity. You almost had me sign a confidentiality clause. So, you talked about the readers' trust, more freedom of movement and of course her safety."

"And? Something you don't understand?"

"Well, uh... blame my journalistic instinct," Leonardo said, "but I have the distinct feeling that you talked about Sibilla's safety for a very specific reason. As if she had already been compromised at least once before. But that's not the only thing I've been wondering about..."

Leonardo leaned forward, being careful not to put any pressure on his wounded knee, and took one of Maria's cigarettes. Impressed by her reporter's gravity she did not say a word.

"When did the column on the supernatural start? I mean, when exactly did a paper famous for its seriousness become interested in weird phenomenon? Because you don't do things by chance..."

Maria Carpi kept silent for a few long seconds, then stood up abruptly. Leonardo thought she was going to send him off on some trivial assignment. But she locked the office door, unplugged the telephone and turned on a huge coffee maker that sat near the window. While the water started whistling softly she sat back down.

"I hope you've finished your work, Verga, because it's a long story to answer your questions."

She leaned back in her chair.

"Before Sibilla came here, *Flash* published a column on crimes and cons that used the supernatural to swindle the gullible. It was written by Lucia Drago. I didn't know her for long but what we went through together made us friends for life. So, here's the story of our adventure a few days after I was first hired by *Flash*."

At that time, she was barely grown up, 22 years-old, a little bit awkward, always fidgeting with her hands. She started smoking to put up a front. Leonardo would have laughed at her long straight hair and the thick black bangs that covered her eyebrows. Besides ignoring her slightly pudgy physique, Maria was careful not to mention to her employee that after a particularly disastrous experience as a novice at a big magazine in Milan, *La Tromba*, she had set her sights on Sir Wilson's group because her former editor-in-chief hated with a passion this media mogul and his "whole court of kiss-asses".

After she sent in her job application to get some revenge, she found herself in the office of the man who would hand her the reins years later: Toni Gambardella. He was an absolutely wonderful man with the sparkling eyes of a 60 year-old who loves life. The little hair he had left was carefully combed into a silver crown around his smooth head. Stuck in his mouth was a cigarillo that smelled strangely of cinnamon. Maria learned later that he had them made special by a company in Tuscany. But at the moment the scent was not unpleasant as the editor of *Flash* gazed at her kindly.

"You know, Maria… I can speak to you informally, I hope, because if you join us you'll see that our formalities consist of hello, goodbye and a kiss on the cheek without any of those bows and curtsies that your old boss probably told you about."

"He did mention that, yes."

"I figured. Anyway, I just want to tell you that it's not the same ambiance her as at *La Tromba*. I mean, we don't treat our young recruits like flunkies, but we expect from them the maximum thoroughness, even in jobs that might seem pretty frivolous."

"You mean like the column 'Honey Trap' by Lucia Drago?" Maria almost hesitated to ask.

She was fidgeting with an unlit cigarette. Gambardella finally offered her a light.

"Exactly," he said. "Behind the whimsical name lies hard, serious investigative journalism. Lucia is our best reporter and an incredible writer. Our readers love her."

The editor had a sudden inspiration and snapped his fingers.

"Why, the best thing would be for you to spend a couple of days with her! She leaves tomorrow for France. The Oise. A mysterious case of hunting a ghost that's been terrorizing someone there. If you agree I'll give you the day off to pack your things and water your plants while I take care of your tickets. And Lucia will brief you. She's that beautiful brunette behind you."

Maria almost fell off the chair when she turned around: a woman was standing right behind her. She had come into the office without making a sound and now she was standing there with a file under her arm and a big smile on her face. The journalist was wearing a long, leather coat and her soft, brown, wavy hair cascaded over her shoulders. She was pushing 40 and there were crow's feet in the corners of her eyes.

Lucia Drago held out her hand to the new recruit who jumped up and blushed at the thought of shaking that graceful hand with her own sweaty palm.

"Signora Drago, I... I'm..."

"Maria? Nice to meet you. You can call me Lucia. I hope you're not too sensitive because you're going to see some really astonishing things."

Her voice was warm and energetic. Maria's questioning eyes went from Gambardella back to the reporter. "But I... I thought your column was about denouncing all the scams..."

"The cases of unexplainable phenomena are not talked about in Lucia's column," the editor-in-chief said. "Keep this to yourself, Maria, and consider this like a token of trust, but *Flash* is going to start up an imprint specialized in the study of irrational events and our star here will be writing the first book."

"I've made notes and carefully arranged all the really supernatural stories that I witnessed," Lucia added enthusiastically. "I don't know if all our readers believe it but I aim to prove that there are hidden forces in this world, magical, protective and menacing forces. I'd love to open the people's eyes to what's around us."

Another doubtful look from Maria to Gambardella who grinned at her, pleased as pie, holding his cinnamon cigarillo between his fingers.

"I know what you're thinking, young lady, and I, too, am a little skeptical, but what better way to form your own opinion than to take a trip with our Lucia?" He clapped his hands. "Ladies! I picture you in one of this American films that are popular now where they pair up a veteran and a rookie. I can't wait to read the article from two different points of view."

Maria had already been to France. She had seen Paris and the Côte d'Azur and she hated both trips. The capital felt like an overpopulated, open-air prison where you couldn't talk to the guards without speaking perfect French unless you wanted to be snubbed. As for the metro, that huge, underground maze, it was like traveling through the clogged arteries of a monster whose cranky corpuscles fed on rotten food. The feeling was not much better in Cannes or Nice. You really had to be very rich, very old or both to appreciate the charms frozen in the concrete.

The greenery of the Oise, ornamented with golden leaves at the start of Fall, gave her more hope. She had heard about some castles that were the pride and joy of this part of Picardy. She figured her getaway would be a little more inviting than her two previous visits.

Lucia was driving a small car rented at Roissy airport, taking sharp turns and cruising down streets without a trace of hesitation, as if she knew the place. Maria had offered to play copilot but her older colleague politely refused. The younger woman was secretly thankful for the rejection: despite her warm and friendly manner, Lucia intimidated her. The newcomer would have died of shame if she got them lost because she could not read the map.

As their journey wound through a thickening forest, the pretty scenery ended up affecting Maria and stirring her imagination. What woodland creature might be stealing through the mist? Maybe no elves or dryads but it was not uncommon to cross a rabbit on the road, hopping over the dead leaves. Lucia slowed down so that she would not run over any careless stragglers.

At last they came to a little, open area and she parked the car on the side of the road.

"We're going to go the rest of the way on foot. Watch out for your heels."

Maria looked down at her ankle boots disappointedly. She had not thought of hiking through the woods on wet ground.

"Don't worry," Lucia said, opening the door, "it's not a long walk."

The columnist went to get her big bag from the trunk along with her notebook. Maria just had a handbag with a memo pad and a Dictaphone.

The two women entered the woods. Lucia walked slowly to stay with her young colleague who felt her high heels sinking into the loose soil. The branches shook as a crow took flight with a screech. Birds sent secret messages in their melancholy warbling. At times they caught the furtive movements of a squirrel watching them but for the most part they just heard the quiet ambling of animals and the murmur of leaves. The ambiance filled Maria with the pleasant realization that she was far away from everything.

"We're here," Lucia whispered, seeming to share the same feeling.

She slowly moved a branch of a hazelnut tree and Maria could not hold back a hoot of utter delight: sitting in the middle of a pond was a beautiful medieval castle mirrored in the lazy ripples. A couple of ghostly white swans floated peacefully near the high wall.

"It's the castle of the Lady of the Lake from the Arthurian legends!" Maria exclaimed.

"Truthfully, it's the castle of the White Lady of Viarme," Lucia said. "It was built in 1420 by a duke who was madly in love with her. According to what I was told, the ghost hunt stops right here at the edge of the pond. It could be the Duke, who died in a hunting accident, trying to get back to his beauty."

"But the lady prays every night that her cruel lord not be able to reach her."

Surprised by this strange voice, the two journalists turned around. Maria even let out a little yelp of fear. An old man stood before them. Tall and thin, his skin turned pink from the fresh country air, he wore a checkered cap and in his gnarled hand he held a cane whose knob was sculpted into a horse's head.

"Stay calm, ladies, I'm not the ghost of the Duke of Oise. My name is Jacques Choiseul and I'm the former game warden."

"Hello," Lucia said. "I'm…"

"You're Mademoiselle Drago," the old man said calmly. "I know. My son Christophe is the one who wrote to you."

He held out a hand to the two women and they each shook it. Choiseul's grip was firm, almost painfully firm, and Maria felt a little squeamish being clamped by the long, bony fingers.

"I heard you telling a short version of the history of this place," the old man pointed at the castle. "Like a lot of legends this one is tragic and cruel. The Duke was very much in love with the White Lady, but he couldn't stand the idea of other men admiring her beauty, so he locked her up in the most beautiful room of this pretty castle. A room without windows and with a strong, solid oak door. He treated her like a precious treasure but was deaf to her pleas, blind to her tears when she asked to be free. Until the day he died in a hunting accident, gutted by a boar. They say it was a superb beast with shimmering fur and silver tusks, sent by the beautiful prisoner who thought she could thus rid herself of her jailor. Unfortunately for the fair Lady, the evil Duke was the only one who knew she was locked away in the castle."

Maria shuddered, horrified by the end she could already guess.

"You understand, mademoiselle, this pretty castle became her tomb. She died without food or water, imprisoned forever in her luxurious bedroom."

Lucia and Maria were escorted by the old game warden back to their car and got directions to his family abode. After twisting through narrow roads for a good twenty minutes, they finally arrived at an old farmhouse with thatched roof and white walls, tucked into a quiet nook of the forest. The trees around it seemed to have already suffered the rigors of an early autumn. They raised their bare, black branches toward a pale sky with only a handful of crows as ornaments.

Lucia took the bumpy dirt road that rocked the car from left to right and then parked near the front door whose upper part had a pane of glass that was covered by a very rustic, checkered curtain.

The rain started falling at that very moment.

As she got out of the car Maria noticed a weird little statue near the corner of the house that she figured was a crude carving of a saint. She barely had time to see that the tiny, moss-covered man of stone had his hands buried inside his open belly when the door opened. A huge black dog snuck out silently, crept around the rented car, sniffing every tire, and then planted itself between the two women, gazing at each of them with its yellow eyes. Someone whistled in the house and the dark-furred dog sauntered back inside.

"Good old Kerry," Choiseul said. "Can't ask for a better guard."

"He's impressive," Lucia smiled.

Maria followed them in silence, her heart racing in her breast. She liked animals but the eyes of this dog... It was absolutely ridiculous but those yellow eyes had stared so hard into hers with not a hint of puppy dog kindness. She scolded herself: being too sensitive could ruin her career as a journalist.

This severe but logical conclusion was immediately put to the test when she entered the farmhouse. A death mask came floating towards her in the half-light. The puddles of shadow that served as eyes opened wide in the middle of the whiteness that almost shined in the darkness.

Maria stifled a cry.

"Don't stand there in the dark, Christophe."

Jacques Choiseul flipped the light switch and brightness suddenly flooded the rustic dining room, revealing a tall, emaciated, young man with black hair and clothes. Like all people who grow too fast he stooped, as if he was afraid the dark, spiky hair on his head would hit the rough beams on the ceiling. He looked uncertain as he leaned both hands on a rectangular table covered with an oilcloth.

"Sorry," the young man spoke in an oddly hushed voice, "I need to stay in the dark…"

"I don't blame you, but look who I found in the woods?"

Christophe suddenly started to tremble and his lower lip dropped onto his chin, unveiling some crooked, yellow teeth. Maria thought he looked like a junkie being offered a needle full of heroin and she held back a shudder. She hated where this was going. Lucia, however, did not lose her radiant smile but her eyes were not sparkling with the same warmth. Maybe because the hunched over guy was devouring her with his eyes and now stumbling towards her holding out his bony, trembling hand.

"Lucia Drago… you came!"

He almost tried to hug her but stopped himself only inches away from the journalist. A subtle change came over him. He straightened up a little and the death mask of his face took on a little life.

"You came. You got my letter. It's such a relief…"

"I couldn't pass up such an interesting investigation, Christophe. Your letter was extremely intriguing. So, I hopped

215

on the first plane for Paris and here I am along with my colleague."

Christophe turned the black puddles in his eye sockets toward the younger woman. The future editor-in-chief of the Flash tensed up. She would not dare say it but she had the feeling that this young man was giving off dark, creepy, hostile waves. She was not welcome here and this was backed up by the low growl from the black dog staring at her as it sat next to Jacques Choiseul.

"But I…" Christophe's voice was strained. "It's just that I can only trust you. It's you and you alone who… whom I need."

A vein started pulsing on his forehead and his lower lip was twitching. Maria thought he was wavering between breaking down in tears or jumping on her and tearing her to pieces.

"Maria helps me in my investigations," Lucia stepped between the two of them. "You see, I'm more and more in demand and I need an assistant."

The journalist spoke calmly, confidently, but with a hint of authority. The message was clear enough: Maria stayed or they left together. But this did not seem to appease the lanky young man and it was Choiseul who defused the situation.

"I'm sure this young lady won't pose any problems because Mademoiselle Drago trusts her. Come on, Christophe, sit down. And please, ladies, sit down as well. Would you like something to drink?"

Choiseul offered them a glass of frênette, cider made from the leaves of ash trees. Maria had never drunk anything like it and the sweet fizziness was not unpleasant. But a kind of moldy aftertaste kept her from fully enjoying this discovery. Then the old game warden insisted that the two women stay for dinner. A pot full of coq au vin, which he had to prepare in advance, was simmering in the kitchen.

As if the man knew that he'd be having guests, Maria thought, becoming more and more suspicious. She was sure that Lucia had not written ahead that she was coming, proof enough was Christophe's total surprise on seeing her.

216

She wished she could act like her companion who stayed friendly and warm but her bright eyes watched the father and son attentively when they were not glancing over the bookshelf and other pieces of furniture. The hardened journalist was suspicious but did not let it show. At least, this is what Maria was hoping.

They sat at the table and despite the appetizing smell she did not eat much. She did not like old Choiseul's smug little smile. Nor did she appreciate the crude manners of young Choiseul who attacked the dinner like he had not eaten for months, swallowing half the chicken by himself and lapping up the wine sauce and fat with an entire loaf of bread. From the looks of his emaciated figure you never would have suspected such a voracious appetite.

The unnerving picture is not complete without the big black dog. Its blazing topaz eyes were glued on Lucia.

Under the influence of the paranoia she felt creeping up on her for the first time in her life, Maria tried to detect the faintest suspicious odor in every tiny mouthful, fearing poison or drugs. She tried hard to get over her fear of the beast by sneaking a piece of chicken under the table for him but the dog did not budge. Its indifference only reinforced her suspicions.

Even though her fear kept growing, she did not miss a word of Christophe's tale, which culminated in Lucia coming here.

"I've lived like a recluse in this house for a long time and my only distractions are taking long walks in the woods and reading. I get newspapers from all over the world so I can pretend to travel. And thus I've learned many languages. The Flash is by far my favorite. I gobble up every one of your articles. That's why I thought of you when I saw strange things in the forest. It happened twice and always in the same way: as I near the little castle on the pond I hear a hunting horn in the distance. The sound seems to want to go on forever, as if whoever is blowing it never runs out of breath. The first time I got so scared that I climbed up the nearest tree. From my perch I saw them pass by—a pack of dogs straight out of hell, dozens of huge hounds with their blood-red tongues hanging out of their mouths full of glistening fangs, and their bulging eyes flashed like lightning. Right behind them was a gentleman dressed in black and gold, the horn still on his lips and as he held tightly to the reins in his pale hand he spurred on his horse whose gallop made the trees tremble. But I was really disturbed by the blood gushing out of the open wound in his belly. The horseman and his infernal horde were quickly out of sight. I had all kinds of trouble getting back down since my arms and legs were shaking in fear. Once on the ground I noticed that there was not a sound in the forest. Even the birds were silent. My mysterious horseman was nowhere to be seen. However, the dead leaves that the apparitions had trampled on were as black as soot. I followed their trail up the path to the pond and saw their muddled tracks on the wet ground of the riverbank. They disappeared into the water. I looked up at the pretty castle, puzzled, and saw a white figure standing for a brief moment in the top of the highest tower."

"When Christophe told me about his supernatural encounter, I immediately thought of the tragic history of the Duke d'Oise and the White Lady," old Choiseul broke in. "I really think my son saw the cruel lord of the legend. That's all it took to get obsessed. He spent weeks on end wandering through the woods, coming back in the darkest hours of the night, tired and trembling. You can imagine how worried I was for his health. I tried to talk him out of going but he was stubborn, determined, so I ended up going with him, bringing food and blankets, you know, provisions for cold and hunger that my son never thought of…"

"Yes, but we both saw them! We saw them!" Christophe exclaimed. "This time we were a lot closer to the pond. We were hiding behind the trees. The phantom crew was even more frightening than the first time, maybe because it brushed by us. It gave off a nauseating, metallic odor, like blood. In spite of the terror knotting my guts, I got up and ran after them, despite my father's protests since he was as scared as I was. What I saw when I got to the pond has haunted me... kept me awake for weeks. The hellish cavalcade of the Duke d'Oise marched straight into the water and it boiled on contact. At the top of the tower, clearly visible now, a lady with skin and hair as white as her dress was watching the spectacle. In spite of the distance I was struck by the expression of pure panic on her face, that beautiful face. The Duke and his dogs tried swimming to the castle. The ghost howled curses at the lady, accusing her of bewitching the pond, then he sank and the water became as smooth as glass. When I turned back to the White Lady our eyes met. I felt like my heart would burst in my chest and I fell unconscious onto the muddy bank.

Christophe's lower lip was trembling as he sucked in a mouthful of air.

"Help me, Lucia!" he almost yelled. "Help me because I'm madly in love with a ghost!"

"There you go," old Choiseul knocked over his chair. "If you can free my son from this insane crush, I swear I'll buy stocks in your paper."

Christophe rapped his fist on the table. Maria and the silverware jumped.

"It's not just a crush!"

"OK! OK!" Choiseul lost his composure and put his hand on his son's arm, murmuring words of consolation.

"Have you thought of a plan of attack?" Lucia finally asked when Christophe seemed calmer.

"Of course. My son and I observed that the Lady's ghost only appears when the Duke came with his hellhounds. Exorcising the place and sending the phantoms back to the hell or heaven they come from seems to us the best thing to do, but Christophe wants to declare his love to the ectoplasmic cru... lady before she's freed of her earthly burden."

"I see," Lucia sighed. "But you know, Christophe, to let your beloved go free is an act of true love. You don't want to be selfish, do you?"

The young man shook his head. His cheeks quivered as if the skin was barely holding onto the bones. "No, no, you're right, Mademoiselle Drago. And my father too, he's right. I just want to say a real goodbye. Out loud."

His lower lip fluttered and his strange voice was choked and broken. But his eyes, so deeply set in those hollow sockets, did not glisten with a single tear.

"Don't worry," Lucia said, "we'll see to it that both of you are at peace."

"Great!" Jacques Choiseul blurted out. "I'll go get some flashlights and sweaters. It gets cold at night. I'll also make a thermos full of coffee. Ladies, I'm so glad you're with us to finally put an end to these ghostly troubles."

"Now don't you go…" Lucia started to say but Choiseul was already in the other room, leaving them alone with the black dog and its young master who was just as frightening. The dark lakes of his eyes stared unblinkingly at the two women.

After a few nervous heartbeats that felt like hours, Lucia, too, stood up as full of energy as old Choiseul. "Stay here, Maria. Keep our host company while I get some stuff out of the trunk."

She opened the glass door and dashed out into the rainy night. Christophe's pouting lip hung down to his chest as he opened his mouth to stop her.

Maria knew right away that she had a job to do: she had to keep the Choiseuls and their dreadful dog busy while her partner was outside. She just hoped that the older journalist did not try to hit the road and leave Maria alone with these weird men. But for some strange reason the young lady trusted Lucia.

As Christophe unfolded his gangly carcass to stand up, Maria did the first thing that popped into her head to distract him—she knocked over the half-full bottle of red wine. The purple nectar spilled over the tablecloth and onto the big boy's black pants.

"Oh, no! I'm so sorry!"

Blushing and sincerely ashamed by such a crude trick, Maria grabbed a napkin and started dabbing the wine off

Christophe's clothes. He waved his long arms in the air and said it was no big deal and for a minute Maria thought she was in one of those comedies with Roberto Benigni, but something weird happened that put an end to the comedy: under the double layer of napkin and pants Christophe's flesh felt spongy. Maria had the impression that the pants were full of jelly.

The dog suddenly growled loudly and deeply, which made the stuffy air of the farmhouse vibrate. The young journalist stopped moving. To top off this vaudeville scene old Choiseul chose that moment to come back with his things. His inquisitive eyes scanned the room quickly and fell directly on Maria holding the wine-stained napkin in her frozen hand.

The old man swiped the cane that was leaning against the table and stuck it under her nose. "Where's Lucia Drago?"

His voice was cold and forceful. The sweet-toned kindness of the game warden was gone.

"She... she'll be right back. She said she needed to get her camera out of the car..."

With her mind still reeling, Maria moved over to the front door when Choiseul headed for her.

"No, no, don't worry, she'll be right back!"

The black hound barked loudly. Maria felt like her eardrums had been punched. She covered her ears and groaned. Choiseul shoved her aside and threw open the door.

The rental car was still parked in the mud with the trunk open, but there was no sign of the journalist.

"She's gone!" the old man yelled, losing his temper. "Kerry!"

The dog bounded outside, sniffed the ground and turned its shining eyes on its master, apparently waiting for orders.

"He's got her scent," Choiseul said. "Come on!"

"What about the lass?" Christophe asked.

He, too, had changed his attitude. His voice was more hollow and he stood up straight almost touching the black-beamed ceiling. He walked oddly, wobbling like a balloon filled with helium.

Jacques Choiseul turned to Maria who backed up against the table, trying to hold back a river of startled tears. The old man nailed her down with a cold, pitiless stare. She could not decide who scared her more, the father, the son or the dog Kerry. How did things get so weird? Where did everything go wrong? What did these people want that they needed Lucia Drago so badly? As for her, the little, awkward apprentice journalist, she was of no use to them.

"There's more important business at hand," Choiseul scowled at her. "We'll deal with her when we get back."

The two men joined the dog and the door slammed behind them. Then the lock turned.

At last, Maria was alone but locked in. She jumped when the bulb in the ceiling light sizzled and flickered. Even without Choiseul there to scare her she was trembling in fear. She went to the door on her wobbly legs and turned the handle to no avail.

The bulb flickered again and she had the feeling that the shadows tucked away in the corners of the kitchen were moving, stretching out during every split second of darkness to creep closer to her. Choked by terror she shook the door on its hinges but could not open it. Then she knocked as hard as she could on the window that formed the upper part.

The light kept blinking on and off and now Maria could clearly hear something scraping on the tile floor. She imagined claws crawling over the smooth surface and she really started panicking. She rattled the door handle and whimpered like a trapped animal.

Whatever it was it was getting closer and waiting only for a moment of darkness to pounce.

Suddenly a voice she had given up hope of ever hearing came from outside: "Maria! Move away!"

The young woman obeyed automatically and flattened herself against the wall. A big rock smashed the window. With her hand wrapped in her coat Lucia cleared away the sharp edges and motioned to her partner.

"Quickly, Maria! You have to get out of there!"

The light bulb buzzed and blinked. In the flashes of light and darkness the room seemed to transform. Only Lucia's shape standing behind the door and her arm sticking through the broken window stayed unchanged. Maria grabbed her hand. At that very moment the light went out with dry pop.

"Don't turn around!" Lucia warned.

No need to tell her twice. The grating claws were scary enough. Maria grabbed the edge of the window and hoisted herself through while Lucia helped her from the other side. She scraped her belly on the edge but she paid no attention to it because she felt an icy touch brush her legs. One final push and she landed on Lucia, almost knocking her over. The two women caught their breath in the rain.

"Now," Lucia whispered, "you can turn around."

Maria hesitated at the idea of what she would see but her curiosity got the better of her. She looked.

A ruin of black stones, covered in moss and ivy, stood in place of the farmhouse.

"I... I don't get it," Maria stammered.

"It was a hunting lodge of the Duke d'Oise," Lucia said.

The journalist took her scared apprentice by the arm and handed her a brass ring engraved with animals. "Come quick, we're going to the Lady's castle. Keep hold of this, it's a talisman. It won't protect you from Choiseul but if any ghosts show up tonight, you don't have to be afraid of them."

They headed into the forest that hummed with the drizzling rain.

"But... it took us twenty minutes by car," Maria objected softly. "Shouldn't we drive?"

She was trying to keep her balance on the slippery ground. She felt like her nightmare had ended only to plunge her into another dream. The rain blurred her vision and her legs were limp. Only the pain in her muscles and her belly convinced her that it was the real world that had taken a strange turn.

"No need," Lucia replied. "I studied a map of the area before coming here. The castle is only a quarter mile away."

"But… But… all that way in the car…"

Lucia gestured to her to lower her voice. "Choiseul messed with us to get us lost but my late husband always said that I had a compass in my head. When I saw the farmhouse standing where the map showed ruins, there was no question about it."

Lucia guided Maria over a path that snaked between the trees.

"Sorry I left you with those guys but it was me they wanted to get alone. It was a risky play but at least I got them to go out looking for me."

Maria gripped her colleagues arm, "Who are they? Why did they scare me like that? And how did they get us to see the ruins as a… a…"

Lucia put her finger on Maria's lips to keep her quiet. She whispered, "We're almost at the castle and this isn't the time. What you're about to see will be even more confusing and scarier too, probably, and I'm sorry, but not another word…"

Three figures suddenly appeared in front of them at the edge of the trees, going the same direction as the two women. Maria and Lucia dropped down behind the wet bushes. They could see it was the Choiseuls and their big dog. The elder was holding a weird, old-fashioned hurricane lamp and squinting in the rain. Christophe was sliding silently over the carpet of soaked leaves.

Lucia gestured to her friend to follow her and they snuck slowly through the undergrowth as the patter of the rain covered the squishing sounds of their feet.

The two men and their dog stopped in sight of the castle. Maria's eyes were wide open: a light was shining at the top of the highest tower of the abandoned building.

"Always there as ever," Choiseul's jubilant voice was heard over the rain. He raised the lamp and shouted across the pond, "Lady Luna! Look here! I've brought the Duke and his pack of hounds from the dead!"

As he shouted Choiseul threw his lamp violently to the ground. A flame shot out and formed a circle around him. And he was changed, suddenly appearing taller. His cap and coat vanished into smoke and he was now dressed in a black robe.

He tossed his cane to Christophe and when the young man snatched it out of the air both he and the object went through a spectacular transformation: the horse-head knob whinnied and grew. Hooves and legs and a black breast swelled out and exploded the wooden walking stick. Christophe straddled it like a witch on a broom. At the same time his face was covered with a thick beard and the black pools of his eyes lit up with red flames.

Maria did not know where to look because the big, black dog metamorphosed as well. It twisted around on the ground like a big bag full of angry cats, then a new head sprang out of its back, then two more, baring their fangs. In no time a whole pack of dogs was popping out, the terrifying result of a division of canine cells. The six howling beasts, all with the same dark fur and blazing eyes, gathered around Christophe, who was sitting on his horse that snorted smoke.

Maria knew that she was looking at the Duke d'Oise and his pack of hellhounds. She bit her tongue to make sure she was not dreaming and was disappointed to find that this was all very real.

She grabbed Lucia's arm as her legs and the entire world started slipping away from her. "What do we do? What do we do?"

"Let the professional journalist get the better of your fear," her colleague said, holding her up with a strong hand. "This is your first assignment and you're going to write a bang-up story!"

In front of the castle Christophe kept calling the White Lady. A figure was leaning over the summit of the tower. Maria thought she saw two black eyes watching the scene with dread.

On the bank the Duke made his horse stomp as he spat out threats and curses. His voice was strong like a furious wind striking a stone wall. "Maleficus, you swore to me that I could finally cross this enchanted pond and take back what belongs to me."

Maria felt Lucia suddenly shuddered and it was her turn to hold up her friend. The woman's face had turned pale.

"Sorry, Maria, we're in greater danger than I thought. Let's get out of her fast!"

She did not have to say it twice. But the two women only made it a few steps when the voice of the man who had called himself Choiseul rang out:

"I always keep my promises, Duke! And I feel the presence of Lucia Drago nearby. I just have to call her by name…"

Maleficus turned around with an evil grin on his face, which only grew bigger on seeing the two women hurrying away through the bushes.

"I just have to call her because a name is a solid bond: LUCIA DRAGO!"

She halted. Her feet were welded to the wet ground. An expression of absolute terror warped her face. "Maria! Maria, he's got me!"

Her friend was about to grab her hand when she was yanked back as if by an invisible cord. Her feet slid over the mud while she tried to reach out for her friend's hand.

"Lucia! Lucia, no!"

Maria finally lunged forward to help her friend but she was already in the arms of Maleficus. He put his fingers on the eyes of his prey and Lucia's body went limp.

The Duke whistled at his dogs and pointed to the other woman. "Cerberus, Titan, Typhon! Devour the damsel! Go!"

Three of the dogs ran at Maria. Then the infernal knight took Lucia in his arms and laid her over his horse in front of him.

This was the last vision Maria had of her friend. She could do nothing for her. The dogs were coming fast, their jaws open, ready to tear her to pieces. She turned and ran through the forest. Louder than the furious barking of the hell-hounds she could hear Maleficus' demonic laugh.

A jaw snapped at her collar and scraped her neck. Even driven by panic and terror she knew she would never make it to the ruins where the car was parked. A heavy weight struck her back and she fell into the mud as the big dog attacking her tried to sink its fangs in her neck. The young women rolled over and shot her arm out in a defensive reflex.

Her fist met the dog's face. Instead of swallowing it in its slobbering jaws the beast yelped and backed off of Maria's body. A sulfurous smoke arose from the weird wound where the journalist hit it. In a daze she realized that she had not let go of the talisman Lucia had given her.

When the two other hounds reached her Maria held out the small metal disk in her trembling hand. The phantom hounds pulled up short at the sight of the object and lingered at a respectable distance. The other beast, which had been hit by Maria, slowly disintegrated while whining like a sad puppy. Such an unexpected result gave her courage.

I have to help Lucia!

The two dogs circled her and growled. They backed away when she pointed the talisman at them. All of a sudden she had an inspiration and ran at the closest one.

"Go back to your master!"

The black beast yelped and pulled back its ears. The closer Maria got, the more its aggressiveness melted and it looked like a big, panting puppy which turned tail and bolted. Maria ran after it.

"I'm coming, Lucia!"

The dog started running so fast through the trees that its feet did not even touch the ground. Maria felt an icy wind strike her: the two other dogs had passed her to help their co-hort but the one Maria had struck with the talisman was nothing but a blurred shadow whose shining eyes were losing their light. Dark fumes drifted up from the vanishing fur like oil bubbles from the depths of the sea.

When she finally got back in sight of the castle Maria almost fainted with relief. She had to lean against the trunk of an old oak tree to catch her breath. The wounded dog vanished completely before reaching the water but the two other dogs jumped into the pond and swam toward the castle.

There was no sign of the knight or Maleficus.

Maria went to the water's edge. Her burst of bravery dwindled at the thought of the old man who had tricked them.

Lights dancing in the windows, on the roofs and at the top of the tower attracted her attention. A wail filled with deep despair startled her. The noise seemed to bounce between the trees before slowly rising up through the leaves and fading away.

Who was that? It wasn't Lucia's voice. Was it the woman whose figure she had just seen in the tower?

With her throat choked with anguish Maria hurried along the shore toward the majestic castle. She stopped when she saw a gigantic shadow spring forth from the front door. And she screamed when she recognized the Duke on his horse holding a lady dressed in white by her hair. The poor lady's long dress dragged behind the sinister team like a pale banner of death. The demon had spurred his horse over the stretch of water and was heading straight for the scared journalist.

This vision terrified her so much she forgot about the talisman. She jumped aside and fell into the pond and her head hit a rock sticking out of the water.

Maria woke up the next evening in the hospital in Creil. It was there that she learned of the castle of the White Lady crumbling to the ground and that they had found Lucia's body in the ruins.

Leonardo did not know how to react. Finding out that Sibilla's mother had been killed in such mysterious, unexplained circumstances by the same man who had almost killed him was a shock. A deep sadness overcame him at the thought of his friend becoming an orphan so young. But he was also frustrated that so many things were left in the dark.

Maria Carpi stood up and opened the window in her office. She leaned on the sill and stood there a moment contemplating the traffic in Milan. Leonardo took a sip of coffee and winced because it was cold. He finally decided to say something when Maria returned to her chair and lit a cigarette, the first since she had started her story.

"How did Lucia Drago die? Is the Maleficus the same one we saw in Florence? And why Lucia?"

"One step at a time, Verga. You'll get your explanations when I get to the end. When I regained consciousness Toni Gambardella was at my bedside along with another man I had never seen before. If you'd seen my old boss' face you'd say he'd aged ten years overnight. As for the stranger, he introduced himself as Count Saint-Germain, a friend of Sir Wilson and Gambardella. He was very nice and broke the news of Lucia's death with a great deal of tact. I know you're going to accuse me of being too sensitive because I didn't know my colleague for long, but really my heart was broken. In fact, no, I know that you liked Sibilla a lot from the moment you met and I felt the same way about her mother. I knew right away what an incredible person she was."

"I can understand, sure," Leonardo mumbled, a little embarrassed by the fact that he was so attracted to Sibilla from the start. "I've heard of this Count Saint-Germain. He makes a lot of noise with the hoity-toity for his philanthropy and his incredible fortune. What relation is he to Lucia that gave him the right to break the news? Did he tell you how she died?"

"Don't badger me with questions. I'll tell you our conversation word for word. Get yourself another cup of coffee and listen. I left the hospital the next day but it wasn't time yet to go back to Milan."

"Do we really have to go back there?" The young journalist expressed her reluctance in a trembling voice that made her ashamed.

Count Saint-Germain understood. "It's normal not to want to relive those awful experiences, Maria, but for your safety you need to understand what happened. You see, I'm very familiar with the man who cooked up that nightmare and he won't hesitate to strike at you when he gets the chance."

Maria was alone with the Count who was taking the country roads through the woods to bring her back to the ruins that Maleficus had transformed into a farmhouse for a while. Toni Gambardella had gone back to Milan with Lucia's corpse. The police had concluded that the neglected castle collapsed naturally and the funeral was going to take place the following afternoon.

The Mercedes finally stopped in front of the old hunting lodge. The car that Lucia had rented was still there. Maria stepped out very carefully. She could not help thinking that Kerry the hellhound was going to come running around a pile of stones with its eyes ablaze.

Even in the middle of the day the ruins looked sinister with their sharp, black stones like a jaw full of giant fangs. A solid door was the only thing recognizable among the chaos of rocks.

Saint-Germain, who had already taken a few steps toward the building, turned around and smiled reassuringly at Maria. The young woman admired this man who could instill courage in her with such a simple, friendly gesture. She caught up to him with her heart pounding and her head still spinning but she knew that the Count would protect her. The two of them went through the door, stepping carefully over the debris. Normally ruins are covered with clumps of weeds, vines and bushes, as evidence of how nature never misses an opportunity to reclaim what man has abandoned, but here there were only stones.

In the middle of the rubble they had cleared a circle. As they got closer Maria and the Count could see an ancient circular stele, a tombstone stuck into the ground and on top of which was carved a weird shape, worn away by the ages. Saint-Germain stiffened and scowled. With obvious disgust he cleared off the rest of the rocks around the grave.

Maria turned pale on seeing the piece of snow-white fabric sticking out from under the heavy slab.

"Here lies the Duke of Hell and his cursed hounds. May they leave this land in peace," the Count translated.

He took hold of the white fabric and pulled gently but it would not budge.

"Last night Evil triumphed in many ways," Saint-Germain sighed. "Come on, Maria, we can't do anything for the spirit haunting this place."

"Was it really the Duke d'Oise and the White Lady?" Maria asked timidly behind the Count.

"Yes, the black demon that Maleficus invoked in the shape of that clumsy young man was buried here and the list of his misdeeds is so abominable that History has hidden it. As for the White Lady, she was the Duke's victim and the guardian of certain magical knowledge that Maleficus has desired for a long time."

"Who is that man? And what did he want with Lucia?"

Saint-Germain took a long, deep breath and let it out slowly in harmony with the wind blowing through the trees.

"Maleficus is a dangerous being. I have to do whatever it takes to defeat him because I am in part responsible for his crimes. He holds a very old grudge against the Drago family. Centuries-old. In fact, a freebooter named Dragut once cheated him and Maleficus swore to get his revenge on all the descendants."

Maria said nothing. She felt dizzy and dug her heels into the soft ground in a tangible attempt to keep a footing in reality. She believed the Count unquestionably after the events she had witnessed that put an end, once and for all, to her faith in a rational world.

"He would've killed me too," she said.

"Did you tell him your name?"

Maria shook her head, "Just my first name."

"Good. The adepts of ancient magic believe rightly in the power contained in a name. In some countries they chose a name just for how it sounds, but in others they still hold a

231

deeper meaning. They are the alchemical essence of our nature. Add to this the name of your ancestors and your whole identity rests in the combination of those letters."

Maria pictured Maleficus throwing off the rags of Jacques Choiseul and calling Lucia Drago by name to trap her in his magical snare.

She stopped suddenly when she recognized where they were going. "This is where the hellhounds attacked me." The ground was scattered with trampled leaves. "I fought them off with an amulet that Lucia gave me." Maria flinched when she remembered the small disk. She must have lost it when she fell into the pond.

Count Saint-Germain pulled the object out of his pocket and handed it to the young lady. He smiled, "Keep it with you always."

Maria took the talisman and felt comforted immediately. Closing her fist around the disk she marched the rest of the way to the pond and saw the remains of the castle. Cars were parked near the ruins and she could see a few uniformed police. Civilians were also roaming around the collapsed building.

"What magic was protecting the Lady?" Maria asked. "And how does Lucia fit in? The Duke seemed happy she was here, as if he needed her to cross this pond."

"Exactly the case. I have no idea what was in the castle. And it's my ignorance that allowed Maleficus to do this behind my back. I don't know how Lucia's presence got them to their goal. Maybe they needed a human sacrifice to neutralize the Lady's protective magic. Many things remain unexplained.

"I went to the funeral the next day. Of course I saw Toni and the Count there but I also saw a woman who looked a lot older than she actually was—it was Lucia's sister. She was holding her niece's hand. The little girl had her back turned to me so I only saw her red curls. The following week I went back to *Flash* and offered to take over Lucia's column under the name Sibilla."

232

Leonardo almost knocked over his coffee. "What? Sibilla was your idea?"

"More or less. Denis gave me the idea for the pseudonym."

"Denis?"

"That's the Count's first name."

"Really?"

"I don't know what you're thinking, Verga, but don't say a word. I don't have to justify my friendships. Anyway, I continued Lucia's paranormal column and I changed the theme. It was no longer about scams but about real supernatural events, which Lucia had witnessed and reported respectfully. I wrote it for twelve years. In the meantime Toni offered me to become the assistant editor-in-chief, so when he retired he handed the reins over to me. The day after, by some weird chance, a very young woman with red hair walked quietly into the newsroom. I almost had a heart attack because I thought it was Lucia come back from the dead."

"And the young woman was Elena, *our* Sibilla."

"On the nose, Montalbano. She told me how she had studied journalism to take up her mother's flame and how her aunt taught her about magic. She showed me a few articles she had written and I thought they were great. Just like her timing to come here. I saw a sign and offered her a job as Sibilla. I've never regretted it."

Leonardo shook his head, amazed by the revelations. "You were the first Sibilla. It's hard to believe…"

"It was better to keep my identity secret… with the help of Toni and the Count, to avoid any retaliation from Maleficus. When I married Salvatore Carpi, may he rest in peace, I came out of hiding because I was protected by his name."

"This story of names is beyond me. Like the rest of the story, to tell you the truth."

"Oh yeah?" Maria leaned forward like a kind professor faced with a slow student.

Leonardo went on, "I know the reputation of your good Count Saint-Germain. A seducer disguised as a kind of clever con artist. All his good deeds were just a smokescreen. And except for you buying into the confused explanations about hundred-year-old wizards, we know nothing about what really happened to Lucia Drago. No, I think Jacques Choiseul was a psychopath who drugged you, which would explain the nightmarish visions you suffered."

Maria listened to him rant, her smile becoming more and more cynical. When he stopped to catch his breath she pulled out her necklace with a small pendant hanging from it.

"This chases away ghosts but I don't know if it works on bores like you. God knows I'd love to hammer a little reason into that thick skull of yours."

Leonardo recognized the amulet from her story. Maria unhooked the gold chain and handed it to her reporter.

"Your skepticism could cost you your life some day, Verga, believe me."

The journalist had a bitter laugh but he accepted the gift and held it in the palm of his hand. "I know, Maria. Sibilla tells me the same thing. And that's why…" He coughed loudly and jumped up out of his seat.

"What happened with Sibilla?" Maria asked.

He held the talisman tightly and grimaced. In Florence, then in Thailand… I almost died… twice. I think that's what made Sibilla decide to… to…" Leonardo sighed, took a deep breath and spit it out. "We're no longer working together, Maria. Sibilla decided to cut her ties with me. The day after we got back she came over to my place and told me that she didn't want me around in her investigations. Because… cause she liked me and couldn't stand the idea of me dying because of her. She also said that my skepticism would get me killed."

The journalist fiddled with the amulet, thinking to himself for a minute, then he put it around his neck. Maria and he stared at each other in an uncomfortable silence broken only by the sound of traffic on the streets of Milan.

Lenoardo & Sibilla by Bernasconi

EXPLORE THE WONDERS OF THE HEXAGON UNIVERSE AND ITS HEROES IN OUR COMICS:

Bob Lance #1: The Round Table. Carpi & Bernasconi. 64 pages b&w. $12.95.

Bob Lance #2: To Seek the Holy Grail. Carpi & Bernasconi. 54 pages b&w. $12.95.

Bob Lance #3: The Ghost of Rasputin. Carpi & Bernasconi. 54 pages b&w. $12.95.

C.L.A.S.H. Frescura & Trevisan. 248 pages b&w. $20.95.

Dick Demon: Vanishing Point. Lofficier, Arden & Peniche. 108 pages color. $26.95

Dragut/Scarlet Lips. Lofficier & Macall. 68 pages color. $19.95

The Frontiersmen/Codename: Glory. Lofficier, Martin Peniche & Mayorga. 48 pages b&w. $9.95.

Galaor, Warrior of Mû. Lofficier, Macall, Xavier & Peru. 68 pages color. $19.95.

Guardian of the Republic #1. Mornet & Roncagliolo. 48 pages color. $12.95.

Guardian of the Republic/Barbarella. Lofficier & Ruiz. 48 pages color. $12.95.

Guardian of the Republic/Dragut/Scarlet Lips/Time Brigade. Lofficier & Macall. 48 pages b&w. $9.95.

HEXAGON COMICS: THE FIRST 70 YEARS. Lofficier et al. 300 pages b&w. $22.95.

Hexagon Group : The Dark Hive (Vol. 1). Lofficier, Roncagliolo & Ruiz. 76 pages b&w. $12.95

Hexagon Group : Hexagon vs. Heptagon (Vol. 2). Lofficier, Roncagliolo & Garcia. 96 pages b&w. $12.95

Hexagon novel #1: Dark Matter. D'Huissier. 300 pages. $22.95.

Hexagon Spotlight on... Alfredo Macall. 68 pages color. $19.95

Kabur #1. Legrand, Lofficier & Bernasconi. 252 pages b&w. $20.95.

Kidz. Lofficier & Macall. 52 pages b&w. $10.95

The Lunatic Legion. Lofficier, Bouquet & Lafuente. 52 pages b&w. $10.95.

Morgane. Lofficier & Lirussi. 48 pages b&w. $9.95.

The Partisans #1. Thomas, Lofficier & Guevara. 48 pages b&w. $9.95.

Phenix #1. Lofficier, Bernasconi & Roncagliolo. 248 pages b&w. $20.95.

Scarlet Lips : Crimson Dawn. Wolfman, Lofficier & Guevara. 48 pages b&w. $9.95

Strangers Origins: Homicron. Buffolente, Lofficier & Dzialowski. 364 pages b&w. $24.95.

Strangers Origins: Jaydee. Grossi. 260 pages b&w. $20.95.

Strangers Origins: Starlock. Legrand & Bernasconi. 256 pages b&w. $20.95.

Strangers #0: Omens & Origins. Lofficier & Various. 128 pages color. $29.95.

Strangers #1: Strangers in a Strange Land. Lofficier & Various. 160 pages color. $34.95.

Strangers #2: Of Blood and Fire. Lofficier & Various. 160 pages color. $39.95.

Strangers #3: Of Gods and Men. Lofficier & Various. 160 pages color. $39.95.

Tales of the Hexagonverse #1 (prose anthology). 244 pages. $20.95.

Tales of the Twilight People: Dr. Despair. Lofficier & Agapit. 148 pages b&w. $12.95.

Tiger and The Eye. Lofficier & Ruiz. 136 pages b&w. $12.95.

Time Brigade: The Grail Wars. Lofficier & Green. 48 pages color. $12.95.

Wampus #1. Frescura & Bernasconi. 232 pages b&w. $20.95.

Zembla #1. Oneta & Oneta. 280 pages b&w. $22.95.

TO ORDER: pay by credit card/paypal direct from our website: *www.hexagon.comics.com/shop.html*

or pay by check to the order of BLACK COAT PRESS sent to: BLACK COAT PRESS c/o Mr. Greg M. Seigel, 18321 Ventura Blvd., Suite 915, Tarzana, CA 91356. E-MAIL INQUIRIES: *info@blackcoatpress.com*

E-MAIL INQUIRIES: *info@blackcoatpress.com*

www.ingramcontent.com/pod-product-compliance
Lightning Source LLC
Chambersburg PA
CBHW060354030726
47497CB00003B/710